FAKING CHRISTMAS

CINDY STEEL

ALSO BY CINDY STEEL

Pride and Pranks Series

A Christmas Spark

That Fine Line

Stranded Ranch

Double or Nothing

To Lisa — thanks for another one.

CONTENTS

TRIGGER WARNINGS

This book deals with the loss of a parent from cancer. Light themes of grief are written throughout.

The email exchange on the following page contains light grammatical errors for the purpose of this story. The author, as well as her editors, are aware of their existence. Hope you enjoy!

PROLOGUE

THE INCIDENT

DATE: NOV 16

To: miltaylor@stantonhigh.edu

From: oliwilson@stantonhigh.edu

Subject: The WORST

Dear Millie,

Per our discussion at lunch, I've compiled my argument in regard to your leaning to the dark side, AKA letting yourself believe that Miles Taylor isn't the actual worst. That is, indeed, the case, and I feel compelled to inform you that the man with the "fine pair of hams" just spent the past ten minutes berating me in the hallway. It's time you know the truth about "the hottest attraction this school has ever seen."

I almost threw up in my mouth just typing that.

Once you peel you're eyes away from the "sexy forearms" and the "hair a girl could run her fingers through" (side note: you *really* need to start reading higher quality books), you'll see what I see, which is NOT anything like Wade Kinsella, okay? Your Hart of Dixie comparison is crap. Wade Kinsella was a charming bad boy with a heart of gold. Miles is a self-righteous, know-it-all, arrogant adrenaline junkie with a heart of coal.

'Tis the season.

Just in the last week, he has forced completely unsolicited advice down my throat, criticized me and all my life choices, made fun of my volunteering to help at the staff meeting, and made snide comments while I was kindly helping out Mr. Johnson in the copy room, all while inviting me to have one of his stupid Friday donuts like he was doing me a favor by being in his company.

These are the facts. Now that you've joined the Miles Fan Club along with every other person at this school, I would like you to explain to me his alleged appeal outside of his "sweet as sugar personality," because I don't get why he's got the whole school eating out of his hands while only I can see what he really is:

A stinking, rotting fish in a sleazy, younger Brad Pitt-esque package.

Love,

Olive

P.S. In case you're wondering. I've never been a fan of Brad Pitt, so that wasn't a compliment. More of a Bradley Cooper girl myself.

P.P.S. Feel free to debate. I'll go down swinging.

DATE: NOV 17

To: millankin@stantonhigh.edu

From: oliwilson@stantonhigh.edu

Did you get my email from yesterday? I'm losing my steam over here. Very disappointed in your counterattack.

DATE: NOV 17

To: oliwilson@stantonhigh.edu

From: millankin@stantonhigh.edu

What email? The one you sent with the dog and the balloon? That was hilarious. I showed it to Hank and the kids when I got home.

DATE: NOV 17

To: millankin@stantonhigh.edu

From: oliwilson@stantonhigh.edu

No. The one I sent about your "friend" who works across the hallway from me.

And yes…funniest dog video ever.

DATE: NOV 17

To: oliwilson@stantonhigh.edu

From: millankin@stantonhigh.edu

Oh, you mean that incredibly hot single man who works across the hall from you? That hunk of eye candy who brings donuts for the school every single Friday out of the sheer kindness of his heart? Never got anything. Checked my spam, too. Stupid server. Maybe send again?

DATE: NOV 17

To: oliwilson@stantonhigh.edu

From: millankin@stantonhigh.edu

Hello? Now I'm dying to know what you sent. Must have been good. SEND AGAIN.

DATE: NOV 17

To: oliwilson@stantonhigh.edu
From: millankin@stantonhigh.edu

Hmmm. It's Friday. School's almost out. I'm really in the mood for a good donut…

Know of any place I can get one today?

DATE: NOV 17
To: oliwilson@stantonhigh.edu
From: millankin@stantonhigh.edu

Mark my words, you have five minutes to spill everything or else I will be eating a donut from Miles, and I don't want to hear any crap from you.

DATE: NOV 17
To: millankin@stantonhigh.edu
From: oliwilson@stantonhigh.edu

I sent the email to Miles.

I SENT THE EMAIL TO MILES.

Not YOU.

I'm freaking out. I'm freaking out. I'm freaking OUT.

WHAT DO I DOOOOOO?????

DATE: NOV 17
To: oliwilson@stantonhigh.edu
From: millankin@stantonhigh.edu

WHAT? How did that happen??? What did it say?!

DATE: NOV 17
To: millankin@stantonhigh.edu
From: oliwilson@stantonhigh.edu

Somehow it autocorrected to his email. DANG you for having the same first three letters as the worst person ever!! WHAT DO I DO???

DATE: NOV 17
To: oliwilson@stantonhigh.edu
From: millankin@stantonhigh.edu

I don't know the level I should be freaking out at. WHAT DID IT SAY?!

DATE: NOV 17
To: millankin@stantonhigh.edu
From: oliwilson@stantonhigh.edu

WORDS. LOTS AND LOTS OF WORDS THAT HE WILL DEFINITELY TAKE THE WRONG WAY. I mentioned his hams. I remember that. I MENTIONED HIS FINE PAIR OF HAMS.

I will be switching schools immediately. It was nice knowing you.

DATE: NOV 17
To: oliwilson@stantonhigh.edu
From: millankin@stantonhigh.edu

GIF of woman spitting out her coffee

DATE: NOV 17
To: millankin@stantonhigh.edu
From: oliwilson@stantonhigh.edu

You did this to me. You got in my head! They were all *your* phrases. I was throwing all the things you said about him back at you. SARCASTICALLY.

DATE: NOV 17
To: oliwilson@stantonhigh.edu
From: millankin@stantonhigh.edu

In my defense, it *is* a nice butt. We both agreed on that.

Maybe this should be a lesson for us to text each other instead of emailing.

DATE: NOV 17
To: millankin@stantonhigh.edu
From: oliwilson@stantonhigh.edu

I can type faster in an email.

What do I dooooo?

DATE: NOV 17
To: oliwilson@stantonhigh.edu
From: millankin@stantonhigh.edu

FOR THE LOVE, send me a copy of this email. I am DYING to read it. It sounds...JUICY.

DATE: NOV 17
To: millankin@stantonhigh.edu
From: oliwilson@stantonhigh.edu

You're dead to me.

I just sent it. Double-checked the name seven times before sending it.

DATE: NOV 17
To: oliwilson@stantonhigh.edu

From: millankin@stantonhigh.edu

Just read it and…I just…I…

WOW.

DATE: NOV 17

To: oliwilson@stantonhigh.edu

From: miltaylor@stantonhigh.edu

Celery Stick,

I was surprised to get your email. Regardless, it was a most insightful read.

I was a bit shocked by all the errors, however. I thought the English Department at Stanton had a higher standard of quality. I've taken the liberty of pointing these out to you, for your own study. You'll find the corrected document scanned and attached to this email.

Your man with the fine pair of hams,

Miles

DATE: NOV 16

To: miltaylor@stantonhigh.edu

From: oliwilson@stantonhigh.edu

B+

Very enlightening. Great use of description. The rules of writing still apply to emails.

?

Subject: The ~~WORST~~

Dear Millie,

Per our discussion at lunch, I've compiled my argument in regard to your leaning to the ~~dark~~ bright side, AKA letting yourself believe that Miles Taylor isn't the actual ~~worst. That~~ is, indeed, the case, and I feel compelled to inform you that the man with the "fine pair of hams" just spent the past ten minutes ~~berating me~~ chatting me up in the hallway. It's time you know the truth about "the hottest attraction this school has ever seen."

Great description

I like that

I almost threw up in my mouth just typing that.

Who is this handsome fella?

Her books sound great.

Once you peel you're your eyes away from the "sexy forearms" and the "hair a girl could run her fingers through" (side note: you *really* need to start reading higher quality books), you'll see what I see, which is NOT anything like Wade Kinsella, okay? Your Hart of Dixie comparison is crap. Wade Kinsella was a charming bad boy with a heart of gold. Miles is a ~~self-righteous~~ sweet, ~~know-it-all~~ smart-as-hell, ~~arrogant~~ dashing, adrenaline junkie with ~~a heart of coal~~ hands of steel.

Italic

'Tis the season.

Just in the last week, he has ~~forced~~ offered completely ~~unsolicited~~ cordial advice ~~down my throat~~, ~~criticized me and all my [illegible]~~, ~~made fun of~~ He questioned my volunteering to help at the staff meeting, and made ~~snide~~ interesting comments while I was kindly helping out Mr. Johnson in the copy room, all while inviting me to have one of his ~~stupid~~ delicious Friday donuts, ~~like he was~~ doing me a favor by being in his company.

Run-on sentence

Too many 'ly' words can make for weak writing

These are the facts. Now that you've joined the Miles Fan Club with every other person at this school, I would like you to explain to me his alleged appeal outside of his "sweet as sugar personality," because I ~~don't~~ get why he's got the whole school eating out of his hands while ~~only~~ I ~~can~~ also see what he really is:

quotation marks in this sense are only meant to be used with sarcasm.

~~A stinking, rotting fish in a sleazy~~ Tall, striking and more handsome than a, younger Brad Pitt ~~esque package~~.

Love,

Olive

P.S. In case you're wondering. I've never been a fan of Brad Pitt, so that wasn't a compliment. More of a Bradley Cooper girl myself.

interesting

P.P.S. Feel free to debate. I'll go down swinging.

ONE

ONE MONTH LATER

"I have not the pleasure of understanding you."
Jane Austen - *Pride and Prejudice*

"Olive."

I looked up from putting the end-of-semester grades into my computer system to find Mrs. Barnes, the school counselor, poking her curly blonde head into my empty classroom.

I smiled, leaning back in my chair and stretching my back for a moment. "Hey, Jill. Excited for the break?"

Her long skirt swished against the floor as she approached my desk with papers in her hand. "So much. This past week has been crazy getting everything lined up for next semester. I had so many kids wanting to switch out of classes at the last second, which makes for one tired and annoyed counselor."

"I'm sorry," I said. I didn't envy her job in the slightest. And that was with me having just survived two and a half weeks of teaching in December—that magical month where all of the students get high on some sort of Christmas crack they must filter through the hallways, leaving the teenagers overly hyper with zero attention spans. The Christmas music the secretary insisted on blasting through the intercom in between classes didn't help. Students somehow struggled to concentrate on the poignant words of William Shakespeare with "Jingle Bell Rock" stuck in their heads after their walk from Spanish class.

"It's all over now, thank goodness," she said, handing me a small stack of papers. "I emailed all the teachers their classes for next semester a week ago, but with all the last-minute changes, I decided to print everyone off a fresh copy."

I glanced through the papers, about to toss them onto the corner of my desk, when something made me pause. My brows furrowed as I flipped to the next paper.

"My British Lit class is so small. Only fifteen?" I looked up to meet Jill's sympathetic gaze, then shuffled through another page. "Seventeen in Basic English?" I was used to nearly twenty-five in each class. A sudden thud hit my stomach. Were *my* classes the ones kids were transferring out of?

"Apparently, there was a spike of interest in creative writing for next semester."

I rifled through the papers again. Attendance was down in all my classes, not just the electives. Embarrassment heated my face as I tried to make sense of the numbers in front of me.

Jill spoke again, her voice soft and kind, which made my face burn even hotter. "I think Miles is having his class study *Harry Potter* this year."

I held back the snort, desperately wanting to scoff at that. *Harry Potter*? What was he going to teach the kids about *Harry Potter* that they wouldn't already know? I loved the books as much as any other Potterhead, but for an English class? What kid hadn't already read it? Or at least seen the movies? How about broadening their literary horizons just a tad? Miles was stealing my students through nostalgia. My kids had to work for their grades while learning the classics—the OLD classics.

Jill cleared her throat and began to edge toward the door. "Well, things are always crazy the first week of school. I'm sure you'll have a few more join your classes than are listed here."

I took a deep breath through my nose and gave Jill a smile. "I'm sure." Laughing lightly, I added, "Fewer kids, fewer problems, right?"

Her eyes lit up, relieved at my acceptance. She made a beeline for the door. "Right. Well, I'd better go deliver the rest of these lists. Have a great Christmas!"

I sat in stiff silence after Jill left, trying to rein in the mountain of feelings threatening to escape from inside of me. Over the past few years, I'd had ample opportunity to really fine-tune my skill of suppressing all emotion. I knew from painful experience that the key was to act quickly when you felt that first rush of overcharged, hot-blooded energy. You had to tamp it down with some fierce self-talk. Be firm and resolute. It generally went something like this:

"You'll be fine."

"Just smile."

"It's not worth the drama."

"You're a grown woman. This shouldn't matter to you."

"Suck it up, buttercup."

"Do. Not. Cry."

"Life *is* pain, Highness." (*Princess Bride* quotes worked, too.)

I'd become rather an expert at smiling even when it hurt, which certainly helped reduce the level of unnecessary drama in my life. Like when I started my first job teaching English four years ago and, in my naiveté, began dating another teacher. He broke up with me months later and got hot and heavy with the PE teacher a week after that, but I still smiled at them in the hallway like everything was just fine. Unrelated, I happened to discover a job opening at Stanton High the next year. Two hours away. A happy coincidence that I accepted gratefully. Life goes on.

Even when my dad lost his battle with cancer a year ago, my chin was always up—helping, writing the obituary, picking the headstone and the flowers, organizing the funeral, and being the solid rock for my mom to lean on. Oh, I did my share of crying, too–he was my dad, after all. But it was always in the quiet of the night, alone.

This past year, I'd dedicated my energy to being fine—in all aspects of my life. It was so much easier to just smile and nod instead of putting up a big fuss over everything. Getting things done and keeping my head down was the key to life. The world was full of people making a lot of noise over things and not enough willing to put in the work to make things right. I was determined to be the latter.

I smoothed my skirt down my knees as I sat in my desk chair and held my breath when I heard the door across from mine open and close. Only when I heard footsteps going down the hallway, away from me, did I relax.

Of course, as all great literature can attest, every good plan has a few obstacles.

I had two.

No matter how hard I tried to smile and put the world to right, these two annoying barriers used every tactic in the book to foil my attempt at stoicism.

The first was Miles Taylor.

With Stanton being such a small school in upstate New York, there was only room for two English teachers. Miles had recently taken the place of, the beloved Mr. Grady, whose health complications, unfortunately, necessitated an early retirement. At first, I'd been just as excited as everyone else about the handsome new addition to Stanton High's staff. But when this complete stranger had the nerve to come into my school and steal half my students with his cool guy persona and maple bars, all while publicly critiquing my life choices, a girl could only be pushed so far before she broke. I put up a good fight, attempting to smile through it all, but my lip had started doing this weird quiver thing anytime Miles smirked at me in a faculty meeting. It was impossible to ignore him completely or smile him away when his classroom was directly across from mine and when I was convinced, he spent most of his free time trying to find new ways to tick me off. Thus, obstacle number one.

The second obstacle was my mom's new husband.

Yes, you heard that right. My dad was not even a year in the ground, and my mom had been remarried for four months. There were no words or smiles to make *that* all right in my head, no matter how much I tried.

"Olive."

I lifted my head toward the door at the sound of my friend's voice.

Millie was an art and drama teacher at the school and looked every inch the part. Today, she wore dark-blue bell bottoms with an orange-and-brown bohemian top. A rag tie lifted her exotic auburn hair off her neck while the loose curls cascaded down her back. She was like an eccentric Disney princess. In sharp contrast to her exotic spice, I was vanilla. I had medium-length dark brown hair, my closet was a concise mixture of three colors—black, white, and gray—and I had exactly two hairstyles: straight down or some form of a ponytail. Millie was just quirky enough to set her apart from the other staff at Stanton High, and the students loved her for it.

"You coming?"

"Where?"

"The auditorium. Right now. Staff meeting." Millie's hands flailed about with each clipped phrase. She was animated and dramatic to a fault. She also had a laugh that could be heard down the entire senior hallway. Basically, she was everything I was not.

I glanced at the time on my computer screen and rolled backward in my chair, banging my knee on the bottom of my desk in the process. I sucked in a breath and waited for the pain to abate only to discover that the desk had ripped a gash in my tights right across my knee. I resisted the urge to snarl at my leg or the cute gray A-line, high-waisted skirt I'd donned in celebration of this being the last day before Christmas break. Though I wasn't remotely excited about the week ahead of me, I'd be lying if I said I wasn't looking forward to a break from school.

"It's so nice of them to not make us go home yet," I said as I stood and began walking toward the door. Millie's eyes widened at my leg, but she kindly let it go. "Being gone for two weeks seems like torture right now."

"I know. I just spent the last hour cleaning paint off all the desks, so yeah, I'm with you. Christmas break sounds terrible."

"Do you know why it's in the auditorium?" I asked, closing my door behind me.

Millie and I fell into step beside each other down the hallway. Out of a habit of self-preservation, I glanced at the classroom across from mine. Miles's door was closed, and the lights were off.

"Maybe Harris arranged a musical number for us?"

I smiled at that. Our shy and stoic principal was generally well-liked among the small staff at Stanton, but a musical number was definitely not his style. (Thank goodness.)

"Or maybe they're getting us presents this year, and they're so big they need the stage to pass them all out," I suggested, smoothing my skirt as we walked.

"I'm sure that's it. So, who's excited to spend a week at a beautiful lodge in Vermont with her mom and her new husband?" Millie's over-exaggerated voice couldn't help but make me laugh, even though very little about my upcoming trip felt humorous.

I made a face at her. "I guess that's me—unless I get a better offer from my best friend to be the fifth wheel at her family's holiday celebrations."

Her face dropped. "You know you'd always be welcome with us. You're like a second mom to my kids, but I think you need to be with your family this Christmas."

"I just feel like avoiding my problems has served me really well these past few months. I'd hate to ruin that now."

"This will be good for you," Millie insisted as we reached the end of the hallway and turned right, leading us to yet another hallway. "I promise. You can't avoid your mom and Russ forever."

"I could sure give it my best effort." We walked a few moments in silence before I added, "But thanks again for telling me about the lodge. Even with my bad attitude, I know it will be better than going home."

She nudged my arm. "You're welcome. It comes highly recommended. I think it will be perfect for your family this year. Like a fresh start. Nobody has to step on anybody's toes or worry about blending traditions. Is your sister's family coming?"

"Yes, thank goodness."

The thought of spending time in my childhood home with another man in my dad's place had been more than my heart could take. When I explained that to Millie, she suggested a Christmas lodge in Vermont that she'd heard about from a friend. It seemed the perfect solution. There were separate cabins and plenty of holiday activities to distract us all. I was a little surprised my mom had agreed to the change, though. We were staunch traditionalists when it came to Christmas, but then again, that was before my dad passed away. For whatever reason, she seemed excited about Vermont, and I wasn't going to argue. Having my sister and her family there would be my other saving grace. Anytime I wasn't locked away in my own cabin, reading, I could play the doting aunt card, which would get me out of any unwanted family time—or at least keep me appropriately visible at gatherings but unable to converse much. The plan was perfect.

When we entered the auditorium, my eyes scanned the room. The faculty had spread out among the first six rows closest to the stage. We began to make our way down the aisle but were stopped by Pamela, the school secretary. Pamela had the heart and demeanor of someone meant for bigger things than a high school secretary. With her loud voice and excitable nature, I could easily see her being some sort of radio announcer or one of those women who MC a beauty pageant. She was originally from Texas, and her accent was her trademark, which meant she worked hard to keep it thick, even after ten years of living in the north. Her hair was as big as her heart, and both were bursting at the seams.

"Hey ya'll. We'll announce what's going on in a minute. For now, grab a cupcake, and then go sit with your department, okay?" She cheerfully motioned us forward and went to greet the teachers following behind us.

My stomach dropped. It might have been fine if my department included even one other person to serve as a buffer between me and Miles, but it was just the two of us.

"Don't leave me," I whispered to Millie, anxiously scanning the aisles. After the email incident from a month ago, Miles had been insufferable. He made himself very available at all times for a snide comment, a teasing reminder of my mistakes, and just...flaunting his...whatever.

"It must really be hard to be single and have to sit with the hottest attraction this school has ever known."

"Don't even start. He never lets me forget that."

She laughed, unrepentant as always.

"And it really doesn't say much for our school if *he's* the best we've got," I hissed. Not that it was important, but for the record, I used to be the hottest attraction. Me. And not all that long ago. I didn't mean that in a conceited way, but I was once the young, cool teacher who everybody planned their class schedule around. Me. And now, because I drew the line at turning my classroom into a donut-eating, *Harry Potter*-reading, student-stealing circus, I was a forgotten old has-been—at the ripe old age of twenty-five.

"Go sit by him. Hold his hand. Tell him he's pretty. And then call me later."

"Millie," I whispered frantically as she inched away from me.

She only laughed. "Go give those hams a little pat hello."

I made a very convincing gesture of threatening to cut her head off, but she only gave me her signature eyebrow waggle and waved as she made her way toward the art department. The traitor.

He was sitting in row six, behind the rest of the faculty, three seats in from the aisle. He leaned forward, talking languidly with the coaches, aka history teachers, sitting in front of him. They were laughing and conversing easily as I trudged toward them as though death was imminent. When I reached the aisle, Miles turned and looked at me. His eyes skittered down my body, landing on my torn tights. It figured that my flaw would be the first thing he noticed. My skin flushed with his gaze, which immediately set me on edge.

"Get in a fight over the Oxford comma again?" he asked, looking at me as though something amused him.

"I'm surprised you've heard of the Oxford comma," I replied pleasantly.

"Some of us take our grammar seriously in this school, Carrot Stick." He paused, making a face. "Nope, scratch that. I've tried out all the vegetables on you, but Celery Stick is just my favorite. It really rolls off the tongue."

"You haven't tried Olive yet," I said, sitting down warily,

keeping an empty seat between us, and smoothed out my skirt so that it covered my knee.

"Too on the nose."

"It's not even a vegetable."

"And yet, it's always on the veggie tray."

I blew out a breath. "So funny. I'll bet all ten fans on your author newsletter get a kick out of your impressive wit." Did I not mention that Miles was an author? He'd recently been picked up by a publishing house for his middle-grade adventure series.

When Miles laughed, his entire face showed it. From the laugh lines on his upper cheek to the golden inflection in his eyes, it was everywhere. If I liked him, I would have been proud of the effect of my words, but I didn't, so I just sat there…unaffected.

He leaned closer, his proximity almost begging me to allow just a quick scan of his strong jawline, long eyelashes, and annoyingly confident smile, but I stayed strong. Eyes on his. No need to stroke his already inflated ego.

"How'd you know I was up to ten? Don't tell me you're englishteacherbuttsdrivemenuts at Gmail?"

I racked my brain for a quick comeback, but all I could think of was Millie's wildly inappropriate ham comment, and I felt my face flush.

Mr. Piper, the middle-aged balding man in front of us who was paid to teach American history but was really just there so he could coach football, turned back to Miles, picking back up on the conversation my arrival must have interrupted. "Hey, did you ski any black diamonds this weekend?"

Miles turned his attention toward him with a friendly grin. "A couple. I was almost too chicken to do that run you were telling me about. I was white-knuckling it the whole way down."

A laugh exploded out of Mr. Piper as he turned back around in his seat. "Somehow, I doubt that."

A large shadow suddenly loomed over us, blocking one of the harsh auditorium lights. I turned, grateful for more interruptions which would mean I wouldn't be stuck talking to Miles—until I saw who it was: Kenneth Harvey, one of two biology teachers at Stanton. His light-brown hair was balding on top, which resulted in an impressive comb-over to the side. His fingernails were about half an inch too long for comfort. And he had breath that could kill a small rodent, which was perhaps fitting for a biology teacher. There had been rumors that someone once saw him eat something with a tail from the lab. I didn't let my mind or my up-chuck reflex go there at that moment, however, and forced myself to smile up at him.

"Hey there, Olive—er, uh…Miss Wilson." He threw me a shy grin. "You're looking nice today."

Did I mention that he had a massive crush on me? His eyes roamed curiously down my body, and I automatically folded my arms across my chest. He was a fairly harmless male species, and my discomfort stemmed mostly from him being socially clueless as to how long he allowed himself to ogle at a person.

Miles leaned across the empty seat, looking up at our visitor. "How's the thesis going, Harv?"

Harvey's attention shifted to Miles, and I felt my body relax, though it wasn't long before his eyes flitted back to mine.

"Well, that's what I came to talk with Miss Wilson about. Are you still okay to edit my thesis? You mentioned a couple of months ago that you wanted to."

My heart sunk deep into the abyss of horridness. I had completely forgotten about agreeing to help with his thesis. That was months ago. And for the record, I hadn't said I *wanted* to. I believe my exact words were, "Um…sure," which, looking back, I could definitely understand the confusion.

With some effort, I smiled up at him. "Sure. I can do that. That's great you got it finished."

He grinned. "Thanks. I was having so much fun doing all the research I almost didn't want it to end."

"What did you write about?" Miles asked, seeming way too happy to be a part of this conversation.

"The reproductive habits of the African dung beetle."

My face dropped.

"I know what you're thinking," Kenneth said, raising his hands up while he grinned at Miles and me.

"I doubt it," Miles answered cheerfully.

"You're thinking there's no way I could get a hundred pages of material on the topic, but you'd be very wrong. There are actually a few different species of dung beetle, and they all mate in different ways. Did you know that the dung beetle actually buries its eggs in dung?"

"Fascinating," Miles agreed while I shrunk further down in my seat.

"It really was." Looking at me, Kenneth said, "Anyway, I finally finished and put it on your desk before coming here. I guess it's a good thing we've got Christmas break coming up, so you'll probably have lots of extra time."

Yup. Extra time. I would definitely have that. Though, it would be hard deciding which was worse between spending Christmas with my mom and her new husband or the African dung beetle's mating habits.

"I left my number on the first page in case you needed to call me about anything...or meet up sometime," Kenneth said, staring at me hopefully.

Call him? Was it 1995? *If* I needed to ask him any questions—and I wouldn't—I would text him like a normal human of my era.

"I'll be out of town for most of the break, but I'll let you know if I have any problems," I said evasively.

The room was finally beginning to settle down. Pamela had moved onto the stage and was shifting boxes around near the microphone. Kenneth said thanks again and moved to sit in the middle of the room with the other science teachers.

We sat in silence for a moment. I held myself tense, begging Miles not to say anything for once in his life. But, of course, Miles could never NOT say something.

"One hundred pages all about the African dung beetle's mating habits," came the obnoxious voice beside me. "You're a lucky woman with a fellow like that."

"I think it will be fascinating," I lied, brushing a piece of lint off my skirt before staring up at the stage, begging Pamela to begin whatever the heck this meeting was.

"Out of curiosity, how much do you charge for edits?" His low voice filtered into my ear, and my defenses immediately rose.

"Nothing. He's a friend."

"Really? I had no idea you two were so close."

"Well, we are," I clipped with a tight smile. "I'm happy to help him."

Miles rubbed his face for a moment, looking toward the stage as though contemplating something. "Listen, it's not my business, but just so you know, that many pages of a book to an editor costs me at least a couple hundred bucks. If you're putting in the time, I think you should definitely be charging."

"I'm so happy to have your opinion on something that's, like you said, none of your business." I leaned in closer to him and batted my eyes for effect.

He chuckled. "You know…you're a lot nicer to everybody else but me. Why is that?"

Maybe it was because he stuck his nose in my business constantly. Or because he always made sure to tell me how I was living my life wrong. Thankfully, we were interrupted by

Pamela, who was now on the stage, rainbows beaming from her round face.

"You're all probably wondering why we called this staff meeting." She paused and looked out at her audience, likely expecting more than the blank stares she got, but she wasn't deterred. "Principal Harris and I were talking about how we appreciate you all so much. Every day, you show up and work so hard. The students here are so blessed..."

I zoned out after that. Pamela was a gusher. She oozed emotion. Not just emotion, but flowery emotion. Normally, that was great. She was a friend of mine, and her positive nature was usually contagious. But today, my patience was spent. Miles seemed to have zoned out as well. He leaned back in his seat with his head resting in the palm of his left hand. I'd bet if I listened closely enough, I'd hear some light snores eventually. He had to snore, right? He needed some sort of outer flaw to show the world he wasn't perfect. Since I was almost certain he had his eyes closed, I allowed my side eye to trail disdainfully across his long, folded body squished in the auditorium seat. It pained me to admit it, but those ripped jeans fit him like they would the mannequin at one of those hip teenage stores in the mall. A store that was too cool for me even when I was a teenager. He also wore a flannel shirt rolled at the sleeves. My eyes lingered on the veins in his forearm. Miles was tall and lanky, but I suddenly wondered if there were muscles hidden underneath all the flannel.

Alright, Olive...move along. I couldn't afford to be distracted by forearms if they were attached to Miles Taylor. Millie would die if she found out I'd even had the thought.

"Should I just take the shirt off?" Miles suddenly whispered.

My breath hitched, alarmed that he was not dozing off like I had originally thought. "Excuse me?"

"You looked like you were undressing me with your eyes. I could make it easier for you."

My mouth gaped open, very much aware of the pompous smile growing on his face—and my traitorous heartbeat.

"I'd rather not have nightmares tonight," I said, swallowing.

He leaned in close. "You look like you're sweating." He scanned my face, a hint of laughter in his eyes. "Flushed face." He scooped up my hand and held it in his palm before I could react. "Clammy hands. I'll bet your pulse is tumultuous."

My heart spiked as I yanked my hand out of his grasp and pushed a laughing Miles away. Immediately, I regretted the touch. I could now confirm there were definite muscles underneath the annoying remarks, and I didn't need to know that. I forced my brain to get back in the game.

"Tumultuous. That's a big word. Have you been sneaking into my classes again?"

"No, just reading your journal," he said, laughing.

I opened my mouth to reply but caught only air. He had won this round, and it hurt a little. As if he knew that, he flashed me an irritating smile. I was happy to report that the lines that crinkled around his eyes did nothing to soften me toward him. I turned back toward the stage, tucking my hair behind my ear as nonchalantly as possible.

"The school board, as well as Mr. Harris and I, tried to look at all of our wonderful staff's excellent contributions over the past year," Pamela was saying, her bright face animated. "And we wanted to honor you all. So, for the first year ever, we are doing a Teacher's Appreciation award ceremony!"

She looked like she wanted us to clap. It was almost 4 pm on the last day of school before our Christmas break. We just wanted to go home. However, when Miles joined the handful of gracious souls giving a few half-hearted claps, I clapped as well.

"We'll start with the art department. Come on up here, art department." Pamela waved her hands excitedly. Millie and her colleagues stood up and made a show of rushing toward the stage in mock excitement.

I slunk down in my seat and began making a mental list of the things I needed to do before leaving for Vermont the next morning. I had to clean my house, do one last load of laundry, pack, buy a new bottle of Tylenol, find a red pen for Kenneth's thesis, water my plants, wrap my Christmas presents…

"What are you hoping to get?" Miles's voice infiltrated my thoughts. *"Most organized? Friendliest doormat?"*

My toes curled, but I forced myself to smile, even as his burn began leaving its mark. "Better than *Easiest A,* which is what you'll probably get."

His brow furrowed. "What?"

"Aren't you planning to read *Harry Potter* in class? Nobly teaching the kids everything about a book they already know?"

"I'm using it to study story structure, Celery Stick. Not to read it to them in class."

My reply (which was actually non-existent) was thankfully interrupted when Pamela called the English department up to the stage. We both stood and slid out of our aisle. When we reached the stairs leading up to the stage, Miles motioned for me to go before him. I did so, putting on the careful mask of pleasantness across my face as I turned toward the crowd.

"The English department, as you all know, had a big change this year," Pamela said into the microphone as she watched us approach. Her voice was animated and robust as if she were entertaining millions instead of a crowd of tired teachers being kept past their normal school hours. "We welcomed a brand-new teacher into our midst this past March. He stepped in and took over while our dear Mr. Grady completed his cancer treatments, and we loved him so much we decided to keep him. Miles Taylor has been a wonderful addition to our school. The reviews from the students as well as the staff have all been glowing." Pamela turned and looked at me. "Isn't that right, Olive?"

The smile on my face dropped for a moment before I rallied

again, giving the audience two semi-sarcastic, enthusiastic thumbs up. Millie's gaze found mine from the audience, and even though she looked like she was very much enjoying herself, I still clung to her like a lifeline. Miles stopped next to me, his shoulder brushing up against mine. He would have definitely appreciated the statement, and I kept waiting for him to nudge my arm, but he never did.

Pamela checked her paper at the podium and bent over, fumbling around in a large box full of trophies, looking for one in particular.

"Any last wagers?" Miles whispered, keeping his gaze forward. "Five bucks yours has something to do with forcing *Jane Eyre* down the throats of impressionable young high school boys."

"Five bucks yours is for *almost* reaching the maturity level of your students. Did I hear that you had a philosophical discussion on *The Terminator* in one of your classes last week? Was that teaching the structure of story as well?"

His mouth twitched as he leaned toward me ever so slightly. "It was the first *Terminator*. Arnold Schwarzenegger. Very classy stuff."

"I'm terrified of the minds you're corrupting."

"My guy blows people up. Yours keeps his wife chained in the attic. So far, we are equals."

For some reason, unbeknownst to me, my lips seemed to want to smile at that. "So far, we are equals," I repeated slowly. "Did you just quote *Pride and Prejudice*?"

A spot of color formed on his face, and I could see the sheepish grin beginning to appear when Pamela stood up, a trophy in her hand. "Okay, first up, Miles. From his interactive classes, to the way he scales rocks and jumps out of planes like it's no big deal, and the fact that he's a real live published author…the kids just love you, and so do we, which is why we've given you the Coolest Teacher Award." With excited arms flailing, she motioned for him to step forward to take his trophy.

After he accepted his award with over-emphasized smiles and laughter, he scooted back to my side, bumping into me ever so slightly.

"You owe me five bucks," he whispered.

"I'll pay you *ten* to stop talking." I kept my face benign. Pleasant. So, Miles just won an award for being the coolest teacher. Great. Good for him. But for some reason, my body wanted to sink to the floor and disappear. It was all so stupid. Awards for doing our jobs. I didn't need a cheesy trophy as validation that I was a good teacher, even though, apparently, kids were now exiting my classes in droves.

"Okay, Olive, your turn. Come on up here!" Pamela looked back, motioning me to join her at the podium. I strode forward, a plastic smile on my face as I waited.

"Now, I can't count how many times I've asked Olive for writing advice over the past year. Every letter I have to send to the school board, I run it by her red pen, that's for sure. I know she's helped many of you, as well. Her grasp of language is unmatched, which is why we've deemed her the Grammar Queen!" She held the trophy up as if she had just announced the winner of the Super Bowl.

My face felt like a balloon deflating. There was a collective hush in the audience before Millie began giving me a pity clap, the rest of the audience joining in soon after.

Do. Not. Cry.

I pinched myself hard under the elbow, hoping to shock my system into not crying. Smiling numbly, I accepted the trophy with a mumbled, "Thanks."

Miles and I made to leave the stage when Pamela stopped us both.

"Hold on! We need to grab a picture of you two for the school website."

We stopped moving and turned to face Pamela as she fumbled with the camera on her phone. I shifted my weight and dared a glance toward Miles. Brown eyes tucked behind long dark lashes met my gaze before I looked away. My chest tightened.

Pamela raised the phone up in front of her, looking at us through her screen. "Okay, squeeze in a bit closer. Yes, that's great! Miles put your arm around Olive. There you go. Just like that. Hold your trophies out in front and...smile."

TWO

"I care for myself. The more solitary, the more friendless, the more unsustained I am, the more I will respect myself."
Charlotte Brontë - *Jane Eyre*

GRAMMAR QUEEN.

It was fine. Not a big deal. I followed rules, tried to help everyone, happened to be good at grammar, and this was my reward. My trophy. What I'll be remembered for.

Most of the teachers mingled in the auditorium after the awards. Miles tried a couple of times to speak to me, but I cut him short. I flew from the room the second Pamela relinquished the mic. Not in a weird way that would make anybody think I was upset, but in a way that suggested I had places to be, like any other busy but emotionally balanced person. I pasted on a smile, pretending to look at my watch, waved to a few friends, and acted like I was headed home to put my new trophy on the mantel.

I didn't have to be the favorite. When I set about getting my teaching degree, I originally thought I'd make a great second-grade teacher. But I fell in love with English. Reading and literature had become passions, and I knew that I needed to teach them. After my dad's passing, I had thrown myself into the work, craving the distraction it provided. I found my rhythm, and the students responded to my efforts. It was the best kind of feeling when your hard work began to pay off. My kids were studying the classics like *Jane Eyre* and *Taming of the Shrew* and, for the most part, enjoying it—even the boys, thank you very much.

At least...I had thought they were.

I didn't become a teacher to win popularity contests. That wasn't the problem. But something about this cut deeply. My job was the one thing I'd had in my life that brought me an escape. Helping teenagers discover the joy of literature and connecting with them over that shared love had kept me going this past year on those days when I didn't want to get out of bed. I thought I'd been shaping lives, at least to some small degree. But Grammar Queen? It felt like a slap in the face.

I needed to clean something.

I stopped in the teacher's lounge to grab my half-eaten lunch bag from the fridge and frowned at the crumb-topped tables and dirty dishes piled in the sink. For some reason, unbeknownst to me, there was a group of older teachers, all male, who refused to eat their lunches in their Tupperware or take-out boxes like the rest of us. They preferred to use a plate from the school's 1960's collection in the cupboard, completely bypassing the stack of paper plates I purchased and put in front of said cupboard. Then, they would either finish and leave their plate in the sink for "later" or cover their half-eaten scraps in plastic wrap and place them in the fridge where they were left to die and grow fur until somebody (me) couldn't stand it any longer and washed them. Glancing back at the still-empty hallway, I hesitated. I needed to get out of here, but my hands itched to do something. To make something right again. I didn't want to get caught by anybody, but maybe I could just wipe the counters down really quick.

Yes. Just the counters.

I was forearm-deep in dirty dishwater at the sink when Miles strode into the room.

He stopped when he saw me and raised his eyebrow. "What are you doing?"

By this time, I had worked through a sufficient amount of my feelings by way of plunging and scrubbing. So, I looked down at the plate of crusted-over sweet-and-sour chicken in my hands and then smiled sweetly back at Miles. "Why don't you give me your best guess."

"Taking out some deeply hidden aggression on dishes that you shouldn't be washing." He strode to the refrigerator and took out a small lunch cooler.

I ignored the jab. "If I don't wash them, nobody will."

"But that's not your problem," he said, leaning against the counter.

I gave him a frozen smile. "If everybody had an attitude like that, nothing would ever get done. Some of us have to put in some elbow grease. It's how the world turns."

Turning back to my scrubbing, I tried to ignore him, which was a little hard to do when he just stood there, watching me. Fine. I was happy to play this game.

"Congratulations on your award, by the way. Are you going to make a special shelf for it?" My attempt at sarcastic humor fell flat, even to my ears.

Still, he said nothing. I rinsed off the dish and placed it on the drying rack. He was still looking at me, but his eyes seemed deep in thought, which was, honestly, more unnerving than him just criticizing me. I reached for another plate.

"You know, Olive, the awards don't mean anything. Nobody

voted. It's just for Pamela and Harris to feel good about themselves, more than anything."

My fingers dropped the plate in my hands, and it splashed into the water, sending droplets all across the front of my shirt. He called me Olive, maybe for the very first time besides our initial meeting nine months earlier. I wasn't sure he even realized that he had.

"I know," I said as I grabbed the plate once more. "I'm not upset about anything."

He nodded his head toward the sink, where I was attacking the dish with hostile fury. "I can see that."

"I'm serious." I slowed to a carefree scrub before rinsing the dish and placing it on the drying rack next to the others, then picked up the washcloth hanging on the faucet and began wiping the counter. Maybe if I said it slowly and with conviction, he would believe me. Most people didn't want to dig too deep; that usually just left everyone feeling uncomfortable. Not Miles. He was watching me with his arms folded like a puzzle he seemed vaguely interested in piecing together.

"Well, that's good because I almost feel a moral obligation to contest the whole thing. If I showed them the love note you sent me, they'd take away your trophy for sure."

I gave him a scowl, which only made an annoying grin spread slowly across his face. "That was a casual email to a friend, not an English paper. And I was in a hurry when I wrote it."

He went on as if he hadn't heard me. "When I saw that our very own Grammar Queen didn't even know the difference between the possessive 'your' and the contraction, I felt a deep sense of worry for the education of our students."

"It was probably spell check. It's always getting it wrong." I wiped the counter, boldly moving closer to force him backward to wipe in front of where he stood. He chuckled and took a step back.

"Whatever you say. I'm not the one that has the whole school fooled."

Ironic. He most certainly did have the whole school fooled.

I opened the refrigerator door and wanted to cry at all the plates and old Tupperware containers filled with leftovers. I knew for a fact most had been in the fridge for weeks. Why were people like this at work? It was disgusting.

Miles grabbed my arm, moved me aside, and pushed the fridge door closed. "You're not cleaning in there."

Extracting myself from his grip, I responded with a mature, "I can do whatever I want." Suddenly, I wanted to clean the whole room. I'd clean all night if that was what it took.

He looked at me incredulously. "Give me two minutes, and I'll go to the office, get on the intercom, and tell everyone to come grab their crap from the kitchen and wash their own dishes. It's not your job."

"I don't mind doing it."

"Why?"

I shrugged. "It's a little game I like to play. First I imagine that every dish has your face on it, and then I get to half drown it in water."

I didn't have to look directly at Miles to know that his mouth lifted in his trademark (annoying) grin. "I knew you liked me, deep down."

"How did you get that from what I just said?"

"You're thinking about me while doing mundane tasks. I think my heart just melted."

Miles Taylor was looking at me as though something amused him, and it made me want to claw his eyes out.

"Want to know what I think?" he asked.

"Nope."

"You're a martyr."

I folded my arms as I glared up at him. "I like things clean, so sue me."

He shook his head, mirroring my body language as we leaned our hips against the counter, facing off. "Just like in the staff meetings when suddenly you've been assigned five more tasks than everybody else, and you act like it's Christmas morning. Or when Harvey asks you to edit his master's thesis for free in all your spare time. Or when Davis stole your idea for the spring project. And you just smile through everything."

"You smile all the time," I accused, fully aware that that particular burn sucked.

"Yeah, I'm a happy guy. But that's probably because I'm not bending over and letting the whole school spank me while I do all their homework."

"Ew."

He laughed, which only made me angrier. I leaned closer, my fingers clenched with fire. "I help out because I'm a team player. And you don't know anything about me."

"Whose fault is that?"

We were interrupted as Mr. Johnson, from the music department, slid into the room. Where Kenneth Harvey was greasy and awkward, Jason Johnson was smooth and slick. He wore a suit like a car salesman, laughed too much, and could talk himself out of just about anything. I took a step back from Miles.

Jason peered at us both, amused, as he slowly raised his arms in the air. "Whoa, where's the fire? I thought the English department settled their differences over books and a cup of tea."

There was a pause in the air as we each put down our weapons to face a common enemy.

"We're fresh out of tea," Miles countered, his eyes never leaving my face.

I smiled and added, "We're just talking." As much as it pained me, I kept my gaze focused on Johnson's gray tie and his well-fitted, monochromatic suit, very aware of another pair of eyes watching me.

Jason noticed his dishes on the drying rack. "Oh, thanks, Olive. I've been meaning to come down and wash those, but I've just been so busy." He strode toward the fridge and took out a couple more half-eaten plates covered in plastic wrap. Checking his watch with a flourish, he turned to me and motioned to the plates in his hand with a sheepish smile—one he probably thought was charming, but it gave me the distinct urge to punch his face. "I hate to ask, but I've got to run and pick up my wife—her car is in the shop—or else I'd wash these myself right now."

I kept waiting for him to ask. But he didn't ask me anything. He just held his containers with a helpless shrug and stared imploringly at me, waiting for me to offer. "I just don't want to leave it for two weeks like this."

"It will only take two minutes, Johnson. I'll bet your wife would be excited to hear you were doing your dishes," Miles said, his voice a quiet warning.

"She's already waiting for me or else I would. Listen, if you can't get to it, no worries. Hopefully, nothing too green will grow on them while we're gone."

I shot Miles a glance. As much as I didn't want to play Jason's maid, I certainly didn't need Miles thinking he was coming to my rescue. My smile wavered only slightly, knowing Miles was watching incredulously as my hands moved to accept Jason's dirty plates and Tupperware.

"Sure. I can do that," I found myself saying.

"You're a gem, Olive." Jason moved toward the doorway, pausing to face us again. "And hey, congratulations on your award. I keep meaning to have you edit a few things for me. I've been dabbling in writing, too." He sent a meaningful glance over at Miles, who gave him nothing in return but a passive stare.

"Welp, have a good Christmas! Thanks again, Olive." He strode out of the room, leaving a tension-filled tsunami in his wake.

"Such a team player," Miles murmured, his disappointed eyes

roaming over my face. I burned hot with indignation. I wasn't sure why it rankled more that he was disappointed in me than actually doing Johnson's stupid dishes.

"I'm happy to help him." I lifted my chin and placed his dishes on the counter.

"This isn't the first time he's done this to you, is it?"

I said nothing as I opened the Tupperware and immediately gagged as the smell of musty split-pea soup filled the air.

Miles's warm body brushed up against mine as he plucked the container out of my hands, closed the lid, and stuffed all of Johnson's food back into the fridge.

The smell had taken my nose hostage, and for several long seconds, I stood over the sink, willing myself not to throw up.

"Why do you say yes to everything?"

"Why do you feel like you have the right to ask me personal questions?" I asked, standing up from my crouched position over the sink and striding toward the front door—away from Miles.

"I don't know. I figured us working together in the same department the past nine months might have warranted a personal question or two."

"Nope." Almost to the door.

"Storming out after an argument? You're such a cliché, Celery Stick."

"I'm not storming out," I clipped back as I walked with light and not-at-all-angry steps down the hallway. "Have a good Christmas!" I yelled as my parting shot.

I ground my teeth as I marched down the hallway, pausing only to give Mr. Young, the social studies teacher, a friendly hello and ask about his children's excitement for Christmas. When I reached the door to my room, it was all I could do not to slam it behind me. I took a deep breath and leaned against the closed door, trying to calm my nerves.

He's not worth the drama.

He wasn't. Miles was a shiny new object. That was it. Was this how Mr. Grady felt when I showed up here two years ago?

No.

Grady was beloved. He had old-man wisdom and wit and decades of experience under his belt. I'd never been any sort of a threat to him. He was practically an institution at Stanton and might very well have stuck around until the day he died if he hadn't been diagnosed with cancer last fall. He'd gotten sick around November and by February had to drop out of the rest of the school year for chemo treatments, leaving a large void in his place—unfillable, in my opinion. Thankfully, unlike my dad, his treatments were successful and his cancer was officially in remission, but instead of coming back to work, he retired early and was currently on a Caribbean cruise with his wife.

When the school board finally found someone to take Mr. Grady's place in March, I'd been conflicted in my feelings but was determined to be welcoming. Since Miles had arrived in the middle of the semester, I graciously offered advice and lesson plans to help get him caught up. He politely listened, took my plans, but then proceeded to do nothing with them. Instead of reading *Jane Eyre,* he chose *Oliver Twist* and then bought his students' interest with cheap gimmicks like movie clips and donuts. Which was fine. Really. It suited him better. To each his own. I couldn't tell you exactly why it nettled so badly. Maybe it was the constant jabs he threw at me about *Jane Eyre* or *Pride and Prejudice,* (my other beloved piece of literature). But still, throughout all this, I attempted to keep my face passive and cheerful. Helpful. Except, he clearly didn't need my help.

FINE.

I could be the classic to his modern era. We could make it work. But I was finding that I couldn't compete with his modern pop culture. Mr. Grady and I had a similar understanding with teaching English. We wanted to make the classics relatable. There was so much to learn from history, even historical fiction, and we wanted to teach it. But *Jane Eyre* was having a hard time competing with wizards to a modern audience.

When I first met Miles Taylor, I thought he was cute. There. I said it. At that first hello, our relationship had all the beginnings of a perfect romantic-comedy plot. We were both under thirty, we both loved English, and we taught at the same school. Seriously, I was waiting for Hallmark to call me for some insider info.

Unfortunately, THAT was where our similarities ended.

I packed my school bag, adding Harvey's one-hundred-page thesis to the weight, and locked up my room. I couldn't help but think that for all the ways I buried emotion in my life, it flew out of me like a sprinkler in the grass on a summer day whenever Miles looked at me wrong.

Which happened daily.

THREE

"Angry people are not always wise."
Jane Austen - *Pride and Prejudice*

I WALKED INTO MY MESSY HOUSE, FLIPPED MY SHOES OFF BY THE doorway, and dropped my purse and keys on the small table by the door. Hanging my coat on the rack, I collapsed onto the couch. For all my prim and proper at work, home was where I let my hair down. While I kept a clean house, it was messy. Lived in. There were my morning dishes in the sink (okay, one bowl and a coffee mug), my laundry piled up on the far side of the couch (one load, which I was planning to pack most of tonight), and on the kitchen counter, next to the sliding door leading into the small backyard, sat a pile of mail and magazine clutter (a pizza coupon and a magazine I wanted to leaf through before throwing away). If I went into the bathroom, I was pretty sure my towel was still on the floor.

Take that, Miles. It was pure chaos in here. I could handle mess. I helped out at school not because I couldn't stand the mess, but because I *wanted* to. Like a decent human who cared about other people.

I fought with Miles in my head for a bit longer, and in my relaxed state, all the things I should have said came flying out—genius zinger after zinger. Let's just say, he would have felt like crap after I was done. Eventually, I forced myself to think of something else. From my position on the couch, I stared contentedly at the two floor-to-ceiling bookshelves that were on either side of the fireplace in my living room, filled with classics from Jane Austen to Charles Dickens to Charlotte Bronte. It was hard to describe just how much the words in those books had taught, comforted, and inspired me throughout the past few years as a teacher and during the dark times of my dad's death.

Eventually, I peeled myself up off the couch to microwave a Hot Pocket for a quick dinner. Pulling out the rest of my half-eaten bag of salad, I ended up with a well-rounded meal of cardboard carbohydrates, imitation dairy, and lettuce drenched in ranch dressing. I ate my dinner standing over the kitchen sink, looking out the window at my snow-filled backyard. Moving to Stanton two years earlier, I had planned on finding an apartment to rent. But on the way to scout out an apartment complex, I passed a single-level, honey-butter-yellow house with painted blue shutters that sat quietly at the end of a cul-de-sac, with a For Sale sign in the yard.

There was nothing to decide. The price was good, and my credit score was excellent, and thirty days later, I was unpacking boxes in my new home. Instantly, those four walls became my oasis. My safe space. The place where, even when parents pass away, or moms get remarried, or mentors leave the school, I had somewhere that the day could fall away. The two neighbors next to me were of the elder-grandparent variety. They were also a safe space in my life. No drama whatsoever. Over the fence, in the summertime, you could often find us chatting about our gardens, the books we read, the disrespectful youth of today, and how much we all appreciated an early bedtime. We understood each other perfectly.

I spent the next hour packing for Vermont. Though my mom still lived in New Hampshire in the house I grew up in, it was no longer my home. It was the house my mom now shared with Russ. Which meant that the one time I had been home since the wedding, it was Russ in my dad's easy chair, watching TV. Russ at the head of the dinner table. It was Russ sleeping in my dad's bed with my mom. Hurt burned in my chest until I grabbed the remote on my bedside table. I turned the TV on and was soon sucked away by a medical drama.

The forecast on my phone made it clear that I would basically be a human popsicle for a week, so I packed a couple pairs of thermal underwear (a staple in the northeastern states) and clothes with lots of layers. Though, if I were honest, I mostly planned to bunker down in my cabin, alone, most of the week. I threw my Kindle on top. There were benefits to being single. I'd have my own cabin, and everybody else would be so wrapped up in their kids and family and...new husbands, they'd hardly notice I wasn't there.

My phone buzzed on the table.

"Hey, Chlo," I said to my sister, Chloe, when I picked up, folding another sweater neatly into my suitcase.

"Ivy, don't pull your sister's hair. No. Stop." I pulled my ear back from my phone as the muffled sound of a child's wail pierced the airwaves between me and my sister. "Nope, honey. We don't act like that. I'm putting you in the time-out chair." Ivy's little voice became louder before Chloe spoke into the phone again. "Sorry. Of course World War III broke out the second I pressed your number."

"You're fine. How are my favorite twins today?" By this time, I had moved into my bathroom, cleaning and wiping down the counters with the phone pressed against my cheek.

"Nope, honey, you sit there until the timer goes off. You're in time out." Once she had put out the fire, my sister's focus turned back to me. "They're crazy today. They could really use some Aunt Olive time."

I smiled. My nieces were three, mispronounced everything, threw down a tantrum like a boss, and had my heart wrapped around their sticky little fingers. "I can't wait. When are you guys getting there?" My sister and her husband also lived in New Hampshire, a few streets over from my mom and Russ.

"We're leaving as soon as we get going in the morning. Ben doesn't have to work tomorrow. How about you?"

I stared into my closet and wondered if I should bring snow pants, but I couldn't think of a scenario where I would be doing anything that involved me playing in the snow. I could help the twins build a snowman in jeans. Experience taught me that they wouldn't last that long in the cold. I left the pants in the bin at the bottom of my closet. If one didn't have the right equipment, one couldn't participate.

"I'll leave late morning. It will take me a couple hours, I think, depending on the roads. How are you feeling?" Chloe had just told the family she was three months pregnant and, from what I gathered, was definitely still in the woes of first trimester nausea and sickness.

"It's a little better in the afternoons, but for some reason, morning and evenings are the worst. This baby is trying to kill me." She sighed into the phone. "You all ready for this week?"

"No."

She paused for a moment. "It's going to be weird without Dad. And not being at home this year."

"Yeah," was all I could say without breaking. My mind went back to last year, when Christmas morning was spent crowded around my dad's bedside because he was too sick to move to the family room. We even moved the Christmas tree to his bedroom. That was probably why I couldn't stomach the thought of putting up my own tree this year.

Chloe sighed. "So, I just talked to Mom. Do you want the bad news or the really bad news first? And it's actually the same thing."

I groaned, grabbing all my toiletries I'd need for the week from my bathroom drawers and dropping them onto my bed. "No news. I'm not interested in any news if it relates to Mom and her new husband." In our own private circles, we referred to Russ as the new husband.

"You might want to be warned of this one."

"UGH. What?"

"You know the Fosters?"

"The family that's been our neighbors our entire lives? Yeah. I've heard of them."

"You can cut the attitude. Trust me, I am doing you a favor right now."

Instantly, the tension in my shoulders reappeared. "I'm sorry. What?"

"Turns out…Mom and Russ invited them to come with us this week."

I groaned.

"That's not the bad part."

My breath caught. "Don't even say—"

"Glenn's here for the holidays, and from the impression I got talking with Mom this morning…she and Virginia Foster are planning this week to be a romantic re-awakening of sorts for the two of you."

"Shut your face."

"I believe the schedule is for you two to fall in love by Day 3 and start having babies within the next six months."

"That math doesn't even make sense."

"I know."

I sank onto my bed in shock as dread began dripping through my veins like an IV.

Chloe went on. "I tried to tell her that it was over between you two and that you have no interest in him, but Mom's pretty convinced that you ruined your life by breaking up with him all those years ago."

The more she spoke, the more weight her revelation put on me. Glenn Foster was going to be at the lodge. All week long. Unfiltered panic began to race through every vein in my body.

No.

NO.

I had my whole week figured out. I was going to fake it all. Smiles. Hugs. Friendliness. And then I'd go back home and cry my eyes out. I did NOT need the added complication of an old flame (and not even a real flame, more like a match you strike once before you realize you'd rather just freeze) trying to make a move. And he would. He never got over the fact that I had broken up with him. I could honestly see the week going one of two ways: him following me around, making sure I was aware of all the things I had missed out on while not being with him, or acting too cool and aloof to talk to me at all, which wouldn't last long if our mothers were behind our supposed reconciliation. Either scenario had too much Glenn Foster for my taste.

"Say something," Chloe said.

"I have no words."

"Alright, plan B. We find you a hot lumberjack at the lodge. There are going to be other families there. Odds are somebody hot and single will be around. Give Glenn some competition."

"This is not one of your Hallmark movies. Hot single men are never where you need them. Also, are there still legit lumberjacks living in the world today?"

"Mmmhhhmmm," was the only dreamy reply my romantic sister could muster.

"We've got to get you reading different books. I'll bring a Jane Austen for you tomorrow."

"No. Listen to my latest I just finished. Even you'd love this one. This hot, reclusive lumberjack rescues a beautiful woman he found in the woods. She'd hurt her leg and lost her memory. So obviously, he had to take her back to his secluded cabin to help her heal and figure out who she was. It was the right thing to do."

"I'm sorry. You're right. It does sound like an American classic."

"I'll text you the name of it. You're gonna love the cover."

"Please tell me his shirt's unbuttoned."

"You'll have to wait and see. Hopefully, we'll find the real thing when we get there." She paused, then added soberly, "I just…I'm not sure what to do about Glenn."

My stomach began to tighten. I did not want to be set up, and I really didn't need an unwanted ex-boyfriend hanging around with my family all week. I would soon be seeing my mother cuddled up with somebody who wasn't my dad. I'd have to act normal around Russ all the while keeping my chin up and my smile in place so as not to ruin Christmas for everyone. I couldn't handle the thought of some awkward setup. Not when I was just trying to survive the week with a smile still attached. Trying to keep my emotions civil would be a full-time job.

So, on a whim, I pulled out something I thought might save me…a harmless white lie.

"As good as a sexy lumberjack sounds, I've actually been seeing somebody the past few weeks, so I think Glenn and his mom might be disappointed."

A long pause and then, "Wait, WHAT?" An explosion of excited words burst across the telephone from where she stood in New Hampshire and where I stood in Stanton. I pulled the phone away to save my eardrums. "When was this?! Why didn't you tell me? What does he look like? OH MY GOSH, Olive, this is HUGE!"

"It's all pretty new." *Extremely new. So new it's almost not even worth mentioning ever again.* "It's not a big deal. I promise."

"Tell me everything," Chloe demanded. "Unless you're lying. Wait. Are you lying? This sounds too convenient."

I hesitated. If I was going to sell this, Chloe couldn't know the truth. She and my mom were too close. Chloe would accidentally spill the beans, and I'd be tricked under the mistletoe with Glenn before I could stop it. No. I'd tell Chloe the truth after Christmas, when my imaginary lover got kicked to the proverbial curb. And she would understand. Actually, now that I thought about it, she *had* to understand. She owed me one. She lied to me for three weeks about dating Dirk McCoy in high school. So...yeah. That didn't make me sound petty at all.

"I'm not lying," I lied.

"Okay, hold on. I'm putting on a show for the kids so I can listen uninterrupted in my bedroom. First love, yay!"

My eyes widened. "No, Chlo, I'm not in love. I just...we've gone out. Like on dates and stuff." I stood and began pacing the floor, stopping at my chest of drawers near the window.

"Is he your boyfriend?"

My mind quickly did the math. Casual dates did not a boyfriend make. What was the saying again? Date as many guys as you wanted, but kiss only one? (Or in my case, none. A very big, fat none.) If I was going to play the fake-other-man card, I would need to put a title on it.

"Yup. He's my boyfriend."

"Who is he? How did you meet him?" This time, her voice had lowered a few octaves. Much less squealing and maybe a smidge suspicious? Like she was sniffing around and smelling something that didn't quite add up. I needed to add a few irons to the fire.

"It's all happened fast. The boyfriend title is…new. But I really like him."

"Who is he? What's his name?"

My hands stilled in my underwear drawer. Shoot. Who *was* he?

I racked my brain to come up with a name. Some name. A name. There were none. NO names. I could think of no guy names. My brain was an empty sheet of paper. Men didn't exist in this world. My life was at my school, and at school there was only…

No.

But suddenly my brain latched onto the name Miles and wouldn't let go.

NO.

Miles. Miles. Miles. Miles.

Mr. Grady! My brain detected another male human. He was in his seventies, but it was fine. I just needed a name, and his name was Ralph!

Ralph. I opened my mouth to say the name, but the word refused to release its death grip on my tongue. Even though men no longer existed in my brain, I knew for certain that Ralph was not a name from my generation.

"OLIVE. Spill."

"It's Miles!"

My heart rate slowed as the pressure of providing a name melted off my shoulders. Though I did feel lighter, my body was immediately filled with remorse. I hated lying to my sister, especially since this type of news had the potential to put her over the moon in the happiness department. It also felt a tiny bit disloyal to use Miles in this way. Not because I liked him, but because I *didn't*. I was disappointed in myself that I had sunk so low as to use him like that. Oh well, he would never know. And Chloe didn't know him, so hopefully it—

"Wait? From your school? The hot new teacher you can't stand?!"

My grip on the phone tightened. Had I told her about him?

"How did you know?"

"You complain about him all the time."

I *so* do not. Do I? Okay, maybe a *few* horrible things said in passing, but nothing anybody should have remembered.

"How'd you know he was hot?" I knew for certain that I would have *never* told her that.

"I don't know, I guess I just assumed. With how you talked about him, I think I just filled in the blank in my mind. So are you for real? This is CRAZY! How did you two start going out? I thought you were never going to date somebody you work with ever again. And WHY didn't you tell me?!"

Her intrusive questions swirled in the air as my brain attempted to pick one to answer. *This* was why people warned you about lying—even little white lies told for the simple reason of saving your sanity. Already, my sanity was null and void, and now my anxiety was through the roof. Maybe I could backtrack.

"I'm just kidding. It's not...it's a different Miles."

"There can't be more than one *Miles* in Stanton."

"Why are you more apt to believe me when I told you that it was Miles, the guy I didn't like from my school?"

"I'm not saying I believe you yet. But please. You liked him. You wouldn't whine so much about him if he didn't get under your skin."

I made a face in the mirror across from me. "That is NOT—"

"Tell me how it happened!" she interrupted. "Did he ask you out first? I had a feeling he liked you. Guys don't tease like that unless—"

"He just asked me out to coffee one day after school. To talk about a mutual student." My eyes widened as more words expelled from my lips. "And there you go. Simple. I didn't want to make it a thing with everyone until it was more sure." There. That sounded pretty good.

"And what about your no-dating-anybody-you-work-with rule?"

"That's why we're being so casual and taking it extremely slow. I don't want to relive the whole Brian fiasco." Correction. I would *never* relive the whole Brian fiasco. Now I was kicking myself that I'd used Miles's name and that, at some point, I had told my sister about him. *UGH. Bad Olive.*

I moved all the toiletries from my bed into the pockets of my suitcase. The truth was, I wasn't against dating. I wanted to date people. A hot, flannel-wearing lumberjack sounded great to me. But not this week. And not Glenn Foster.

"So anyway. There you have it. My dating life in a nutshell. I guess one of us should mention this to Mom so she can warn the Fosters before they get there."

"Mention to Mom that you're suddenly dating somebody that nobody knew about? Somebody who nobody will see during this trip? And that your relationship is so abnormally casual and the timing is just perfect enough that it doesn't sound quite real?"

"Well, maybe not with that tone."

She snorted.

Her voice was now riddled with wariness. But I had made my bed, and I now had to jump in.

"Listen. You don't have to believe me, but I am dating Miles Taylor." The words came off my tongue with frightening ease, but it still hurt to say them out loud.

She spat out a dry chuckle. "Fine. I'll tell Mom so hopefully it will get Glenn off your back, but I will need to see your eyes when you tell me this is real. If I still feel like something isn't quite right, and if you're lying to me, so help me, you'll pay for it."

"I just got chills."

"Thank you. And when I say pay for it, I mean by way of a sexy mountain man that I *will* find in Vermont. And when I find him, you have to go on a date with him."

"Not when I'm dating Miles." I would now take this to the grave if I had to.

Chloe snorted. "I want to believe you, and I'm halfway there, but listen, Ben just got home, so I'm going to go talk to him, but we will definitely be revisiting this tomorrow."

I smiled. "Fine." I had twenty-four hours to come up with some details. And then lock myself in my cabin.

When I got off the phone, I sat on my bed in a stupefied silence. It was weird thinking about Miles like that, even if he would never find out. This was a lie. And lying was wrong. But this was also a lie that wouldn't hurt anybody else. If anything, it would save me. I'd lean into this idea of a boyfriend back at home to get me through the next six days and get everybody off my back. I'd wait a couple weeks and then tell Chloe. She'd forgive me because she really did owe me one. Then we'd all move on.

Miles would never find out.

FOUR

"My life is a perfect graveyard of buried hopes."
L.M. Montgomery - *Anne of Green Gables*

THE NEXT MORNING, THE SPOTLESS TRUNK OF MY GRAY HONDA Civic held my luggage, books, and an extra pair of winter boots. I slammed the trunk closed and ran back toward my house to lock the front door, with my hood covering my face as the snow pelted down. The next house I bought in upstate New York WOULD have a garage. That was the only downfall to my otherwise steal of a house deal. Once everything was locked and secured for the week, I tucked myself inside my car and slowly made my way toward the highway.

My phone rang as my tires trudged through the slushy mess of snow on the road. I briefly glanced at the ID on my phone and debated answering. Eventually, I flipped the phone on speaker.

"Hey, Mom."

"You're dating someone?!" her voice demanded into the phone.

Well done, Chloe.

"Why didn't you tell me?" she continued. "Chloe said it's been going on for weeks."

A bolt of regret struck me as my mom obviously seemed crushed by the news. Since she had gotten remarried, the frequency of our calls had dwindled in number, which was a far cry from speaking two to three times a day the past year.

"To be fair, I didn't tell anyone." Including myself.

She made a noise that sounded like my excuse did nothing to alleviate the hurt I'd caused.

I checked the rearview mirror for cars as I inched my way through the tiny town of Peru just north of Stanton on my way up to the northeastern tip of the state before I could cross the snow-covered Lake Champlain and enter Vermont.

"I'm sorry, Mom. I just wanted to test it out a bit before I said something."

Guilt seeped into the cracks of my resolve to see this through. Just because I could talk myself into thinking I owed Chloe a lie, that didn't mean I owed my mom one. The last time I lied to her was in the sixth grade when we watched an R-rated movie at a friend's house. The guilt had run so rampant in my mind that I ended up confessing the whole of the misdeed two days later. I reminded myself again that this was different. Mom thought my dating life was non-existent in Stanton. Mom loved Glenn Foster. I did not. Glenn and I would be thrown together all week long, under the mistletoe and on horse-drawn carriage rides, unless my heart was promised to another.

"How about I bring him home for a weekend sometime in January so you can all meet him?" Unless of course, our relationship experienced an unfortunate explosive demise before then.

"Fine. But promise me you'll at least be nice to Glenn. You'll both be there with no families of your own."

"Mom. Please call off Virginia Foster and any plans you two have regarding us. Our relationship didn't work then, and it won't work now."

"But I still don't understand what happened between you two. You never told anybody. He's such a nice boy. And he has a great job."

I didn't want to get into it about Glenn. Even I had a hard time putting into words what exactly went wrong. The thing I did know for certain was that Glenn had two very different personalities. One for public and one for private. He wasn't a bad guy, but he wasn't for me, and I would not be coerced into spending time with him.

"I'd better go. It's getting foggy, and I should focus on the road." The roads were at that questionable icy stage, where I wasn't sure if they were just wet or if I was driving on black ice. "I'll be nice to Glenn, but I'm not hanging out with him alone. I have a boyfriend," I said firmly, clinging to that lifeline now. "Are you and Russ already there?"

"Yes, we just unpacked our things. It's so beautiful here. Seems like we jumped right into a Christmas card. Russ wants to take me cross-country skiing here in a bit."

Cross-country skiing? Who was this woman?

"Drive safe, honey. Take it slow if you need to."

"No problem there," I said, inching along the highway.

After I hung up the phone, I began to wonder how much weight I should give this fake-boyfriend thing to be sure Glenn and our moms would get the hint. Should I get a fake ring? A promise ring?

No. Too soon.

Three long hours later, my GPS led me to a long driveway. I stopped my car just underneath the wooden archway that held a sign saying, The Lodge in the Hills. I peered down the snow-covered drive for a moment, wondering if my Civic could make it all the way. My mom was right. It was like something out of a postcard. Snow-topped maple trees lined both sides of the driveway, but since it was the middle of winter, they did almost nothing to block the snow from piling up into a slushy mess.

The drive from Stanton to Montpelier had been slow going. There were some patches that I had to grip the wheel to keep my car on the road. Now that I was so close to my destination, my limbs felt heavy, and I was impatient to just get there, which is how I found myself plunging forward down the driveway with snow slushing around my tires. I instantly regretted my decision. The car swiveled while the tires tried to find their grip on the slushy snow, then it began slowing down. I rammed my foot into the gas, hoping a quick burst of speed would save me. After fishtailing grandly for a couple yards, the car came to a complete stop.

I tried reversing, but the tires only spun. I couldn't see the lodge from where I sat on the road, and I suddenly wanted to cry. The perfect start to this week in purgatory. I was about to call my mom when the sound of a motor caught my attention. A big, red tractor with a plow was coming in the direction of the lodge, right toward me. Looked like if I would have waited one extra minute, I could have avoided the whole thing. A few moments later, the tractor pulled to a stop in front of me. The door swung open, and a tall, lanky man dressed in a red-and-green flannel shirt, a black vest, a baseball hat, and knee-high rubber boots jumped to the ground and made his way to my car.

I rolled down the window, almost sheepishly, as I met the gaze of a handsome man who looked to be in his mid-fifties, with salt-and-pepper hair sticking out from under his hat and wrinkles around his eyes—no doubt due to laughter, I noted, as he grinned at me widely.

"Well, dang. Not bad for a Civic. You should be impressed with your driving skills, young lady."

A smile broke out across my face, deeply appreciative of the fact that he wasn't going to pull a jerky male card and try and make me feel stupid about what just happened.

"I'm so sorry, I thought I could make it."

"Oh, no, it's our fault. The tractor broke down before we could clear the road. But...it's fixed now. Do you mind if I finish clearing to the end of the road, and then I'll come around and pick you up? So the whole driveway gets cleared? It'll just take me a minute."

"No, go ahead."

He nodded, and within seconds, he was back in the tractor, edging around my parked car to finish the driveway. By the time he circled back, I had changed into my snow boots, which looked funny with my skirt, but I stepped out of the car, determined to help with something. Snow fell in large pellets onto my coat. To my surprise, the man got out of the tractor along with a teenager who looked to be around sixteen or so—definitely a son, if I guessed right.

The man motioned to me. "I'm Jack Taylor, the owner of The Lodge. This is my son, Jett." He squinted his eyes at me, appearing to look me over. "Now let me guess, are you with the Ellis family?"

My first instinct was to say no. I was a Wilson. Walt Wilson's daughter. But instead, I smiled and said, "Yes. I'm Olive."

He gave my hand a hearty shake. "Nice to meet you, Olive." Motioning to my car, he asked, "Any kids in there or just you?"

"Just me."

"Great. If you want, Jett here can steer your car while we pull it. It gets a little tricky in the snow. You're welcome to hop in the tractor with me. Or you're more than welcome to drive your car. Whatever you're comfortable with."

I looked toward Jett. I'd probably be teaching him in my class if he lived in Stanton. His light-brown hair was partially hidden underneath a black beanie, his hands stuffed casually in his coverall pockets and a shy smile on his face. I immediately felt right at home with him. Teenagers were my favorite. "Maybe I'll let Jett bring my car in. He looks like he *might* know what he's doing." He smiled, a flush rising across his cheeks at the teasing challenge, and he took my keys.

A few minutes later, the men had a thick chain hooked up, connecting my car to the tractor. I climbed the steps of the tractor and settled in next to Jack Taylor. It smelled faintly of hay and dirt. Christmas music played softly in the background. For a while, I kept turning to check on my car but quickly found there was nothing to worry about. It was clear that I was in very capable hands.

"So, Olive, huh? That's not one you hear too often. I'm guessing you get some interesting nicknames. Like carrot or broccoli?" The man gave me a cheeky smile. He had one of those personalities that you couldn't help but smile along with him, even if the joke had run its course over the past twenty years. More specifically, the past nine months, but who was counting?

"You could say that. Lately Celery Stick seems to be the most popular."

He laughed. "I like it."

"So, what all do you do here at The Lodge?" I asked, motioning toward the large red barn and a handful of other wooden buildings looming in the distance. "I'm guessing it's not just open for Christmas time, right?"

He tugged at his hat, his hand steady on the wheel as he plowed the other half of the driveway. "No, we farm about two thousand acres. We do hay and grain for our cattle. We make our own cheese and sell it locally around Vermont. We have a small dairy where we milk our own cows. You might say we're a jack-of-all-trades type of operation."

"I love that. Did you start this place?"

"No, my dad started it about fifty years ago now. Of course, it was just a small farm back then. Times were tough for quite a few years, as you might expect. But slowly, we kept adding to it, and then our luck really changed when we opened it up for tourists. Ten years ago, we built the village of cabins, and it's been a lot of fun ever since. We have all kinds of different programs, depending on the season. But my favorite is Christmas time. All the farm work has slowed down, and we can concentrate on just feeding our animals and making Christmas special for our guests. It's a pretty great gig. Now, enough about me. What do you do for a living, Olive?"

"I teach English to high schoolers."

His face lit up. There was something so familiar about him, but I could not put my finger on it. "Well, isn't that something. My son is an English teacher, too. He's coming home tonight." He suddenly eyed me, brimming with mischief. "You dating anybody?"

I gave a startled laugh, ready to tell him no when I remembered. "Oh. Uh, yeah, I am." I'd better stay consistent.

At his disappointed face, I added, "Should I be on my guard? Is he as charming as you?"

"Eh, he does alright for himself. He looks just like me, though, so you know he's a handsome son of a gun." He shot me a sly grin.

I laughed. Jack then busied himself with showing me all the points of interest.

"That big red barn is where we milk the cows by hand twice a day. Once at 7am and then again at 5. You're welcome to come and watch or even try your hand at it anytime you'd like. Around back are the stables where we have about a dozen horses. Let us know if you ever want to ride. That big wooden building in the middle is the lodge. That's where all your meals will be and any other group gatherings. During the day, we have lots of crafts available and movies to watch, and we hold the Christmas dance here." He pointed toward a group of small buildings lining both sides of the cutest pretend Main Street I'd ever seen. "That place is open twice a day and will serve you free hot chocolates, coffee, or an ice cream cone."

"Ice cream? In the winter?"

He eyed me suspiciously. "Well, now, maybe I ought to reevaluate my initial view of you. Any visitors at the lodge need to appreciate ice cream in all the seasons."

A grin split my face. "I assure you, my freezer is full of Ben and Jerry's at this very moment."

He laughed a deep rumble as he clutched his chest. "Attagirl. Don't you scare me like that."

I re-focused my gaze out the window, still smiling. This was one of those surprising moments when I found myself completely at ease with someone in a matter of minutes. It didn't happen to me often, but when it did, I was always blown away by it. What was it about people like that? How did they give you the feeling that you could be fully yourself, no holds barred, and that you'd be happily accepted? The dark cloud above my head at my arrival had evaporated into a light, contemplative gray as he continued to point out different buildings and recount funny stories about farming. Deep in my little baby Scrooge heart, I could see the magic of this place. I could feel it from the pride in Jack's voice. It was like a picture perfect little Christmas village in a snow globe. Next to the tiny ice cream shop, there was a small building boasting a sign that read *General Store*. Squinting closer as we passed, I saw the sign in the window stating the four hours each day that it was open. A small white church with a steeple sat across the street, with a sign out front boasting that all were welcome. Each building was snow-covered and had Christmas lights strung along the outside, and wreaths hung on every window in sight.

"You know, with the exception of this humongous tractor, it feels like we just stepped into a Thomas Kinkade painting."

Jack laughed. "Good. That's the goal."

He nudged my arm and pointed a couple hundred yards down Main Street. "That's where all the guests stay. We call it the village."

Roughly fifteen cabins were littered around the base of the tree-covered hills. They weren't in any linear order but seemed scattered in more of a circular manner, giving each cabin a more secluded feel as opposed to being directly across the road from its neighbor. The cabins were different sizes, but they were all constructed from rich, dark wood. Chimney smoke rose up to greet the sky, lending a sense of warmth and coziness to the atmosphere, and like the rest of the buildings in this charming place, wreaths adorned each of the doors and windows.

"Wow," was all I could say.

Jack circled back toward the barn and stables sitting on the other side of Main Street, past the general store, and parked the tractor. He stood and leaned forward to open the door for me to exit.

The men made quick work of unhooking my car. Jack pointed toward the lodge just up the sidewalk and said, "I know your parents and sister are here already. My wife, Sandy, should be in the lodge and can get you all checked in."

I took my car keys from Jett. "Thank you for not wrecking this priceless heirloom."

He grinned, the braces on his teeth gleaming. "Don't know how you drive in something that low to the ground. I'd recommend getting a truck."

I laughed. "Every winter, I put that in my letter to Santa, but he never comes through."

Turning to Jack, I shook his hand, "Thank you for the lift and for my personal tour."

He chuckled. "My pleasure, Olive. It will be fun to have you around. And if there's any way we can get rid of that pesky boyfriend, let me know. I'd love to introduce you to my son."

"I don't think so." I grinned and waved, making my way toward the lodge. If his son turned out to be anything like Jack, I was going to be sorely disappointed in my fake-boyfriend situation.

A light sprinkling of flakes drifted down from the sky. The air was fresh, and for a moment, I almost decided to keep walking instead of facing my family. But I forced myself to be a grown-up, put a pleasant look on my face, and opened the lodge door.

The place seemed empty at a glance. The doorway opened into a large foyer with a hallway that seemed to round the perimeter of the building. I moved forward and passed through another doorway and into the sprawling main room. The pitched ceilings were high, and the floor was concrete. Long, wooden picnic tables were placed all around the open room with chairs tucked neatly underneath. Front and center, a stage with a red, velvet curtain drew my eye, and directly across from the doorway was what looked like a large kitchen with a long bar top coming out from the wall, connecting the kitchen with the main room—probably where they served the meals. I took a few steps inside, scanning the room with interest. A front reception area sat off to the left side. There seemed to be no one there to greet guests. I was about to turn and leave when I noticed a small yellow light shining out of what looked like an office just behind the front desk.

A moment later, a thin woman with short blonde hair peeking out from underneath a cute red beanie stepped out of the office. She gave me a wide smile, and I couldn't help but smile back as I took in her black leggings, long red sweater, and snow boots. She looked like a walking ad for Vermont tourism.

"Hi! I'm Sandy. How can I help you?" She leaned against the reception desk separating us and glanced over me and my luggage. "Oh wait, you're the spitting image of two other brown-haired beauties I just handed keys to. Are you with the Ellises?"

I clenched my stomach while I smiled, determined not to let the name bother me in public. "Yes. Elaine's my mom."

She leaned over and checked a paper on the desk. "Yes. Cute couple."

Suck it up, Buttercup.

"What's your name, dear?"

"Olive Wilson." I made sure to emphasize my last name. Maybe it was petty, but I was *not* an Ellis.

Her brows furrowed as she looked at her papers. "Is your husband coming? There won't be much room in Cabin 7."

"I'm not married."

She peered up at me. "Oh, I'm sorry. I thought, with your last name..." She trailed off awkwardly and I tried to feign a smile.

"Nope. Just me."

"Okay. That pull-out couch can't be too comfortable, so we do have some cots available if you'd prefer."

"Oh. Are there no beds in there?"

"Well, with your sister's family in there already, it will be a little tight. It has one full-sized bed, and there's a pull-out couch in the living room. It's one of our smaller cabins."

My heart sank. "I thought I had my own cabin."

That statement caused a furrowed brow as the woman shuffled through the papers on her desk. "Let's see..."

My feet began to twitch as I tried not to panic. I loved my sister, but other than offering some babysitting here and there, I hoped to be hidden far away in a cabin all my own. A place where I could choose when to come out and be seen (i.e., rarely, with a side of mealtime only).

"Oh, yes. Here it is. I'm sorry you weren't told. Your mother called yesterday and had you moved into Cabin 7 with your sister. She said it was because the..." She searched through more papers on her desk. "...the Fosters were now coming." She looked at me with concern in her bright eyes. "Is that alright? I wish we had another cabin available, but unfortunately, everything is booked up this week."

It took me a moment to adjust my face back into some sort of (hopefully) pleasant expression. Of course I wouldn't have my own cabin. That idea was for people with luck on their side. I felt a brief stab of guilt at my disappointment in the new living arrangements. Truth be told, I probably should have planned it like that from the very start. Ben and Chloe could certainly use some help with the girls, and wasn't this whole week supposed to be about spending time with family?

"Would you prefer to stay with your parents? They're in a small cabin as well, but it would have less people."

How to put this nicely? Thank you, but I would rather jab a hot needle into my eyeball. I wasn't sure what kind of love life two newlywed married widows in their fifties had, but I wasn't about to find out.

With a practiced smile, I said, "No, my sister's cabin will be great. Thank you so much."

And just like that, my last vestiges of hope for surviving the week were shattered. There would be no lounging in a bubble bath, reading. No late-night TV binges. No safe place to hide when the strain of my fractured family threatened to overwhelm me. There was no escape. The week I had already been dreading for the past month just went from bad to much worse.

FIVE

Terminators are immune to pain. I am not. Please don't bite me again.
The Terminator

After I left the lodge, I climbed back into my car and drove down the freshly plowed street toward the village, leaning forward to scan the cabin numbers. Although the cabins were spread out quite a bit, the pathways between them had been freshly cleared of snow. Number seven was a small A-frame close to the road, with a porch running across the front. I parked just behind Ben and Chloe's green Subaru and killed the engine.

Here it was. The start of fake Christmas. That's what I was calling it in my head. How could it be real without my dad here? And even more than that, how could we replace him so quickly with…something else? Something so different? This was all just fake. Bright, flashing lights in a store window; aisles and aisles of cheap toys. A distracting excursion while we all tried to pretend that our family infrastructure hadn't imploded.

I thought I had made my peace with it, I really did. But this time of year felt so raw. The snow, the lights, the Christmas music, the baking, and the holiday smells had cemented the last moments with my dad deep into my weary soul. He passed away a week after Christmas. Last year, Chloe and I had camped out at the house, knowing his time was nearing the end. Those last few days, hospice had a bed set up for him in the living room. Though the week was one of tears and sadness, I couldn't deny that it was filled with sweet and beautiful moments as well —the four of us all together for the last time. Mom and Chloe and I would crowd around his bed, playing cards, rehashing memories, and laughing about childhood antics–jokes we'd played, the times Dad had made us laugh, or made us mad, or taught us a lesson. He tried his hardest to stay awake for our visits. Some days, he put in a better fight than others, but oftentimes his eyes would glaze over while we talked around him, looking peaceful, which is exactly how he went. One moment, Chloe was telling us about the time she snuck out of her window late at night to try out her new bike headlights in the dark, and the next, he'd given one last smile and shut his eyes for the last time. His sickness of two years finally coming to an end. And now, it was Christmas again. It was amazing the difference a year could make.

I gave myself another minute of deep breaths before finally opening my door. The crisp air filled my lungs as I hefted my suitcase and duffel bag out of the trunk. I wondered briefly if I should have thrown in a few more books. I had my comfort reads, *Jane Eyre* and *Pride and Prejudice,* and of course my Kindle, but was that enough to dilute the senses for what was surely to come? Probably not.

I climbed the sturdy steps onto the porch and gave the door a quick knock. As I had learned from one unfortunate incident,

Ben enjoyed walking around in his underwear in the comfort of his own home. So now, I always knocked first, and I always waited to be let in. Ben opened the door this time—fully clothed, thank goodness. He waved me in while making an apologetic gesture toward the phone at his ear. His blonde hair was combed stylishly, and he wore tailor-made jeans with a quarter-zip sweater. Closing the door, he threw me a smile and a chin thrust without skipping a beat in his conversation, then turned and disappeared into another room.

A small living room greeted me. It included a brown couch, a chair, and a coffee table. Just past that, tucked into the corner, was a small kitchenette with a fridge, stove, and microwave and four maple cupboards surrounding it. Two small doors on the opposite side led to a bathroom and the small bedroom Ben had just occupied. Though it was about the size of a hotel room suite, the cabin had the appearance of being newly built while still maintaining a rustic charm.

It felt warm and welcoming, or that could have been the three-year-old blonde terrors who launched themselves into my arms the moment they saw me.

"Aunt Owive!!!"

Laughing, I dropped my luggage and pulled both of them into a bear hug. I relished the feel of their little arms, a death grip around my neck, and only let go to tickle their sides.

"I thought I told you two to stop getting so big."

"I tawer than sissy," Ivy stated proudly while Holly began rummaging through my duffel bag.

"You made it!" I glanced up to see my older sister walk out from the bathroom. Standing up, I reached out to greet her with a hug. Though she was four years older, we were at eye level at five foot six. Where my hair was dark brown with auburn highlights like my dad's, hers was light brown like my mom's. We both had Mom's pert nose and a light sprinkling of freckles across our faces, however. Though still thin, Chloe's body had rounded and softened the past few years, due in part to becoming a mother, and it looked good on her.

"Yeah, how are you? When did you get here?" I asked, bending over to redirect Holly's attention to a toy to stop her dragging out all the makeup from my toiletry bag.

"A couple of hours ago."

"So, I don't know how we're all going to sleep." Chloe motioned toward the small bedroom. "When I heard you'd be in here with us, I figured we'd just put the girls on the floor in our room, but there is literally no room on the sides of the bed. It's so tiny in there. I'll have to put the girls on the floor out here in the living room, but that doesn't give you much privacy." She pointed at the couch. "I think it does pull out into a bed, though, so that's something."

I looked at the brown couch. It was newer and honestly didn't look too bad. Perhaps technology had found a way to rid the pull-out couch from the uncomfortable bar running across your back? I guess I'd be finding out.

"This looks great. Don't worry about it," I assured her.

"Ben asked about renting another cabin for you, but the lady said they were all booked up."

"Yeah, I did, too." I smiled at her. "It's really not a big deal. I'm just sorry I'm intruding on you guys."

She shot me a look. "Hey. We love having you. I just want you to be comfortable. The twins still don't sleep great, so I'm worried they'll have a scream fest and keep you up half the night. You could always sleep in Mom and Russ's cabin if it's too much for you."

Nope.

"I promise, I'm fine," I said, ignoring her worried look as I moved my bags behind the couch, where they'd hopefully be less of a temptation to two curious three-year-olds. "Are Mom and Russ back from cross-country skiing yet?"

Chloe plopped down on the couch, emptying a tub of

magnetic blocks she must have brought with her onto the floor. As if by magic, the sound had the twins racing over and they were distracted with the blocks in no time. "I haven't seen them yet. We got here after they'd already left."

I sat down next to her. "Is it weird she's skiing with him? I've never heard of Mom doing anything like that before."

Chloe shrugged. "Russ has her playing on a club volleyball team with him back home, too."

I tried to picture my mom playing sports. Or cross-country skiing. Growing up, my family's wild Friday nights consisted of Monopoly or a movie night.

"I haven't seen your boyfriend yet."

I shot her a look. "Huh?"

Chloe gave me a wicked smile. "Glenn Foster."

"You're the worst."

"He might be your boyfriend again after this trip if you don't start spilling about Miles."

I'd had two hours alone in a car to prepare, so I was ready for her this time. "Listen. I don't want to get worked up over the tiny details yet because it's so new. It will just get in my head."

There. That was smart. And true. If I had actually been in a brand-new relationship, I'm sure I would be mature enough to not want to hash out every little thing, especially with Chloe. She'd be so excited that she'd make too big a deal out of everything. That's the kind of stuff that gets into your head.

"How about just *some* details, then? And look me in the eye."

I spent the next couple of hours being a human jungle gym with the twins on the floor and giving Chloe just enough information about Miles to keep her satisfied, though I wasn't sure she was totally convinced. Ben had gotten a few new responsibilities at work, which explained the phone attached to his ear most of the afternoon, but he did join us for brief intervals.

"What's the schedule for this place? Do you know?" I asked, reluctantly curious to know my fate for the night.

"There's a big welcome dinner at the lodge tonight," Chloe said. "That's all I know."

Ben joined us again a few minutes later, pulling out a chair next to the couch. We spent the next while laughing and talking, and I managed to relax for the first time since I'd arrived. It felt normal, just the three of us. We were just siblings meeting up for a fun winter getaway. No parents allowed. It almost felt like our bubble hadn't burst. The dam hadn't broken. As if Dad hadn't passed away, and Mom hadn't gotten remarried to the first guy she met.

SIX

"I see a woman may be made a fool,
If she had not a spirit to resist."
William Shakespeare - *The Taming of the Shrew*

THE LODGE WAS LIT UP LIKE A BEACON WITH GLOWING WHITE Christmas lights as we set out on Main Street. We passed the general store and the other rustic buildings that were even cuter upon closer inspection, as we headed toward the lodge. Somewhere above us, Mannheim Steamroller's "Carol of the Bells" played softly. The sidewalk across the road was also lit up, and guests from the other cabins bustled along, headed toward the lodge for dinner. I kept a sharp eye out for the Fosters but thankfully didn't see anybody familiar as we walked.

Mom and Russ had apparently gotten lost on their excursion and had to rush back to their cabin to change. Mom texted Chloe that they would just meet us at dinner. I trailed behind our group, holding Ivy's little hand because she insisted on walking.

By the time we reached the lodge, everybody else had already gone inside. Ivy walked over to a large lit-up statue of Santa Claus just outside the building, and I let her look at it as long as she wanted. Every time she seemed ready to move on, I'd point out something else about the statue to attract her attention once more.

"Oh, look, Ivy! Is that a reindeer behind Santa?"

"Look! Is Santa holding a bag of presents?"

"Do you like presents, Ivy?"

"What did you ask Santa for?"

So on and so on. It was mostly for distraction purposes, but I could squeeze the cute stuffing out of her earnest chubby baby face while she mispronounced words and L's for the rest of my life.

"Olive."

I turned to see Chloe peeking out of the doorway.

"You coming?"

"Yeah, sorry. She just wanted a closer look at Santa." Which was TRUE.

Chloe eyed me suspiciously. "It almost seems like you don't want to be here."

"It's not my fault your kid is so curious."

She held the door open for me while I picked up Ivy in my arms and breezed past her into the foyer of the lodge. Jett stood to greet us in front of the door leading into the main room.

"Well, look who it is. Rescue any more stranded motorists today?" I asked, smiling at him.

He blushed, a hint of pink creeping across his cheeks. "Not in the last couple of hours anyway."

We stepped inside to find a sprawling room lit with cozy yellow lights. I had just been here hours earlier, but now the place shimmered with Christmas. Rows of wooden beams held up the high ceiling. Long tables and chairs were lined up and decorated near the stage. Wreaths covered every window, greenery was draped across anything it could possibly be attached to, and white twinkle lights were strung above the tables. A hay bale display in the corner was obviously intended as a backdrop for pictures. It felt like I had just stepped into a Christmas book.

Except for the Fosters, we were the last in our group to arrive. Even my mom and Russ had somehow beaten us there. Crowds of families gathered around the room with a handful of children running wild under everybody's feet. We were directed toward a picnic-style table, while the buffets behind us were being filled by staff members with bowls and platters, heaping with food. The smell of smoked meats and cinnamon had me salivating.

"Ohh, he's cute!" Chloe pointed toward a tall blond, with muscles bursting out of his long-sleeved shirt, sitting on the edge of a table.

My eyes couldn't help but follow her rude finger point, and I settled my gaze on a man who looked to be in his mid-thirties.

"He has a ring on."

"What?" She squinted closer at him. "Dang it."

"Stop showing me guys. I'm dating somebody," I lied, feeling incredibly grateful to have the Miles card in my back pocket, so to speak. Lie or not, it really was genius. Although it was becoming quite evident that, despite my amazing acting skills, a part of Chloe still didn't seem to believe me.

"I'm just showing you the scenery," she said, all innocence. "Just in case you might need somebody here physically to fend off Glenn and his mother."

Chloe motioned toward a long table on the right side of the room. "We're all sitting over here."

I glanced over and saw my mom smiling expectantly at me as she stood from her seat and began making her way over to us. I vaguely registered a blurry blob next to her that was probably Russ, but I didn't let myself look at him yet.

It was go time. Smile on.

Mom came toward me with her arms out and a warm smile. She looked the same as always and yet somehow not. Her brown hair had streaks of gray running throughout and reached just to her shoulders. She seemed younger, but it was probably the cute snow boots, jeans, and flowing floral top she was wearing. She also seemed softer somehow as she pulled me close. I wrapped my arms around her and shut my eyes briefly, soaking in how good it felt to be hugged by her. My mom had always been a great hugger, tight and all-consuming, and she never pulled away first.

Okay, I stand corrected.

She never *used* to pull away first. But since I didn't pull away, she finally had to. I probably would have stayed there all night if it got me out of talking to Russ.

"I'm glad you're here. How was the drive?" she asked me.

"It was slow. You look great, Mom."

Russ stepped forward, one arm around my mom's shoulders and his hand outstretched toward me. "Hey there, kiddo! You ready for the party?"

Party.

Russ was large. Not overweight, necessarily, but he was tall, towering over six feet. His shoe size had to have been at least a fourteen. He looked completely skinny from the back and even straight on from the front, but his side profile showed a decent-sized pot belly. And he had a voice that boomed.

I stared at his hand and waited a beat too long to react. It was petty and made our greeting feel awkward. I tried out a new pep talk in my head. *I am a grown woman, not a bratty teenager.* Summoning up a smile, I managed to reach out and shake his hand.

"Hi, Russ."

A loud piercing through the room had everybody ducking

and covering their ears. The microphone was a perfect excuse to pull my hand from Russ's and focus my attention elsewhere.

Jack Taylor stood on the stage and tapped the microphone three times. A large smile captured his face as all the eyes in the room turned toward him.

"That's our welcome-to-the-lodge noise." A murmur of laughter filled the room. "Welcome, welcome, everyone. If you could all find a seat, we'll get going on dinner, and we'll start breaking down the calendar for this week."

I sat down at the end of our table, next to Ivy, across from Ben, and three seats down from Russ, which meant I wouldn't have to make polite conversation.

"Man, this is a good group here tonight," Jack Taylor was saying. "It's been a great day meeting all of you. We've got three different family reunions going on. We got the ice cream machine working again, thank goodness. And our cow, Snowflake, only kicked me twice while I was milking her tonight." He paused while a low murmur of laughter broke through the crowd.

I looked around, counting roughly sixty people taking up space throughout the large room. Even though it was huge, the rustic wood and brown tones gave the whole lodge a cozy feel.

Jack dismissed the group to get dinner, and the entire crowd began to stand and wander over to the buffet tables along the back wall. Chloe and Ben went before me, each expertly balancing their own plates of barbecued ribs, roasted vegetables, and salad as well as a plate with a dollop of mashed potatoes and a roll for each of the girls. Once we were all back at our tables with heaping plates of food and cups of hot wassail, Jack took the stage once more.

"Alright, keep eating. I hope you're enjoying the ribs from Old Snowflake's mom, Bessie. She was a great cow, but she could have been a lot nicer. I'll bet she regrets that now."

He grinned at the alarm on all our faces. Jack's laughter filled the silence. "I'm just kidding. We'd never feed you a cow we named. The ribs were courtesy of an unmarked cow from the back pasture. She was ready to go. It was her time."

A few bouts of ruckus laughter filled the room, interspersed with soft, undecided chuckling. I decided to eat my mashed potatoes first.

"I'm kidding. Alright, we've got something special to tell you about. When my wife, Sandy, and I started taking over this week of Christmas, we began to notice a theme. It became all about the kids. Which is wonderful. But we didn't want parents to just be here, watching their kids experience the magic of Christmas. We wanted this place to bring back a little magic for them, as well. So, a few years ago, we came up with an idea. This will be the third year we've done our Christmas bingo, and it's been a hit every time."

He held up a card. "Here's how it works. Everybody will get a bingo card. In fact…" He looked around the room until he spotted his wife. "Sandy! Would you come grab this stack of cards and start passing them out? You all probably met my better half, Sandy, when you checked in, but just in case, she's the woman who knows all the things, if you ever have any questions." Sandy bowed theatrically before she reached the stage and took the stack of cards he handed her. "Thank you, my dear. Alright, on the cards are twenty-four things—plus a free space—for you to do during your week's stay. The cards are all the same. It's more like a choose-your-own-adventure bingo. There is an adult version and a child version. Most overlap, so you can do things together as a family, but the adult version has a handful of extra events, for reasons I'll tell you about in a second."

"We are so doing that." Chloe's eyes sparkled with excitement.

"Have fun," I retorted.

Her face scrunched, and she looked like she was about to say something but was interrupted by Jack.

"Alright, for the adults, there's a small prize for anybody who gets a bingo. That means five squares in a row in any direction. As soon as you get a bingo, bring your card to the lodge for your prize. Same with the kids. But if you get a blackout–that's *every* square crossed off and completed–before the Christmas dinner on December 25th, your card will be entered to win an all-expense-paid trip for two on a cruise to Mexico this winter. For a whole week."

A small gasp overtook the crowd. That even had my ears perking up. New England winters were long and dark…a winter trip to somewhere sunny with a beach had all of us interested. When a bingo card made it down to our table, I took one, though only out of curiosity. Most of the card was full of simple Christmas activities, things that were easy to do with kids, like sledding, building a snowman, or decorating a gingerbread house. But my eye caught on the more problematic squares: polar plunge, mistletoe kiss, milk a cow by hand, barn dance, etc. I leaned back in my seat, having seen enough. I'd just save for ten years and pay for my own vacation like a respectable adult.

"Now," Jack was saying, "I'm going to ask my lovely wife to send around our calendar of events. Most of the activities on this list are available through the lodge. For example, we always host a barn dance at some point during the week. We'll have several gingerbread house and Christmas cookie competitions. We can show you how to roast a chestnut by the fire. And we'll have sleigh rides to the big hill for sledding. Keep your calendar handy, and getting a bingo will be pretty easy. Blackout…now…that's another story. There are a few things you have to do on your own. And some things–looking at you, polar bear plunge–sound pretty terrible." He did an exaggerated full-body shiver that made the crowd laugh.

Jack leaned down toward the audience, cupping his ear toward somebody who had yelled a question. He repeated it into the microphone. "Polar bear plunge is where you go from the hot tub to a full jump into the pond behind the lodge, and then back to the hot tub. There's a hot tub located just behind the lodge with a convenient pathway straight to the pond."

If it was the pond I noticed on my drive in, it was completely frozen over. I shivered just thinking about it. Jack went on, explaining a few more of the rules while I stirred the mashed potatoes on my plate. I had no desire to make this week any more of a "thing" than it already was. My body had to be here, but that didn't mean I had to engage more than necessary. Now, thankfully, with the whole boyfriend bit, I wouldn't have to do any of it. I patted my lying little self on the back for that one.

"Hey, hot guy, 5:00," Chloe whispered across the table. She was seated facing the buffet table behind me while I was facing the stage.

"If that's Glenn, I'm going to kill you."

"He looks like he might work here. Holy cow. He looks just like Jack. That's got to be his son. Look at him."

"What? No! Stop being so obvious!"

"Our table's out of butter."

"What?"

She threw me a salty grin. "He clearly works here. I'm going to ask him for more butter. Be right back."

Before I could stop her—not that I could have done anything to stop her except fling myself across the table to grab her arm —she scampered off. Kill me now. I refused to look behind me. I had a boyfriend, for crying out loud.

Okay, I heard it, but still.

While I sat there, painfully unaware of what she might be saying to the poor man, I kept myself busy being a docile mother figure to Chloe's monstrous three-year-olds. Jack seemed very comfortable with a microphone in his hand and began sharing a few corny Christmas jokes. I picked up my fork only to put it back down again, then wiped Ivy's face with a napkin. What was taking Chloe so long? Was she getting his number? Heaven forbid, was she going to point me out to him?

From across the table, Ben nudged my foot, pulling me out of my panicked musing. "Um, is there a reason my wife has been talking to some mountain-man version of Bradley Cooper for the last five minutes?" he asked, his eyes plastered somewhere behind me.

I stilled. I was tempted to ignore him as he was probably just trying to be funny. But the Bradley Cooper part had me casually scanning the room before darting a quick glance behind me by the doorway. Chloe was standing with her back to me, talking animatedly to a man wearing a flannel shirt with his arms folded. A Bradley Cooper dressed in flannel? But upon closer inspection, the celebrity lookalike in question looked an awful lot like—

A gasp, quick and painful, shot out of me as I blinked my eyes a few times, wondering if I was dreaming. Because there was no way—NO WAY—this could be happening right now. The world was too big for a coincidence this horrible.

And yet…

The man dressed in red flannel rolled up to his forearms, jeans with just enough holes that the teenage guys would think he was one of them, and a stupid gray beanie on his head, was none other than Miles Taylor.

SEVEN

"It's delightful when your imaginations come true, isn't it?"
L.M. Montgomery - *Anne of Green Gables*

A FEW THINGS HIT ME AT THAT MOMENT. FIRST: JACK TAYLOR WAS a charismatic delight of a person, but he clearly sucked at getting to know someone. Other than inquiring into what I did for a living, he hadn't asked me anything of value about my personal life during our little tractor ride this afternoon. Not even where I lived. We could have figured all of this out before I ever reached the lodge, which would have left me plenty of time to fake a horrific stomach virus. I could have been in my car driving home as we speak.

P.S. Stomach virus. Why didn't I think of that?

Second: Taylor was a common enough name. I sure didn't imagine that, out of all the schools in and surrounding the state of New York, his son would just so happen to be the guy working in mine. Also, it just occurred to me that I hadn't had a clue where Miles hailed from. I'm sure I must have known at some point, but I suppose when one is trying their best to avoid the annoyingly attractive new teacher, one tends to forget those minor details.

Miles was smiling and talking to Chloe as she gestured wildly with her hands. He moved a bit closer. Any minute now, she would be pointing me out to him. I had to move. Now. Chloe's back was to me, but if Miles looked my way, we would lock eyes for sure.

I scanned the room and found a door to the side of me. It looked like it could lead into a hallway of some sort.

That was my target.

To Ben, I said, "I have to use the bathroom."

His brow furrowed as I stood up. "Listen, I don't need a play-by-play—"

I was already gone. Once standing, I made a beeline for the door, not looking back, feeling like I had a million eyes trained on me, waiting to pounce.

I was so close to my target. The end was in sight, and then I would fake a brilliant illness and go home.

Once behind the safety of the doors, I found myself in a hallway. Praise the heavens. I took a few calming breaths and peered through a crack in the doorway, trying to see Miles and Chloe, but the angle wasn't right. The dark hallway meandered toward the entrance. I crept closer to the exit—the door that would also put me closer to Miles and Chloe inside the large room. Not ideal. But I didn't know any other way to escape. I'd have to risk it.

I slowed my steps as I got closer to the door, peering through the crack, and was startled to see how close Miles and Chloe were to me. Just on the other side. Now was my chance to escape.

"That's so crazy your name is Miles. I'm hearing that name everywhere all of a sudden."

Chloe's muffled words drifted to my ears, and without consulting my mind, my body halted, edging closer to listen.

"Oh yeah?" Miles's voice seemed deep and friendly. "The secret's out, I guess."

Chloe laughed. "My sister is actually dating a guy named Miles."

"I told ya, it's a good name."

Seriously, Chloe, get off the name thing. It's getting weird.

"Alright, well, I'll leave you alone. You just looked so much like an old friend from college I had to double-check."

I at least had to be grateful she didn't use the butter excuse.

He laughed. "No problem. It was nice to meet you."

She turned to head back to the table, and I was just about ready to breathe a sigh of relief when she stopped suddenly and turned back to Miles. "Wait. Where are you from?"

My eyes went bug-eyed. No. NO. Chloe! Your conversation is over. Go back to your children. To your husband.

"I'm from here. My parents own this place. But I live in Stanton now."

I was dead. Floating away. From the crack in the door, I saw Chloe's face cloud over in a puzzle. Miles was starting to edge toward the door—*my* door—probably to get away from this psychopathic married woman who wouldn't leave him alone, when Chloe's voice put the final nail in my coffin.

"New York?" Chloe asked while I bit down on my knuckles and went into full-blown panic mode.

"Yeah."

"Wait. Miles? From Stanton? That's where my sister lives. What do you do there?"

"I teach English at the high school."

My hands flew to cover my mouth in horror. I had no idea how to stop this freight train from splattering me all over the tracks.

"My sister teaches English at the high school there."

There was a pause before Miles said, "Wait. Your sister is Olive Wilson?"

For the first time, I found myself wishing that he *didn't* know my real name. I'd happily answer to Celery Stick for the rest of my life if it would get me out of this absolute catastrophe. Still, I couldn't deny feeling a splash of warmth heating my frozen tundra of a body as my name fell from his lips. It was a mystery as to why, but I had no time to break the code before Chloe struck again.

She laughed. "Yeah." Her eyes brightened suddenly, her voice low as she said, "Are you here to surprise her? She acted like she wouldn't be seeing you during the break."

At what I can only assume was a very confused look on Miles's face, Chloe chuckled again. "Sorry. She told me you guys were dating. I hope that's ok? But I feel like she didn't have any idea that you'd be here, or else she would have told me."

Again. Long pause. I could feel Miles calculating his answer. As for me…my body turned into a frigid hunk of ice, one strong wind away from toppling over and shattering.

"Yeah." His voice was low with a scheming edge. "I definitely came here to surprise her. How long did she tell you we'd been dating?"

"A few weeks." Chloe's eyes widened. "Why? Has it been longer? She's been annoyingly close-lipped about this whole thing."

"No. That sounds about right."

"Omigosh, can I please watch you surprise her? She's going to freak out." Chloe turned her head suddenly, her focus probably going to her confused husband and children. "Where'd she go?"

Miles's head snapped over to where she was looking. "She's here?" Why did his voice go up two excited octaves?

"She was…" Chloe's voice trailed off as she searched the crowd. "Honestly, I thought she was lying about dating you, so I was messing with her by pretending to try and set her up with somebody. I don't think she realized it was you."

Another low chuckle. "Oh, she might have."

She smiled at him playfully. "Should I do my overbearing-sister warning now or later?"

Miles was scanning the room. I knew he was. Santa came early this year, and he had a present to torture. He seemed distracted when he answered her, "Your what?"

"My speech. The one where I tell you if you hurt her, I'll kill you. Because up until yesterday, all I had heard about was how terrible you were."

He chuckled again, seeming to snap back into the real Miles. "Let's see how this week goes. What cabin is she in?"

I shot daggers into Chloe's head, using telepathy to force her to NOT TELL HIM, though I was aware he could probably very easily find out from his mother where we were staying.

"Seven. With us. She's on the pull-out. We had another cabin rented for her, but we gave it up so my parents' friends could come—Olive's ex-boyfriend and his parents, to be exact." She gave him a meaningful look.

Was there NO girl code of honor anymore? She could never resist throwing down some drama if an opportunity presented itself.

"Hey, Chloe, it was nice to meet you, but I just remembered something I need to take care of."

That was my cue. I knew what Miles was about, and I flew into a panic. He would be coming to find me, and I needed to be G-O-N-E.

My intentions were semi-honorable.

My speed was impressive.

The execution was unfortunate.

I was halfway out the main door when the strap of my purse caught on the door handle. My body reared back from nearly clotheslining myself. While I was frantically trying to untangle the strap, I felt a warm body at my back, and a hand grasped my arm. Then I heard the low drawl that filled my heart with dread and my body with chills.

"Hey there, Celery Stick."

My shoulders dropped, along with my head and every ounce of my dignity. The hour of reckoning for all my sins was now upon me.

"Or should I say, girlfriend?"

I turned around. Miles was standing much too close to me, filling my view with flannel stretched across a broad chest and a little peek of hair past the top button. I swallowed, bringing my gaze upward, past the annoying grin, strong cheekbones, and five o'clock shadow, until they met his eyes—brown, crinkly, and full of mischievous glee.

"Did I miss something? I've been a boyfriend a time or two before, but I remember a lot more kissing."

Even though I was embarrassed and annoyed that he was in my space, and my fingers itched to pull that stupid gray beanie over his obnoxious face, I couldn't help my cheeks as they began to warm. Which was ridiculous. It was MILES. My nemesis.

"But I mean…you did email me that romantic love note, so…" he continued.

I felt like I'd been dropped in the middle of a tennis match and somebody was handing me a golf club. I couldn't think how to *begin* processing this entire situation, let alone deciding on a course of action. I was still confused as to *how* Miles was here. In my face. Teasing me. I forced my brain to focus on a response.

"That *wasn't* a love note."

"Sure had an over-abundance use of flattering adjectives."

"It was sarcastic." I scowled at him.

He stuffed his hands into his pockets, looking completely at ease with our entire exchange. "You could have at least added a line in there about wanting to meet my parents."

Granted, I deserved all of this. I had brought this on myself. But still, couldn't he have just a bit of gracious dignity?

"Care to explain a few things, Olive?"

My eyes shot up to his. For the second time in five minutes, he had spoken my name, and for the second time, warmth emitted from my chest.

I peered past his shoulder and was satisfied we were alone. I really didn't want to bring up the whole Glenn thing, and so far, the threat of Glenn seemed pretty mild—as in…he wasn't here. Out of sight, out of mind. But as infuriating as Miles was, I did owe him an explanation.

"Okay, listen," I began, then stopped, my cheeks flushing, mentally smacking my head into a wall. Why did I have to use Miles's name? "To stop my family from trying to set me up with an ex-boyfriend…I might have told them that I was dating somebody."

He put his hand over his mouth as though deep in thought while he nodded. "I see. Understandable. The only problem is that your sister seems to think it's me, specifically."

I closed my eyes and took a deep, cleansing breath through my nose. It did nothing to calm me. But he wouldn't rest until I spoke the words. "When I found out he was coming–my ex…on a whim, I told my sister..."

His eyebrows raised appreciatively, waiting for me to finish the statement. With me standing there…really not wanting to.

"And…" he prodded.

"And when she asked who…your name came out."

"There it is." He sighed happily.

"For the record, it was only because we'd just had that fight in the kitchen yesterday that my mind even went there."

He reared back at that. "Fight? What fight? That wasn't a fight."

I scoffed, folding my arms and glaring up at him. "You yelled at me in the kitchen, trying to make me feel stupid for helping out."

His brow furrowed. "I never yelled. And that's not what I meant."

I tucked my hair behind my ear. "Listen, I just needed a name. For some crazy reason, yours came out, but I never thought that it would ever matter."

He was silent for a moment, staring at me. "Haven't you ever heard me talk about the lodge before?"

I threw my hands up. "I must have missed it in all of our conversations."

He made a noise of disbelief before he folded his arms. "How'd you find out about this place, then?"

"Millie told me—"

I stopped abruptly, my hands covering my face while Miles only laughed. Millie's last text message from this morning telling me to have fun and be willing to embrace the unexpected delights in life took on a whole new meaning now. That little punk. She'd be receiving a strongly worded text from me later tonight.

I rubbed my hand over my eyes. It was difficult to have a fake imaginary boyfriend when the real guy had just shown up. I had to end this now. Glenn would officially be my problem this week.

"It was all so stupid, okay? I'm sorry I dragged you into this. I'll tell my family everything tonight. I can just...deal with Glenn. You are officially allowed to forget this ever happened." I gave him a tight smile and turned to make my escape.

"Wait a sec—"

Nope. I was out of there. I reached for the door handle when my eyes caught movement outside. And then I wasn't moving anymore. Out on the sidewalk, under the lantern-lit walkway, striding toward the lodge, were Glenn Foster and his parents. Though it had been years since I'd seen Virginia Foster, her platinum-blonde bob was impossible to miss. Her husband, Lyle, walked beside her, grasping her elbow to keep her from slipping in her three-inch heeled boots. And in front of them, leading the way and looking as suave as ever in a black trench coat, brown scarf, and a newsboy hat, was Glenn.

And then I panicked.

There were different levels of awful, and I quickly realized that Miles's awful was much more palatable than Glenn's. Flipping around, I found him still there with his arms folded and looking at me with raised eyebrows. With my mouth gaping and no words exiting, I shot another glance out the window.

"Okay, will you pretend to be my boyfriend just for right now? I'll figure something out after this, I promise." My words came out choppy and quick. I didn't have time to overthink my actions. Glenn would be here in seconds.

Miles leaned over me, taking his time to glance out the window. "Ohhh. This must be the ex. He doesn't look so bad. What's the story?"

I was definitely not about to get into past relationship issues with Miles Taylor, but I did need his help, so I had to give him something.

"He's just not for me."

Miles stepped up beside me, rubbing his hands together and cracking his neck as if preparing for a boxing match. "Alright, what stage of dating are we at? Hand holding? Pet names? Making out behind the barn? Not sure what you prefer. I never woke up in time to finish reading how Rochester got the job done."

I mentally forced myself to ignore the attack on my favorite book to address the higher priority. "We will never be to the barn stage, Taylor."

"That's not what your sister alluded to."

I whacked his chest while he breathed out a laugh.

Low murmurs outside the door meant the Fosters were

nearly upon us. Miles leaned in closer, his warm breath a feather on the skin below my ear. "What's it gonna be? Are you going to kiss me? Should I hold your hand? Gaze into your eyes?"

I pretended to gag. "I'm not a PDA type of girl, so just stand there and keep your hands to yourself."

Just before the door opened, Miles wrapped his arm around me, pulling me tight against his body. "The first thing you need to know about your fake boyfriend is that I am *definitely* a PDA type of guy."

Tingles ran up my spine, but before I could shake them off, the door yanked open, and Glenn Foster and his parents stepped inside.

EIGHT

"My courage always rises at every attempt to intimidate me."
Jane Austen - *Pride and Prejudice*

EACH OF THEM DID A DOUBLE-TAKE AS THEY REALIZED IT WAS ME.

"Olive?" Lyle asked.

"We were so excited when your mom told us you would be here," Virginia said brightly. Her smile dimmed a fraction as she eyed Miles's arms around my waist.

Miles released me just before Virginia swooped in for a hug. Her tight embrace and the strong floral scent made it hard to breathe for a second. Lyle was next, giving me a quick squeeze before stepping aside, leaving a clear pathway for Glenn.

Glenn took me in with a wide smile. His eyes scanned my body with a quick efficiency that instantly brought me back to our short time dating years ago. He seemed taller, though I wasn't sure he actually was. He wore expensive-looking clothes, and his dark-blond hair spiked at the front as if he were trying hard to look younger. He was older than me by four years, which meant he was now pushing thirty.

"Hey, Olive Oil." He leaned in and pulled me into his arms, completely ignoring Miles standing next to me. After a moment's hesitation, my hands patted his back awkwardly. He lingered a bit too long, the same expensive cologne infiltrating my nose. His hug was both familiar and unwelcome, and I quickly extracted myself from his arms and stepped back toward Miles.

Glenn finally took notice of the man standing patiently by my side. His parents were staring at him as well, and each set of eyes trailed across my shoulder where Miles's arm currently rested.

"Who's this?" Virginia asked. Her voice was polite, if a bit uncertain.

Miles stuck his other hand out toward her, smiling. "Hi. I'm Miles, Olive's boyfriend."

Chills shot all around my body. His words mixed with that casual low drawl had me suddenly wanting to curl up on his lap while he played with my hair as we watched a movie. Though he was quite a bit taller, our height difference seemed complementary. But I couldn't allow myself to get distracted by thoughts like that, because there was no doubt in my mind that he was going to make me suffer for this. Everything had a price with Miles Taylor. Now the feel of his hand lightly rubbing my upper arm felt different. Ever so slightly, I flicked my shoulder upward, trying to ward off his fingers. They stilled but didn't move.

Virginia's expressive blue eyes bounced from mine to Miles. "Oh! Boyfriend? Your mom didn't—" She cut off, glancing at Glenn.

"It's pretty new," I stated brightly, desperately wanting this moment to be over. "It's so nice to see you all again."

Virginia smiled tightly, sending one more curious glance

toward Miles before saying, "Yes, I can't wait to catch up. We'll go in and say hi to your mom and Russ now."

Lyle and Virginia moved toward the main room, leaving only Glenn standing in front of us.

He stared at us both for a long moment, then finally gave a slightly patronizing smile and stuck his hand out toward Miles. "Glenn Foster."

Miles shook his hand, dropping his left arm to fit snugly around my waist. Even though I knew it was Miles and we shouldn't have been touching like this, I couldn't help but feel a tiny bit more at ease with him next to me. I wasn't alone with Glenn, and I wouldn't have to be.

"Miles Taylor. Nice to meet you."

A glint hit Glenn's eyes as he took Miles's measure. "And what do you do?"

"I teach English with Olive."

He stepped back, looking between us both before he started laughing. "Both of you? Oh geez. I'll bet you have some crazy Friday nights, busting out Shakespeare or whatever those boring books were that Olive used to read all the time."

Miles looked as though he found something amusing—not Glenn so much, but something. Looking down at me, he said, "Sometimes she writes me love notes." I pinched his side, and he did the same to mine.

Glenn scoffed, shaking his head. "I can't believe there are two of you."

My foot twitched inside my boot. Something niggled. I could handle Glenn's comments—the snide, underhanded rudeness covered by a charming smile. I knew to expect them, but it really rubbed me wrong that Glenn was doing the same to Miles. I mean, to me, Miles *was* the worst. But to everybody else, he was beloved. Just because he wasn't my cup of tea didn't mean I wanted my ex-boyfriend to put him down. Although...it shouldn't have mattered. I should have kept my mouth shut. It would only add fuel to Miles's fire later on, but I couldn't help it.

I folded my arms and tried to seem nonchalant with my praise, but my heart was pounding. "Miles is an author, actually. He was just picked up by a big publisher to finish out his series. He's also quite the adventurer–rock climbing in the summer and skiing black diamonds in the winter." I should have stopped there, but all reason left me and I kept going. "And he still finds time to write me love notes."

Glenn raised his eyebrows. "I thought you wrote him love notes."

When I had the nerve to actually look at Miles, he had a grin on his face. "I help her find the right words, so they're actually from both of us by the time we finish." He pulled me closer and kissed me on the temple before I could blink.

I stiffened into a stone statue when warm lips from Miles Taylor touched my face.

Don't think. Don't react. Normal boyfriend behavior.

DON'T THINK.

Glenn stared at Miles, disbelievingly, for a long moment. "What do you write? Romance?"

Miles stared deeply into my eyes for a few too many long, agonizing moments. He seemed to enjoy working over his crowd and making everybody, including me, uncomfortable. The payback had already begun. "Maybe someday."

Okay. We had to reel this in or else Glenn would know something was up. I gave Miles a warning look.

"He writes middle-grade adventure," I said.

"Kid books?"

Miles cleared his throat, this time looking less amused. "What is it you do?"

Glenn smiled tightly. "I'm an acquisitions manager for a manufacturing company outside of Boston."

"Sounds like a mouthful."

Glenn smirked. "Pays the bills."

By this point, both men were still smiling, but it felt more like rabid dogs bearing their teeth.

"Well, it's been nice seeing you again, Glenn." I smiled up at him, giving him a gracious hint that it was time to move on. My body was in a flurry of agitation. I needed Glenn gone, Miles to stop touching me, and this whole miserable night over before my pounding heart went into cardiac arrest.

"Yeah. I should go and sit by my parents for a bit. I hear we're neighbors, though." He gave me a pointed look. "Maybe I'll swing by later tonight and throw some rocks at your window like old times. We have a lot to catch up on."

He shot me a satisfied look before nodding toward Miles and moving past us into the main room. My body felt ten pounds lighter at his exit.

"He seems sweet," Miles said.

I carefully stepped away from his arm. My gaze went to the floor, for some reason unable to meet his eye. This whole thing was nothing I had bargained or prepared for. I had said his name to my sister last night. He was never supposed to know. And yet, here he was. Almost as if I had ordered myself a boyfriend for the week. It was disconcerting, and I needed to end this now.

"Well, thanks for…that. I'm really sorry for this whole weird mess. I'll figure out something to tell my family tonight."

"What are you going to say?"

I shrugged, still finding the floor fascinating. "I'll just tell everyone we broke up."

He snorted. "No way."

My eyes flitted up to his. "Why not?"

He crossed his arms over his chest. "You're gonna let them think I broke up with my girlfriend a week before Christmas? No. I'm not gonna be that guy."

"Fine. I broke up with you."

He shot me an impatient look. "They'd never believe that."

I scoffed, feeling annoyed at the sparkle in his eye. "You know, they really might."

"Nope. I say we're in it for the whole week."

My eyebrows raised in shock. That was the last thing I'd expected him to say.

"No. We're breaking up tonight," I hissed. One thing was for sure–with the way my traitorous body reacted to him, I could only date Miles Taylor when Miles Taylor had no idea we were dating.

"Olive, who is this?" Mom came walking into the foyer with an expectant smile on her face, with Chloe trailing behind her.

Miles and I were suddenly two deer very much in the head-lights. I stood frozen, unsure of what to do given the last bit of our conversation.

Miles shoved his hands in his pockets and eyed me with amused curiosity, awaiting my move. He was going to let me lead, but consequentially, effort-wise, he was going to make me come one hundred percent to his zero.

"You didn't wait for me, Miles." Chloe stood with her hands on her hips, peering back and forth between us. She was looking slightly pale and like a strong wind might topple her, but that didn't stop her from staring at me with an emotion I couldn't quite place. Suspicion? My brow furrowed slightly. Miles was here. By default, she *had* to believe me now, right? She raised her eyebrows at me. Waiting.

Apparently her obsession with true-crime podcasts was paying off. She was like Sherlock freaking Holmes, sniffing for clues. Something inside of me couldn't let her know she was right—not yet, at least. And not in front of everyone. Somebody had to prove to her that I wasn't the liar I actually was.

I stepped closer to Miles and linked my arm through his. He gave me an over-the-top alluring grin. I mentally cringed at what this would cost me later.

"So, you're the handsome boy we've been hearing about?" Mom asked, looking up at Miles.

Okay, gag me. I didn't appreciate her insinuation that I talked about him all the time. And I would never call him handsome—especially to his face. That word was for the romance books hidden secretly on my Kindle. Not for Miles Taylor.

Before I could answer, Miles leaned forward, reaching out to shake my mom's hand. "I'm Miles. I work with your sister."

Mom raised her eyebrows. "You mean my daughter."

I fidgeted uncomfortably as Miles made a big, clichéd show of proclaimed astonishment at my mother's age while my mom blushed and swatted his shoulder playfully. It struck me just then what was so different about my mom tonight. She was wearing makeup. She never used to wear much, if any at all, and now a flattering streak of pink colored her cheeks, and her eyes were highlighted by a dark coat of mascara.

"I think this one's a keeper, Olive," she said, bringing me back to the conversation.

He draped his arm once again across my shoulders, squeezing me in extra tight. "I keep trying to convince your daughter of that."

Mom laughed while Chloe added, "His family owns this place. He kept it a secret so he could surprise Olive when he found out we were coming."

Her voice was definitely riddled with wariness. Which had me wondering if my sub-par acting abilities were to blame. It was time to put on my big girl pants and play this dumb game I'd started. I smiled brightly and turned to my fake boyfriend, piercing him with a private stare so full of pleading he could do nothing while I leaned closer and placed a kiss on his cheek. It was warmer than expected, given the cold. He had a hint of stubble on his face, and the overall feel wasn't as horrible as I had imagined. I refused to meet his eyes, though.

Turning to face Mom and Chloe, I said, "It was the best surprise. What are the odds?"

"You two are so cute." Mom beamed.

"Just a peck on the cheek?" Chloe smiled daggers at me. "After such a romantic gesture?"

My nose flared slightly, but I managed to keep my smile bright as I regarded my horrible sister. "I've already thanked him plenty. Besides, I'm not into PDA."

"I am, though," Miles said, turning to face me, pure devilish mischief on his face. "I don't mind you thanking me again."

My entire body froze. Mom and Chloe watched me expectantly. I had to play this off. There was no way I would be kissing Miles, even though I now knew exactly how he intended to get even with me for all of this.

I squeezed his arm tighter while attempting to laugh off my mom and Chloe. "Don't you two have husbands to get back to?"

"They'll be fine," Chloe said, snapping her wrist in front of her like it was no big deal. "I want some proof that you're actually dating. Since nobody heard about you two before last night."

That little hormonal perv.

I looked at my mom to save me. Surely this was weird for her, too. But this woman was a far cry from the prim and proper mother I had grown up with. She smiled and folded her arms. "She does have a point. A quick kiss might help us all wrap our heads around this."

What was happening?

Miles turned to face me, trying to hide his smile. "Better give the people what they want, Celery Stick."

Fine.

FINE. They were right. It wouldn't hurt anything. The effect of a kiss was all in our heads, blown up by the romantic comedies of the world. An actual kiss was just one mouth pressed against another mouth. Kind of gross, actually. But really no big deal. I could put my mouth on Miles Taylor's mouth and just be done with it. You know what was difficult to wrap *my* brain around? That I was being forced into this position. That Miles was actually HERE right now. I was going to kill Millie.

I turned to face Miles. "Alright, let's do this."

His lips broke into a smile. "So romantic," he murmured.

"Shut up," I whispered just before I grabbed the collar of his flannel shirt, pulled him down to where I could reach, and pressed my mouth against his. I hadn't realized how cold my lips were until they were touching his. How were men always so warm? The attractive pine and spice smell of his cologne immediately tried to weaken me, but I remained strong, like an immovable oak. As far as kisses went, it was what I imagined giving a grandparent a peck on the lips would feel like. Our lips were slightly puckered, but I refused to open my mouth any more, so we just stood there with our mouths pressed together for as long as I could stand. I pulled away and tucked the hair behind my ear, wondering why my heart was pounding. It couldn't have been from *that* kiss.

I cleared my throat and turned to face my executioners. "There you go."

"Wow," was all Chloe could say.

"Huh," Mom said.

We all stood there in a semi-awkward silence for a few moments before my mom put us out of our misery. "Well, Olive, you're still in trouble for keeping him from us,"

I wrinkled my nose playfully. "I'm sorry. I wanted to be sure he wasn't a dud before I told everyone."

Miles chuckled appreciatively, his arm snaking around my waist once more.

Suddenly, Chloe bent over, resting her hands on her knees, and took a deep breath. Her face had grown even more pale since we'd been standing here.

"You okay, Chlo?" I asked.

Another breath. "Yeah. Just nausea."

"We have a general store here with over-the-counter medicines. I can go grab you something if you need it," Miles offered. I looked at him in surprise, but his eyes were on Chloe.

"We have some at the cabin." She smiled at him gratefully. "But thank you."

"So, is this the guy I've been hearing so much about the past…five minutes?" Russ's booming voice broke into our group. We turned to see him and Ben walking toward us, each holding a twin in their arms.

I resisted the urge to roll my eyes as my shoulders sank in defeat. This freaking foyer was busier than a subway.

Miles leaned forward, shaking Russ's hand. "Nice to meet you, sir. I'm Miles."

"Russ Ellis. Has anybody ever told you that you look like a young Bradley Cooper?"

"Right? I thought the same thing," Ben chirped from behind my mom.

A grin split across Miles's entire face. "I have heard that a time or two." The hand that was around my waist dug into my side, tickling me. I tried to casually get out from his grip, but he held me firmly.

"How'd you come to be here?" He eyed us curiously. He must have missed Chloe's explanation.

Mom stepped in, looking at me. "Miles's family owns the entire lodge. I still find it crazy that you were able to keep this secret that long."

"He loves a good joke." I looked up at him and patted his cheek, maybe a smidge too hard.

Mom squeezed my arm. "Well, we're going to get Chloe home." Looking at us, she said, "Good night, you two. I can't wait to chat more with you, Miles."

"Looking forward to it," he replied. We said our goodbyes,

and they all turned to go. To me, he whispered, "Should I call her Mom?"

I elbowed his stomach. "Why does it seem like you're overly thrilled about this?"

Warm puffs of air hit my ear as his lips moved dangerously close to me. "Because now you owe me. Big time."

Before I could protest or demand we cancel whatever this was, Miles claimed he had to help clean up the building and strode off without another word. My eyes narrowed, not sure if I believed him but not wanting to drag this out, so I let him go, hoping that, by tomorrow morning, we'd be on the same page with the whole breakup plan.

NINE

“If she do bid me pack, I'll give her thanks as though she bid me stay by her a week.”
William Shakespeare - *The Taming of the Shrew*

THOUGH I WASN'T FAR BEHIND THEM, CHLOE HAD GONE STRAIGHT to bed by the time I arrived at the cabin. I didn't like to see her so sick, but I couldn't help but feel relieved that I wouldn't get the Spanish Inquisition from her tonight. The twins were eating at the table when I entered, apparently famished after having refused to touch their dinner at the lodge. I set up my pull-out bed and then helped Ben change the girls into their pajamas. We laid out blankets on the floor next to the fireplace along with their sleeping bags. Once the giggles and mischief died down, they drifted off to sleep. Ben said goodnight and snuck into the bedroom. I sighed as his door closed and I finally had the quiet I had been craving since my arrival.

Fluffing the pillows we'd found stuffed in the closet, I tried to get comfortable. Technology had definitely not advanced in the pull-out bed department. A long bar stretched out across the bed frame, protruding through the thin mattress pad. I contemplated changing the bed back to a couch but realized I didn't have the energy. There were more important matters to address. I reached for my phone.

ME: Just letting you know...I will no longer be bringing you double Oreo milkshakes on the second day of your period. And when you have to pee so badly during your fourth hour, when I have my break, I will no longer be coming to relieve you. Ever.

MILLIE: What on earth did I do to deserve that?

ME: You backstabbing traitor. You sent me to Miles's lodge on purpose!

MILLIE: Oh, dear me. Was that Miles's lodge?

ME: MILLIE.

ME: *GIF of Darla from *Little Rascals* crunching a pop can*

ME: You told me you'd heard about this lodge from a FRIEND!

MILLIE: He is my friend. But I have so many friends sometimes it's hard to remember who tells me what...

ME: You knew exactly what you were doing.

MILLIE: Well, as long as you're there, try and make the best of it. I'm sure there are some janitor closets somewhere. You know what to do.

ME: Chloroform him?

MILLIE: Try less felony…more kissing.

ME: We will have words when I get back.

MILLIE: I take chocolate, milkshakes, and wedding invitations in lieu of apologies. Heading to bed! Keep me posted.

I PUT MY PHONE DOWN AND PULLED MY KINDLE OUT OF MY duffel bag. I had almost told her about the whole pretend-to-be-my-boyfriend debacle but didn't want to get into it. It was over, and I'd never have cause to mention it again. Once I spoke to Miles tomorrow, I would apologize and swear him to secrecy. I flopped around on the bed for a few moments, trying to find a spot where the bar didn't jab into me, when my phone lit up again. Expecting Millie, I was half tempted to wait a whole five minutes before responding, to really drive home how upset I was, when I noticed it wasn't from her.

UNKNOWN NUMBER: This is Miles. I am hypothetically throwing rocks at your window.

ME: Why are you doing that?

ME: And how did you get this number?

UNKNOWN NUMBER: I have the numbers of all my fake girlfriends. Come outside.

ME: Is this how you kill your victims?

UNKNOWN NUMBER: I'm about to kill you with kindness. Like Taming of the Shrew.

ME: Wow. Shakespeare? I underestimated you.

UNKNOWN NUMBER: COME OUTSIDE.

HEART POUNDING FOR SOME UNKNOWN REASON, I STOOD UP FROM the uncomfortable bed and pulled on my white parka and gloves. I glanced at the door that led into Chloe's room and suddenly felt like a naughty teenager sneaking out in the middle of the night. The girls were sleeping peacefully on the floor, and I glanced regretfully back at my Kindle. But I guess now was as good a time as ever to break up with my fake boyfriend. I stuffed my feet into my boots by the door and crept silently outside.

Miles stood on the sidewalk just below the front stairs, wearing a dark-blue coat and his beanie slung low across his forehead. Bits of his flannel shirt poked through the collar. I swallowed.

"I have a proposition for you," he said. His arms were folded, and he was staring at me with a calculating expression on his face.

The wind bit at my face, but I moved to stand just in front of him. "What's that?"

"It's recently come to my attention that you might be crazy about me."

My fingers clenched. "Not true."

"I was the first person you thought of when naming fake boyfriends."

"I just said a name, and it happened to be the same name as yours."

He went on as though I hadn't spoken. "You're also not above objectifying my body—my fine pair of hams, to be exact."

"That was sarcastic!" I stamped my foot in the snow, but he only laughed.

"But tonight's got me thinking. This arrangement could be useful to me, too."

"We don't have an arrangement. I'm confessing all my sins tomorrow morning."

"No need. You owe me now, and I wanna do it."

Slow down, heart. He didn't mean it like it sounded. "Do what?"

"Pretend to date you this week."

I looked at him like he was crazy. "What? Why?"

"Have you told your mom or sister anything yet?"

"No. Chloe was already in bed by the time I got home." I rubbed briskly at my arms to ward off the chill.

Miles noticed. "Do you want to move to the porch? It might be warmer."

I shook my head. "No. The windows are right there. Somebody could hear us."

Miles brought his glove-covered hands to his face and blew warm air into them. "I've got three dates my mom is insisting I go on this week. You're the perfect excuse."

I made a noise of disbelief. "Why don't you want to go on those dates?"

"One of the girls I knew in high school. She once made out with another guy while on a date with me."

I mimicked Miles, blowing warm air onto my hands. "And your mom wants you to go out with her?"

"She doesn't know that part. She thinks it's two old flames reconnecting."

"And it's not?"

"Nope."

"Maybe we should introduce her to Glenn."

He smiled, his eyes crinkling. "Not a bad idea."

"And the other two?" I asked, clearing my throat.

"The other one's a big lawyer here in town. She's pretty, but kind of scary. She would eat a sweet, creative soul like me for breakfast."

I scoffed. "A *what?*"

A grin burst across his face, his white teeth gleaming under the glow of the porch light. "You heard me. Very sweet."

"And the other date? Are there really that many women your mom's trying to set you up with?"

He smiled. "Well, you see, this is where it gets good. The other one is you."

I jolted. "Me?"

"Apparently, you made a wonderful first impression on my parents. They both now love you."

Dang it, Jack Taylor.

"I told your dad I had a boyfriend."

His eyebrows raised appreciatively.

"He didn't know it was you. He shouldn't be pushing you toward a date with me."

He laughed and folded his arms. "My dad's a big believer in the whole 'all's fair in love and war' mentality."

"And you can't just tell them no?"

He shrugged. "I could. But according to them, you're exactly my type."

I made the mistake of looking at him just then. My stomach dropped as our eyes were locked in a crosshair battle of wills and...something else. We should have broken our gaze moments ago, but he was still staring at me, and I was having a hard time looking away.

"I figured we could help each other out. We both get away from the matchmaking, and you save face with your mom and sister. Your family already thinks we're together. It wouldn't be hard to convince my parents."

I sucked in a breath. This whole thing was my idea. I knew that I should have been readily agreeing to this crazy scheme. Glenn was here. And he was still a jerk. Miles was actually trying to do me a solid, helping me out in his own twisted way.

For reasons I couldn't define, it was too much to have him see me like this. Too personal. My emotions from being here were too cloudy. I needed to be able to hide away under a passive smile to get me through this week. And Miles had never been one to let me get away with anything. Pretending to date him would mean we would be hanging out all the time. Him seeing me interact with my mom and her new husband? No, thank you. I didn't need him judging my life choices over Christmas break.

"What do you say, Celery Stick?"

"No."

"No?"

"No." Even saying it for the second time, a sliver of doubt pierced through me, but I couldn't let him see that. "I don't think it would be in our best interest to get involved like that. I don't date people I work with—even if it's just pretend."

He gave a tiny smirk of a smile. "No?"

"No."

"Our grasp of the English language is astonishing," he said, grinning.

The smile was out of my mouth before I could rein it in. I bit my lip to tug my unruly mouth back into shape. Did he seem more charming here than usual? I mean…not that I ever found him charming before.

"Alright," he sighed. "Time to pull out the big guns." He cocked his head to the side and studied me. "What do you want?"

My brows furrowed. "Nothing."

"Everybody wants something. Did I hear you're sleeping on the pull-out couch?"

I swallowed before lifting my chin defiantly. "Yup. And I love it."

"Really? Do they still have those hard metal bars across the bed?"

"I wouldn't know. It feels great so far." Wow, the lies were just spewing from my mouth these days.

He smiled. "What if I told you that I had access to a cabin that's not being used right now."

I froze as my eyes flew up to his, trying to determine if he was pulling a fast one. A sudden sense of hope infiltrated my body. "Your mom said all the cabins were rented."

"Not this one. The gas fireplace doesn't work, so they couldn't rent it out."

"It's not heated?" I asked doubtfully. That was a no-deal for me. I had to be warm.

"It has an old wood fireplace, too. Lately, it's more used as a cozy look for website pictures, and the gas fireplace is what's used to actually heat the place up. But I could find you an ax."

He grinned at me. My eyes were drawn to his five o'clock shadow and mysterious brown eyes. I found myself blushing. Hotly. It had nothing whatsoever to do with the sudden vision of Miles Taylor in red flannel outside my cabin, chopping wood.

"You make all your guests chop wood?"

"I'll chop it for the ones I like."

My breath stilled. Did he mean—

"So, I'll be sure to get you an ax."

I glared at him while he only bit his lip, smiling.

"You do this fake-dating thing with me, and the cabin's all yours."

Welp. The stakes were raised, and they were definitely good stakes. Very intriguing. Pretty much everything I could ever want in this place was being offered to me on a silver platter. And all for the low price of one fake boyfriend.

"Where is it?" I made a point of looking around at the rest of the cabins in the village. Every one I could see already had a vehicle parked in front. "Is it run down somewhere and crawling with mice?"

"Last I checked, the mice were tame. Just leave some cheese out every now and then, and they won't cause any issues."

"Miles." I shot him a warning look.

He laughed. "No mice. It's on a trail behind the lodge. It was one of the original cabins before they built all of these." He motioned to the small subdivision around us.

"Do people still use it?" I had sudden visions of furniture draped in white sheets and cobwebs everywhere.

"Yeah. When the fireplace is working." When I said nothing else, he continued. "What's your hold up? Wasn't this *your* plan?"

That I could answer. "My hold up is that you were never supposed to be here. It was just a name to scare people off. Not real."

He shrugged. "It's still not real, though, right?"

I bit my lip. It felt real when there was a warm body to suddenly go with the name.

"Can I think about it tonight? And let you know tomorrow?"

He crossed his arms over his chest and shrugged. "You can, but I can't guarantee the offer will be the same tomorrow. That gives me a whole lot of time to think. You might want to snag this deal while you have it."

What else could he possibly add to this crazy scheme? "I'll take my chances."

I should have been nervous when he just grinned bigger and shrugged at my statement, but I was feeling too rattled to overthink things.

Turning to walk back up the porch steps, I said, "I'll let you know tomorrow."

"Sweet dreams, Carrots."

"Don't *Anne of Green Gables* me," I hissed. A low chuckle met my ears before I closed the cabin door.

TEN

"I'll be back."
The Terminator

Saying no was a good idea. I didn't want to get involved with Miles Taylor, even if it was strictly fake. I certainly wasn't nervous about my feelings getting confused, but I also read and taught books for a living. I knew what happened in every fake-dating storyline. Lots of unnecessary touching and confusion and somebody professing love and real feelings. Not on my watch.

From our brief interaction tonight, we had already kissed once on the lips (although I used the term kiss very loosely), along with a cheek kiss and a kiss on my temple. Which was too much kissing for two people who didn't like each other. Saying no was responsible. It was me taking charge of my life and not allowing Miles to tempt me into something so clearly absurd. It was me making things right with my sister and my mom. Though, I did begin to suspect that my acting skills from earlier still hadn't completely won either of them over. That's it. I was going to say no.

Unfortunately, my plan to be the bigger and better person went completely out the window at 2:30 that morning.

After determining I would turn down Miles's offer, I attempted to read on my Kindle with all the clueless naiveté of a woman unused to sleeping with children in an unfamiliar environment. I had just drifted off to sleep when Ivy began moaning and rolling around in her sleeping bag. Not wanting her to steamroll her sister and wake her up too, I crept over to her and tried several times to get her to curl up on her side of the makeshift bed. Half an hour later, after listening to all the whimpers and moans I could handle, I finally picked her up and carried her into bed with me.

Like a cat, she snuggled up against me, whimpering softly in her sleep. I just embraced the fact that I would be a zombie tomorrow and pulled her close. The response was immediate, her little arm going around me and her hot breath puffing against my neck while her body splayed out across mine. But it was all so sweet, and I let myself relish the feel of those little arms for the moment.

Without warning, hot smelly vomit began erupting from her tiny mouth all down my neck and the front of my pajamas. I sat up, gasping in shock, cringing at the feel of the warm sludge sliding farther down my body. Instantly, my body fought against the smell by dry heaving. I tried to pull it together for Ivy and began breathing through my mouth to keep down my own puke.

"Ivy, are you okay?"

Her retching had finally stopped, but her little head hung limply across my shoulder. She sniffled but gave me nothing else to go on.

"Does your tummy still hurt?"

She shook her head.

Okay. How do I handle this? Do I stand up and get it all over the house walking to the bathroom? Luckily, Chloe's mom ears had clued in, and the door to their room opened. A few moments later, Ivy was extracted from my arms, and I heard the bathtub running. I lay there for the next few moments in my niece's puke before the bathroom door opened and Chloe handed me a towel to wrap around myself.

"I'm so sorry," she whispered as I made my way into the bathroom for a quick shower.

"It's fine," I said. When the door closed, I ran to the toilet, dry heaving for several long, uncomfortable moments.

After a quick shower, I made my way back into the front room. Chloe had just laid Ivy back down in her sleeping bag on the floor.

"I'm so sorry," she said again as I crawled back into a bed now covered in blankets.

"It's okay, I promise."

"I stripped the bed, but I couldn't find any more sheets in any of the drawers. I just put a few blankets over top. I really am so sorry." Chloe's hands flew to cover her face.

I reached out and touched her arm. "Chlo, it's fine. I feel like I've got a mom card now."

Chloe breathed out a tiny laugh.

"How's Ivy?" I asked.

"I'm wondering if it was the hot dog she ate when we got home from the lodge."

My nose wrinkled. "Most likely."

Chloe looked like she was about ready to keel over with exhaustion.

"How are you feeling?"

"The nausea goes away when I'm sleeping, so that's always a plus."

I breathed out a soft laugh. "Go get some sleep. Everything's fine out here. I promise."

"Okay, I'll keep the door open."

"Good night."

ACCORDING TO CHLOE, CHILDREN THROW UP WHENEVER AND wherever they please, no rhyme or reason to it. They wake up in the middle of the night, find their target, explode, and then sleep easily. I peered at Ivy warily as she inhaled the scrambled eggs Chloe set before her, as though she hadn't emptied her insides all over me the night before.

She burped before catching my gaze and throwing me a cheeky grin. I playfully glared at her for a long moment until my smile betrayed me.

Chloe sighed and sat down on a seat next to me at the table. "Ben and I talked, and we're going to switch you beds for the rest of the week. You should totally get your own room. If I'd know my kid would suddenly turn into a crazy puking, bed-stealer, I would have just started off with us out there."

I stared at my sister just then. The way she was hunched over, holding her stomach like she was one step away from throwing up herself. Padding around in her slippers and oversized shirt and joggers. The bags under her eyes. I was the one who felt like an intruder. I could always stay with my mom and Russ, but...no. I knew what I had to do. And I was not looking forward to crawling to Miles with my tail between my legs, believe me. Or even worse, pretending to *date* him. But, even more than that, I didn't want to force my sick, miserable pregnant sister onto the world's most uncomfortable pull-out couch.

"Actually, I think Miles has a cabin he can let me stay in."

Chloe's eyes flashed my way in surprise. "*His* cabin?"

"No. It's empty. The gas fireplace is broken, so they couldn't rent it out."

"Won't you freeze?"

"Apparently, this cabin was one of the originals. The wood-burning fireplace is still there, but they added a gas fireplace for ease. So, there's wood we can chop."

"You want to know my first thought when I saw him?" Chloe's eyes were flashing with a bit of the playfulness she'd had the night before at the lodge, which immediately raised my guard.

"Not really," I said, taking a sip of my coffee.

"He'd make an excellent lumberjack."

"Okay, simmer down. He'll probably make me chop it."

Her gaze turned questioning. "Why?"

Dang it. Any boyfriend worth his salt would probably do the wood chopping for his woman. I decided to appeal to Chloe's feministic side. "He's a big proponent of teaching a man to fish—or in this case, a woman to chop wood."

"You tell him that if he doesn't chop your wood, I'm going to kick him where the sun doesn't shine."

Oh, right, I forgot. Chloe only had a feminist side after she watched any movie set around 1800's England.

"Well...do what you've got to do."

She sputtered out a laugh. "He's hot, I'll give you that."

I straightened in my seat. "Thank you?"

"And I can tell he likes you."

I suddenly felt like a mouse trapped by a playful cat. Maybe Miles was a better actor than I thought.

"I missed the surprise. Were you freaking out when you saw him?"

"Yup. Definitely freaking out."

Her smile took on a pained look. "All right, I want to hear more, but I'm gonna go lie back down for a while. Ben said he'd take the kids to look at the animals this morning while I took a nap."

"Good. Sleep well." I stood from the table, taking one last sip of coffee for fortification. "I've got to go see a man about a cabin."

◆

THOUGH MY SISTER SEEMED SAD ABOUT THE IDEA OF ME changing cabins, I could tell a small part of her tired, pregnant body was relieved to not have to sleep on the pull-out couch. And Ben would probably be excited to walk around in his underwear.

I spotted Miles out chopping wood behind the barn. Of course he would be chopping wood. My steps slowed significantly as I drew closer, watching his tall, lean body bend over to place a log carefully on the stump, lift the ax, and swing. I jumped, hearing the abrupt thunk as his muscles tore through the log like it was a twig. It was too much. Really. All of Chloe's lumberjack jokes, and here I was, about to beg one to be my fake boyfriend. Again.

When I was a few yards from him, he stopped and stood tall, stretching his back. Though he was covered up to ward off the chill, my eyes couldn't help but admire the way the old pair of Levis snugly fit his frame. Turning, he spotted me almost upon him and smiled.

My breath caught. That smile was unexpected. It seemed genuine and didn't look like he was about to tease me or—

"Morning, Celery Stick."

Okay. Yeah. Back to earth.

"I'll do it." Might as well just get down to business before the "offer" could change or whatever nonsense he threatened last night.

His eyes narrowed, and alarm bells began ringing through my head. Maybe I *should* just let Chloe take the couch. No. I had to do this. Also, there was Glenn to consider.

"Do what?" His gleam etched across his face, letting me know we would be doing this the hard way.

I sucked in a breath, allowing myself to revel in the last calm moment before my world would change forever. "Pretend to date you this week." Oh, yuck. I can't believe I was even saying those words aloud. Pathetic and one hundred percent my own fault.

"What changed your mind?"

"A three-year-old barfing all over me at 2 am."

To his credit, his face was sympathetic. "That'll do it."

"I need my own cabin."

"I see." He nodded his head thoughtfully as he leaned over to set another log on the block.

I waited with bated breath for my fate.

"Well, unfortunately, since you waited so long to accept, the offer has changed."

There it was.

"Come on," I whined, taking another few cautious steps toward him.

"I'm sorry. I tried to warn you last night."

"Changed to what?" I asked, folding my arms. Of course he wouldn't make this easy. Except, this time, I had to say yes.

He adjusted his gloves. "Nothing too drastic. But I realized something. I gave you too much. If you get your own cabin, you'll never leave. Nobody would ever see us together."

"That's not true." It was exactly true. A brilliant plan if I said so myself. "I'm sure I'd get hungry."

"There's a coffee maker in that cabin. And it's a good one. So that only leaves two meals you'd consider coming outside for."

I didn't like where this was going, but I couldn't see how to stop it. Miles was looking at me like I was a juicy hamburger, and he hadn't had lunch yet. I felt flushed and agitated and twitchy.

"Doesn't that sound like the perfect way to fake date? Limited time together?"

A small smirk appeared on his face. "It might be easier, but much less realistic. I've got a reputation to uphold. Any woman of mine wouldn't be able to keep her hands off me."

"You're about to be very disappointed, then."

He only stood there with arms folded, a lazy grin on his face as he waited for me.

With great reluctance, I asked, "What do you have in mind?"

"Bingo."

"Huh?"

"I'll only agree to this if you do the bingo game with me." He leaned in closer. "Not just the bingo. The blackout. I could really use a trip to Mexico."

"The blackout?" I didn't remember much about the bingo card, but two things stood out like a glaring neon sign in my brain. A mistletoe kiss and something about a polar bear plunge. Two very strong NOs from me.

"No."

His eyebrows raised. "No?"

"Just the bingo. That's more than enough time together."

"You scared you won't be able to resist me?"

"No. But isn't there some sort of nepotism clause for you to do the blackout stuff?"

"I'm not an official employee. I'm just snagging a few free meals and helping out with the farm. If I was just a boyfriend and you ended up winning, they couldn't stop it."

"There was a mistletoe kiss on that card. No way."

The grin on his face immediately set my heart pounding. "I promise I'll make it good."

My cheeks flushed annoyingly while I tamped down some runaway butterflies.

"We've already kissed," I said, attempting to gain back an ounce of control. "We can just count that one."

He looked at me like I was crazy. "My grandma could have kissed me better than that. And besides, there wasn't any mistletoe."

I guess my grandparent thoughts while my lips were pressed against his weren't that far off.

"A tiny, harmless mistletoe kiss seems like a much better option than sharing a bed with a puking three-year-old," he said, dangling his bait carefully.

My heart thudded to a stop. He was right. I didn't have much of a choice, but the blackout thing was really throwing me. That changed the entire tune of the quiet, hide-away-in-a-cabin vibe I was going for. This would require time. And dates. With *him*.

When I looked up at him, grappling, he only smiled. "What will it be, Oliviana? Five days of luxury cabin living with your sexy new boyfriend, or more puking on a hide-a-bed with the family?"

Curse the day he came into my classroom and found a piece of mail on my desk with my full name. I think I preferred his vegetable tray references. I folded my arms and raised my chin. "You know, I could just blow the whistle on this whole thing and be all the happier for it."

"And resist these fine hams?" He motioned to his back end. "I'm sure Glenn would be excited about that plan."

I wanted to punch him. In the face. Cue visions of his nose bleeding all over that blue coat. My eyes glazed over as I allowed the fantasy to play out in my mind. But the choice was already made for me. I wouldn't be making Chloe sleep on the pull-out couch. And I definitely wouldn't be sleeping anywhere near my mom and Russ. I didn't want to spend any time with Glenn alone. Looked like my Christmas vacation just got worse. And better. But mostly worse.

"Fine."

A slow, Cheshire-cat grin crawled across his face just then, and my heart rate immediately sped up.

He reached out a hand toward me. My first instinct was to jerk away. He gave me an impatient look, and I realized he was holding out a hand to shake. I slowly brought my hand to his. His hand covered mine, giving it a shake. It felt warm, and rough, and manly. And way too excited.

"Why do I feel like I just made a deal with the devil?"

"You started this whole thing. I'm just giving it a better ending." He gave my hand a quick squeeze before releasing it. "I'll pick you up in an hour to take you to your cabin, Celery Stick."

ELEVEN

"Of all matches never was the like."
William Shakespeare - *The Taming of the Shrew*

MILLIE: Have you forgiven me yet?

ME: That's a strong no.

MILLIE: Well, have you two at least kissed? It's been almost twenty-four hours.

ME: I have a Christmas present that I forgot to give to you before I left. I will now be gifting it to myself. I'm planning to watch it with some gummy worms, Ghirardelli brownies, and a carton of Ben and Jerry's ALONE. And I'll be perfectly happy.

MILLIE: Changing the subject?

ME: ...

MILLIE: WHAT is happening there? Did you two KISS?!

A KNOCK AT THE CABIN DOOR HAD ME JUMPING UP FROM THE couch and flipping my screen to black, as though Miles could suddenly see everything. I slid the phone into my back pocket and pulled on my coat and gloves. Ben and Chloe had taken their kids to the lodge for some coloring and crafts, which left me with some time to make the bed, do the dishes, and tidy up the cabin for Chloe so she wouldn't have to worry about the house when she got back.

I tried not to look nervous opening the door for Miles, but I was thankful that my pounding heart was hidden beneath several layers of fabric.

"Planning to stay for a couple of months?" he asked, eyeing my luggage as he held the door open for me to step outside. Once I stepped out into the sunshine (which was misleading because the temperature hovered around eleven degrees), he reached over and took the suitcase and duffel bag out of my hands, pushing the extendable handle down so he could lift the suitcase.

"You should be grateful I left my library at home."

He looked at me in surprise. "You didn't bring any books?"

"Just my Kindle." I decided to leave the two hardback classics I had brought out of this discussion.

"Oh, the famous Kindle. I'd love to take a peek to see what the prim-and-proper lit teacher reads in secret." He gave me a pointed look. "I mean, I already know one special book on your Kindle that you took the time to read."

I made a mental note to make sure my Kindle was nowhere in sight for the next five days in my new cabin.

We hemmed and hawed up the sidewalk, the snow making a crunching sound at our feet with each step.

"Whose house is that?"

Miles lifted his head and followed my point off in the

distance toward a large, two-story, red farmhouse with a wraparound porch.

"That's my parents' house."

I slowed my steps, suddenly feeling unsure about my stay in this cabin. It seemed odd to be so far from everybody else and so close to the owners' home.

"Is this a joke or something? Do you really have a cabin for me to stay in?"

"Well, cabin is a loose term. It's actually more of an underground lair I use for experiments."

When I gave him a dark look, he chuckled. "Yeah, where do you think I'm taking you?"

"I'm not sure. This looks like a lovely place for murder. Why is this cabin so far away from the others?"

"My parents lived here for a few years before they built their big house. Then, they decided to add some more cabins but wanted them closer to the lodge to give them more privacy."

"And this cabin still rents out?"

"People stay here all the time."

"When the fireplace works?"

"Yup."

We walked a bit longer on the sidewalk in silence. After we passed the lodge, I followed Miles to a road leading toward his parents' house. Halfway up the road, he motioned me toward the left and onto a snow-covered driveway I hadn't noticed. A small, wooden cabin sat in the distance, surrounded by trees, a trail of smoke puffing out of the chimney.

The cabin was medium-sized, woodsy, and just gothic enough that it would look at home in a spooky Halloween book for kids. The wraparound porch had rails sticking out in all directions and broken steps leading up to the door.

"Did this house ever guest star in *The Addams Family*?"

He laughed. "I was born in this house."

I placed my hands on my hips. "I'm not staying here by myself."

His eyebrows raised with decided interest, but before he could speak, I cut in. "And I'm not staying here with you either." I pointed toward the cabin, which honestly looked less scary the second time, but still. "I can't be here alone at night. I'd never get any sleep."

He set my suitcase down on the snow, staving off his laughter. "You've got to stop talking. There are so many things I could—"

"Miles."

"Just come and look inside. The outside needs fixed up a bit, but the inside is just your typical late-nineties, dated, over-decorated, wall-papered home, okay?"

I looked back over at the cabin. It was either this or the pull-out couch. Or Mom and Russ. "Fine."

We climbed the rickety stairs to the porch. Miles unlocked the door, and it squeaked open, revealing a cozy, butternut-yellow-painted room with a plaid wall-papered border. Mismatched couches and loveseats of browns and plaids filled the small living room.

"Wow," I said.

"Told ya."

For some reason, I had to bite back a smile. Though the outside left much to the imagination, instantly the home inside felt so warm to me. My parents had had a similar plaid wall-paper in our downstairs living room when I was in grade school, and memories of our home came flooding back. The cabin was small and tidy but cluttered with pictures of moose and bears, and there were knick-knacks everywhere. I took a step inside. Against the back wall was a small oak kitchen with an island covered in a brown, marbled Formica sitting between the two rooms. A hallway jetted to the left and looked like it housed a couple of bedrooms and a bathroom.

"Change your mind?"

"Yeah."

He walked in behind me, set the luggage down, and closed the door. Immediately, he began tinkering with the wood fireplace. There was a small fire already going, but he removed the gate and tossed more sticks inside. A minute later, the fire had cast a cozy orange glow about the room. He stood up, brushed his hands off, and turned around to meet my gaze.

"Thanks," I said, suddenly feeling shy. The cabin felt so small with him inside, much like how my classroom did whenever he felt the need to torture me with a visit. Which reminded me that I had a few things to discuss with him about our whole *arrangement*.

"Alright," I started. "We obviously need to set some ground rules."

"For what?"

"Fake dating."

"Why?"

He had a small smile on his face, which meant he was very much trying to goad me.

"Because I'd hate for you to fall in love with me."

"Such a cliche." He moved toward the island in the kitchen and leapt backward to sit on top. His legs dangled from the side as he leaned back on his hands casually. "I can't wait to hear your terms."

I walked a few steps forward, closer to him, but not too close, and leaned against a wall. For some reason, I needed to feel tall with him in the room, which was why I didn't choose to sit just yet.

"Number one. No unnecessary touching. Obviously." I ticked the rule off with my finger, ready to add another when his voice stopped me.

"Nope."

My startled eyes flew to his. "What?"

A tiny smile quirked at the side of his mouth. "Veto. I disagree."

My brow furrowed in confusion. "No…that's…not up for debate. No unnecessary touching."

He leaned forward and met my gaze unabashed. "If I'm going to be dating you this week—"

"Fake dating," I broke in.

He went on, unfazed, "I can't work under those kinds of restraints."

I shook my head, irritated that he always had to find a way to get under my skin. This wasn't even a hard rule. This was an *obvious* rule.

"No. Any good book or movie worth its salt will tell you that fake dating always has rules. It's the only way it can work. We touch *only* in public, and it's super platonic."

"So…what book have you read where fake dating worked as planned? Should I take a quick peek into your Kindle?" He cocked his head to the side, a smile playing on his lips, his brown eyes diving into mine.

I shifted uncomfortably. "They don't work because people stop following the rules, and things get confusing. We *need* rules."

"What do you mean by confusing?" he asked, his wide eyes the picture of innocence. The rate of my heartbeat kicked up a notch.

Maybe it was a good thing he moved to the island in the kitchen. If he was standing by me, I would have kicked him in the shins by now. "You know what I mean."

"And what does 'unnecessary' mean?" He gave quotation marks to the word. "When do you deem touching necessary?" He leaned back on the island as if he had all the time in the world.

I clenched my fists, eyeing him warily. "If we're around my family, then…you can…touch my shoulder or something."

"The shoulder, huh? Wow." He rubbed his face with his hand. "Both of them?"

"Shut up."

He shook his head, a smile playing on his lips. "Nope. If we're dating this week—"

"Fake dating."

"Then I'm gonna act normal."

"What's normal for you? Making out on the top of a class-five rapid?"

"I'd never make out during a class five, Celery Stick. You need two hands to do both of those things." He regarded me for a long moment. "I'm going to treat you just like any other girl I'd be dating. If I'm having fun with you and getting the vibe you're into it, I'll make a move."

"Well, that's just fine then. I don't plan on giving off that vibe." My smile was crisp, and I stood up tall, away from the wall, about to ask him where the bathroom was, before he continued as though I hadn't said a word.

"I'll start with holding your hand."

A scoff escaped my lips as I brushed nonchalantly at a piece of lint on my sweater.

"And then when that pretty smile of yours starts to feel real, I might pull you in for a hug."

I stilled. My eyes flicked over to him.

"And if your big eyes keep dropping me hints, *begging* for more, then maybe I'll hug you again."

To my utter horror, the mood between us began to shift. I wanted to look away, but my eyes were locked onto his, trying to decide what he was about. He was just messing with me. He *had* to be. But the words were infiltrating my mind and wreaking havoc on my central nervous system.

His eyes never left mine. "After the second hug, you'd be more used to the close proximity—and you'd like it, by the way. I'd probably kiss your cheek next."

I drew in a soft breath, about to tell him to stop when he spoke again.

"And then, I'd move up and down your jawline right about here." He reached up and drew a long finger across the base of his jaw. Goosebumps scattered all around my skin. My eyes betrayed me and followed his every movement from the bottom of his ear to the point of his chin.

"Kissing every little freckle."

The sound of the grandfather clock struck loudly, thundering into the room. I jumped, clutching my chest at the sound, before I looked back at Miles. He ran a hand through his hair and glanced away. When he turned back to me, a smile was on his lips. He had been playing me. That was all. Which was a relief. A RELIEF. *Dang you, Miles Taylor.*

"And then I'd throw up on you," I said. I was trying to save face, to get him back for what he just did to me and my body. So, why did that statement send a pang of traitorous remorse into my gut?

He jumped down from the counter with the grace of a jungle cat and slowly began walking toward me. I lurched backward into the wall in search of an escape, or at least a little space, but he was nearly upon me before I could move. He stopped a few inches away from touching me, but the heat radiated from him.

"And after all that, if you give me any sort of signal that you want more, well…I'm leaving that open. It just makes good sense. For our cover."

His eyes bore into mine as he leaned forward, reaching his hand slowly toward me. I couldn't look away, even as my skin broke out into flames all across my body. Warm fingers brushed my cheek ever so slightly before he grinned and patted it gently, as if I were a toddler, effectively breaking me out of my trance. "So, if you need a no-touching clause, you're going to have to find a new fake boyfriend."

My fingers clenched as he walked past me and made himself

comfortable on the couch. When his back was turned, I took a few deep breaths. He was only trying to get under my skin. I had forced him into this, and this was him sticking it to me. It wouldn't matter. We would never get to the point where I would be giving him any sort of *signal*. The idea was laughable, though the goosebumps were still on my skin, alive and well—a tingling reminder of the power Miles Taylor had with words when he chose to wield them…inappropriately.

He folded his arms behind his head and leaned back on the couch. "So, we've established that appropriate touching is acceptable. Next?"

I sat down warily on the loveseat, diagonal from Miles. "That was my main common-sense rule."

"Didn't take much to convince you to overturn it."

"Contracting a violent stomach bug is still on the table for me. Then, none of this would matter."

He smiled and shook his head. "Nah. I'd be over every morning, acting the part of the concerned boyfriend with chicken soup, and fresh blankets, and *Home Alone*."

"Why *Home Alone*?"

He looked at me like I was crazy. "Because it's the best Christmas movie."

"Agreed."

His expression changed slightly. He looked surprised and mildly impressed. "I thought it would be too childish for you."

I scoffed. "If you're playing the part of a doting boyfriend, why would you bring over a movie you think I'd hate?"

"I'd help you discover the power of a true classic. We could follow it up with *The Terminator*. I'm surprised you like *Home Alone*, though."

"It's my favorite Christmas movie." I didn't want to give him any more explanation than that, so I didn't. "Do you have any rules?" I asked. "Beyond trying to 'get some' whenever you deem the moment appropriate?"

A boyish smile broke out across his face at that. "Look at you, using words like the youth of ten years ago."

I held my hands up in a motion like I was about to strangle him, which only succeeded in making him laugh.

"I don't have any rules. Anything else on your end?"

I pulled my leg underneath me as I sat on the loveseat, wondering exactly how to phrase my demand.

"No commenting on my family. You show up and you play the nice boyfriend, but you don't get to tell me what I can or can't act like with them. You're not allowed to pass judgment." I trailed off, breaking his gaze for a moment only to bring it back again.

He didn't move, just sat in the chair, looking at me with a slightly furrowed brow. My request had clearly baffled him. "Is there anything I need to know about your family before we do this?"

My stomach tightened. It felt weird enough that my coworker, Miles, knew my sister's name. He had met my mom. And Russ. It felt vulnerable and intrusive in a way I hadn't been expecting. He now had the potential to discover way too much personal information about me, and it was disconcerting. But if he was going to be my pretend boyfriend this week, I had to set him straight.

"My dad passed away last year. Russ is my mom's new husband."

A shadow passed over his face, and when it looked like he would say something more, I cut him short.

"Deal?" I asked.

It took him a moment to respond. "How about this? I won't pry or pass any judgment on your family. But if you bring them up or want to talk about them, then the rule's off."

I wanted to argue. That wasn't a concrete deal, but it was probably the best I'd get out of him. Besides, I wasn't worried about me bringing them up. I was a closed book. I'd probably just raised his curiosity about my family even more, which might have been a sore oversight on my end.

"Fine. So, do we shake on—"

"I just thought of one," Miles interrupted, giving me a smile.

I cocked my head to one side. "What?"

"We have to use this time to try and get to know each other better."

For a long moment, I was stunned into silence. "How? Through your necessary-touching clause?"

"No. Through talking."

"I promise I know you exactly as much as I care to."

For a second, his face fell slightly, and for the first time, I wondered if I'd crossed a line with that comment.

"I'm just saying," he said, "we've had some friction between us this past year, and this might be a good opportunity to bury some of your hatchets."

I folded my arms and leaned back into the loveseat. "*My* hatchets?"

He turned, pointing to his back. "Specifically the one or two you lodged deep in my back right here."

I chucked a pillow at him, which only resulted in him catching it easily and both of us holding back smiles.

"What do you say, Olive Wilson? Should we try to be adults about this fake relationship?"

I hesitated before giving my answer. Talking meant connecting, and connecting meant coming to an understanding. I already gave permission for "appropriate touching," but I was not going to get involved with Miles. Besides the fact that we were coworkers, we were complete opposites. This was just exciting to him, some type of weird adrenaline rush. Last time I made the mistake of getting involved with a fellow teacher, I ended up moving schools when we broke up because of how uncomfortable it became. Miles and I worked five feet away from each other.

"It's probably best we don't."

"Why?"

I fingered the fringe on the decorative pillow on my lap. "This is a business deal. That's it. I'm not going to be your kicks and giggles just because you're bored and it's out of season for skydiving or whatever you do in the summer."

He bit his bottom lip, his mind calculating. "What are you so scared of?"

"There's a big difference between being scared and being practical."

"Please?" He cocked his head to the side. His sparkling brown eyes went the way of a puppy dog. "Everybody seems to love you at school. I want to see if I can figure out why."

I scowled at him while he laughed. "You act like I *want* to know more about you."

He held out his hands in mock retreat. "I'd never presume anything like that."

I knew that the mature thing to do here would be to try to get to know him better and put the misunderstandings behind us. But for some reason, getting to know Miles Taylor seemed like it would be the beginning of an end for me. I just wasn't sure what that end would be. But pulling a ceasefire at work did sound like a good idea. And I'd be lying if I said I wasn't at least a little bit intrigued by what Miles was proposing.

"Fine."

He got up from his spot on the couch and made his way over to me, holding out his hand. "So we have a deal, then?"

I stared at his hand before shaking it once, fast and firm. "I guess."

He shook his head. "Now that's the attitude I want from the woman I'm dating. I'll let you get settled. We start at lunch. There's a mirror in the bathroom if you need to practice your 'I love Miles' face."

I scrunched my nose at him, but he continued as though he

hadn't noticed. "And I believe there's a snowman competition at the lodge after lunch. Don't let me down."

He opened the door and passed through the threshold, calling out over his shoulder, "I'll be sure to get you an ax so you can cut your own wood. Don't want you getting any ideas about me." He flashed me his roguish grin, and then he was gone.

TWELVE

"This is my house. I have to defend it."
Home Alone

When I had packed for the week, I hadn't intended to spend much time in the snow. I had a pair of jeans, some thermal underwear, and a pair of loose-fitting joggers. The most outdoorsy I had planned to get was to take a walk at some point every day. And for that, I could get by with what I'd brought. Completing a ridiculous game of ultimate bingo was something neither my wardrobe nor I was prepared for. However, I figured that the more underdressed I was for the occasion, the less I'd be forced to participate, which was why, when Miles found me at lunch later that afternoon, wearing jeans and a sweatshirt underneath my white parka, I couldn't help but smile.

"What is that?" he asked, his eyes on my legs as I made my way toward him. Miles was setting out a large package of water bottles on a serving table brimming with sandwich fixings, chips, and salads. He was definitely dressed for the weather, wearing heavy black snow pants and a puffy down jacket over a green flannel shirt. The first couple buttons of his flannel were left undone with a white undershirt of some sort peeking out from underneath. His usual gray beanie was missing from the ensemble, and my eyes couldn't stop from trailing up to his rumpled brown mop. It looked like he had been wearing his beanie but yanked it off before coming into the lodge. It gave him a charming, boyish look that I needed to forget existed.

"This is the best I've got for an impromptu snow day."

He stared at me in disbelief. "You came to a winter lodge with no snow pants?"

I lifted up my leg. "I brought boots," I said cheerily. There was something about disarming him that was beginning to be rather addictive to me.

He rolled his eyes. His hand found my back and propelled me toward the paper plates. "Grab your lunch and find us a table. I'll meet you there in a minute. We need to go over the calendar to make sure we don't miss anything for the blackout."

"Oh, yay," I mumbled as I quickly filled my plate.

Miles soon joined me at our table. The lodge had been slowly filling up with people, though I hadn't seen Chloe or Ben yet. I should have texted her and told her I was headed to the lodge, but I had been so flustered after Miles left that I hadn't given it a thought. My mom and Russ walked in, holding hands and laughing about something. I immediately turned away as Miles placed the bingo paper on the table between us.

"What kind of sandwich did you get?"

I glanced down at my food. "Ham and cheese."

"Looks good."

I raised my eyebrows. "Thanks?"

"Dare I say, those hams look...delicious?"

I elbowed him in the stomach and picked up the bingo card.

"Did you bring a swimming suit?" he asked a few moments later.

"Why would I have done that?"

He took a bite of his sandwich, which was mostly roast beef with a few slabs of cheddar hanging off the sides. "It says there's a hot tub right on the brochure."

"Well, Millie tricked me into coming here, and I never saw a brochure. Besides, hot tubbing in the winter in Vermont just doesn't sound like a good time to me."

"Trust me, that hot tub's going to feel mighty good after diving into the frozen pond."

Immediately, my palms began to sweat. "Miles. I can't do that. Can we…trade that one in for something else?"

He turned and faced me as I took a bite. "Just think of how awesome you'll feel once you've done it. I say we do it tonight—before you catch that fake stomach bug."

My eyes widened as panic immediately filled my body. "What? No. Why? I…don't even have a swimsuit."

"We shook on it. I'm pretty sure my sister has one she left at my parents' house. I'll find it for you."

"I can't do that. I'm serious. I know this is just another adrenaline-rush thing for you, but I promise it will break me."

His finger found my lips, stopping my panic-induced babbling. My eyes were locked on his, which prevented me from swatting him away like an annoying bug. "Just think, the polar plunge is the hardest thing on that list. Once we get that crossed off, you're home free."

He removed his finger and whispered, "If we do the snowman and the polar plunge today, you can pick what we do tomorrow." He nudged the bingo card to sit in front of me.

"So generous of you," I said lightly, picking the card up to examine it, forcing myself to examine the other items on the list. To my surprise, there were a few things that I wouldn't completely hate.

"Gingerbread house competition," I said.

Miles wrinkled his nose and looked at the card once more. "Of course you'd pick the lamest thing on there. I think they're doing that on Monday."

"You don't like gingerbread houses?"

"It sounds horrible and tedious. I can count on exactly zero fingers how many times I've done one before. I'll let you take the lead on that."

I grinned at him. "All of a sudden, I'm super pumped to make a gingerbread house with you. Now, I'm just trying to decide if I should make you add the sprinkles one at a time, or if I should put you in charge of frosting each individual piece all by yourself."

He groaned, and I loved seeing him uncomfortable for a change. I picked up the bingo card again. "Fudge-making competition? Learning to roast a chestnut? These sound right up my alley."

"The lodge is doing a lot of that kind of stuff tomorrow afternoon, so we can cross a few things off the list easily." He flicked the card out of my hand. "How about milking a cow and drinking fresh chocolate milk in the barn?"

I shuddered. "The word *fresh* in that context terrifies me."

"You two lovebirds going for the blackout, or whatever it's called?"

We both looked over to see that Glenn had plopped himself down across from us. Amid all the strange revelations with Miles yesterday, I had almost forgotten about the entire reason I had gotten myself into this mess.

"That's the plan," Miles said easily, taking a swig of his water bottle. "How about you?"

He waited for a beat before smiling tightly. "No. If I want to go on vacation, I'll just buy my own tickets."

Even though I had originally had the exact same thought myself, hearing it from Glenn's smug lips felt like a mortal insult upon both Miles and his whole family's idea to bring the magic of Christmas back into people's lives.

"It'll be fun. The last thing I'd want to do is let myself be too stuffy to have a little fun now and then." I was very aware of Miles turning his eyes on me just then, but I ignored him and smiled sweetly at Glenn instead.

"Isn't it...kind of strange that your mom didn't know you were dating anybody until yesterday morning?" He looked at us both again, a patronizing look on his face like he knew we were pulling a fast one.

I shrugged nonchalantly, like we got this question all the time, even though, inside, I was wondering how bad our acting skills really were if Glenn was suspicious. I snuggled as close to Miles's side as my conscience would allow. "We wanted to keep it quiet for a bit, that's all."

"I see." He nodded as though considering this deeply before looking up at Miles. "Was there some reason for the secrecy, though?"

Miles smiled, his hand dropping to my knee for a second before it moved a tiny bit higher—my lower thigh, to be exact, if the trail of smoldering heat and fire was accurate. His thumb made a soft back-and-forth motion that caused my breath to catch. "If there was, I guess that would be our secret, then."

Glenn laughed and held out his hands like he had been joking. "Hey, I don't care either way. You guys do you. I just thought it was strange, that's all."

I couldn't help but feel grateful as my mom settled in beside me just then, with Russ next to her and Glenn's parents across from us. Glenn would act much different now. The three of us eased more into the background as the group of four neighbors and friends talked and teased about the actual game of bingo they had just finished playing together in a back room of the lodge.

Miles removed his hand from my knee to eat his sandwich. And…thank goodness. I didn't miss his hand. Not at all. But I couldn't deny a feeling of emptiness his hand had left. It was probably just the warmth that I missed from his touch. As if his thoughts mirrored my own, Miles's thigh suddenly brushed against mine and stayed there, bringing with it another tingling heat wave. I forced my mind to focus in on the conversation around us.

"I'm trying to get Elaine to be more adventurous," Russ was saying. "She's scared to death to do anything fun."

My mom balked, slapping his arm gently, a flush rising to her cheeks.

Miles broke in, nodding toward me. "Must be a family trait." He nudged me gently, almost as if to tell me he was only teasing. "It's been like pulling teeth trying to convince her to do the polar bear plunge."

Every eye at the table was suddenly upon me. I wasn't sure how to handle this level of attention, so I forced my gaze back down to my plate.

"I even told her I'd take my shirt off," Miles said, "but no dice." I cringed as Russ snorted appreciatively.

I had my snarky reply primed and ready until I remembered we were a couple in love—or at least boyfriend and girlfriend in serious like. So then I sat for a few seconds, pondering another type of reply that would match that storyline, and I remained stumped.

My mom spoke first, her mouth slightly agape. "You're doing the polar bear plunge?"

"Maybe," I told my mom at the same time Miles said, "Yes."

Her eyebrows raised. "Good for you." Looking at Miles, she added, "And good luck to you."

He laughed. "It'll be good to get her out from behind her books for a bit this week."

His hand now brushed my back, rubbing lightly.

"My books are more fun."

"We'll see about that."

"Her mom's the same way," Russ interjected. "I practically had to force her to go cross-country skiing yesterday." He looked down at my mom. "And what did you say about it again, hon?"

My mom blushed. "It was fun," she conceded.

"She's spent the last thirty years hardly leaving the house. Not anymore," Russ said. "It's time to get out and see the world. We're hoping for a scuba-diving trip to Jamaica this year."

My nostrils flared with rage at his words. Just because my mom didn't cross-country ski, that didn't make her boring. It didn't mean she wasn't living life. She and my dad had just been that way. They preferred a quiet evening at home to the crowds and the busy restaurants. As a child, when my dad got home from work, he loved to sit in his office and read. He went golfing with friends a few times a month, and my mom had her book club. But other than that, they were quiet people happy to live a quiet life, and my mom didn't need Russ to come in and change that. Change her.

"Some people are perfectly happy to be at home. They don't need to prove themselves to anybody," I clipped, smiling smartly at Russ.

His face dropped, and he nodded. "I know, kiddo. I just... want your mom to experience some fun, is all."

Fun. He thought my mom's past life hadn't been fun. He was trying to make *her* think it hadn't been fun. My toes and fingers curled tightly in a clenched ball.

Miles was watching me curiously, and I expelled a rigid breath, hoping to release my frustrations. My mom could do what she wanted. She was a grown woman. If she wanted to plaster her face in makeup and turn herself into some sort of outdoorswoman, so be it. I just hoped that she didn't allow her new husband to make her think that the past thirty years hadn't meant something.

Because they did.

THIRTEEN

"I'm in the depths of despair!"
L.M. Montgomery - *Anne of Green Gables*

In case there was any confusion, pulling on an old swimsuit in the middle of winter to go jump in a frozen lake was my personal version of hell on earth. How did one dress for that? Miles insisted on picking me up at the cabin because he knew, with certainty, I'd never meet him on my own (points for being correct). After lunch, we'd met up with Chloe and Ben and the girls outside of the lodge and built two epic snowmen. Ivy and Holly's snowman was of the Picasso variety, parts and sticks poking out everywhere. Miles and I went with a more classic look, with rocks and carrots, complete with an old scarf. We didn't end up winning the competition, but one square of the bingo card got crossed off, which was enough for me. The crisp air had been surprisingly refreshing, and if Chloe had been on the fence about me and my supposed boyfriend, watching Miles chase her girls around the snowmen, tossing them into the air and catching them, definitely had to sway her in our favor. I even caught myself smiling at the non-stop giggles I heard from the girls and Miles.

It was only when my mom and Russ showed up that I feigned a headache and made my way back to my quiet cabin for a cup of hot chocolate and a book.

By the time the knock at the door sounded later that evening, I had pulled on Miles's sister's old swimming suit (the one he had kindly dropped off earlier), but it was now covered by my joggers, my flannel pajamas, and my white parka.

When I opened the door, Miles stood leaning against the door frame, a duffel bag strapped across his shoulder. He wore tan, insulated coveralls, his blue coat, and his gray beanie. There were bits of straw in the part of his hair not covered by the hat. He must have come straight here from doing chores.

"Broccoli."

"Miles."

"You skipped dinner."

"I had a headache."

"That sounds like something your boyfriend should know."

He was probably right, but I hadn't cared. "Sorry."

I scooted back to make room for him to come in while I pulled on my boots. He stepped forward, but to my surprise, he headed toward the bathroom.

"I've got to change really quick."

As he walked farther away from me, I contemplated a quick escape somewhere. Outside, a sky full of clouds covered the moon, resulting in a pitch-black evening. If that didn't give me pause, the stiff breeze wafting into my cabin definitely did. But it had to be better than—

"I will hunt you down if you run," Miles called cheerfully as he stepped into the bathroom.

I scowled at his back and closed the front door. Before I

could put on my boots, Miles poked his head out of the bathroom.

"Quick question. How do you like your ham? Board shorts or Speedo?"

I threw my boot toward the bathroom door. Miles was laughing as he easily caught the boot and tossed it back to me. But it wasn't until he was safely tucked away into the bathroom that I let out an embarrassed huff of laughter.

Thankfully, he chose the board shorts. He had a t-shirt on over his muscles, and I couldn't decide whether I should feel grateful or disappointed.

"Is that all you're wearing to walk over there?" I asked incredulously.

"Not all of us are wimps."

"We'll see how you feel on the walk back."

"I'll have my girlfriend to keep me warm."

"If that's your plan, I suggest you find a new girlfriend."

"But I'm having so much fun with this one."

We grabbed towels and fell into step together on the pathway leading toward the lodge, me stuffed inside my oversized parka and Miles dressed for a quick summer dip.

I paused when the pond first came into sight. It was probably about the size of half of a football field. It looked completely frozen over, save for a small dark hole in the ice next to the dock that two people could fit through.

"Looks like we aren't the first to do this," I said.

"We probably are. My dad keeps this section broken so people can jump in."

"Of course he does."

We rounded the corner of the lodge, and both of us stopped in our tracks. Through the steam and fog of the frigid night, the hot tub was already occupied—by one Glenn Foster. I froze, not sure what to do. Why Glenn? And why was he by himself? Next to me, Miles didn't seem to know what to do either, but before we could retreat, Glenn looked up and saw us both. Thanks to Miles refusing to wear anything resembling winter wear, we couldn't pass our appearance off on just going for a walk. We were clearly there for the hot tub.

At least, Miles was.

I began backing away. "He doesn't know I'm here to swim, so…" I whispered frantically.

A warm body stopped my backward movement and began propelling me forward again. "The towel on your shoulders is a dead giveaway. Come on, it'll be fun."

"I didn't realize tonight was the special night," Glenn called out.

Well, with a patronizing invitation like that, how could we refuse? Actually, let me be clear. I could refuse perfectly fine, but the arm that somehow found its way around my waist would have none of that.

Glenn watched us approach in silence. Miles smiled and leaned across the hot tub, holding out his hand.

"How are you, man?"

After the briefest of pauses, Glenn leaned forward and shook his hand. "Good. You?"

Miles flung his towel down on a chair next to the tub, kicked off his boots, and began peeling off his white t-shirt. Though his motions were hurried (it was literally five degrees out), he seemed to move in slow motion to me. I bit my lip as I stared at him shamelessly. So, Miles *did* have some muscles underneath the shirt. He was lean and lanky, so it wasn't like he was suddenly The Rock under there, but he had lines and definition and would definitely be able to unscrew pickle lids or lift a couch or something. The important stuff in day-to-day life would be more than covered by his assets.

Assets.

Yuck.

For a second, I had forgotten just who I was thinking of. It was strange being in a different place together. We were out of the normal, and suddenly, this all felt wrong. I mean…even more wrong. He was a coworker. He pushed all my buttons and annoyed me daily, and I'd do well to remember that. I didn't need to see his muscles. It only messed with my head.

He turned just before entering and met my gaze. I wasn't sure what he saw there, but it was enough that laughter sprang into his eyes. He motioned to a spot on the side of his lip and mouthed, "Little drool."

Hey, look, I'm cured.

After all, one time I had thought Glenn attractive, and now I could hardly stand the sight of him. Clearly, I couldn't be trusted. My five-second ogling didn't mean anything. I glowered at him until he turned away, stepping into the tub and settling in across from Glenn.

Both men turned to look at me expectantly, which made sense as I was the one person connecting us all and I hadn't said a word. But I was currently still dressed for a night in an igloo. If they thought I was going to strip down to a bathing suit while they both watched, they had another thing coming.

As if Miles understood my dilemma, he turned back to Glenn and engaged him in conversation, forcing Glenn to focus on him. I breathed a bit easier and began pulling off my boots and unzipping my coat. I stripped down to the red-and-white-striped one-piece while Miles learned that Glenn's job as an acquisition manager was really just a glorified assistant to the actual manager. He also learned that he was from my same hometown and that we went to college together at the University of New Hampshire. Glenn had finished his degree but had been working and still hanging out in the college scene when we reconnected. Typical Glenn to carry on talking about himself without asking Miles anything in return. It was hard to squeeze anybody else in when his favorite topic was himself.

I climbed up the rickety steps and eased into the hot tub,

causing enough disturbance in the water that both men looked at me. Glenn's eyes immediately inched down my body and back. And honestly…I sit a lot. I do try to get some light walking in three or four times a week, but I'm definitely not any sort of athlete or gym rat. My skin crawled at his approving gaze.

Miles held out a hand to me, and before I could think, I took it and allowed him to lead me into the water. His brown eyes held mine before I glanced away, fearful that the heat now setting my entire body to flames would show. I blamed it on the hot tub even though I was confused by the soft looks he was giving me. He settled me next to him and scooted in close, plopping his hand on my knee.

Oh. That's right. We were onstage. The touching made sense.

I could breathe easier now.

"I'm excited I get to witness the famous polar plunge," Glenn said, eyebrows raised.

"Yup." Miles readjusted his position, and his arm moved to settle around my waist, his fingers brushing at the side of my stomach. I stiffened at the familiar touch. I didn't know what to do with my hands, so I folded them awkwardly across my stomach.

"Relax," Miles breathed in my ear.

Reluctantly, I moved both hands underneath the water. If he was a normal boyfriend, I probably would have let my hand rest on his knee–but he wasn't a normal boyfriend. He was a guy I didn't like, who I worked with, who was now playing the part of my fake boyfriend because he had so rudely and unexpectedly crashed my anti-Christmas vacation. It had been a complicated couple of days. I settled on resting my hands on the hot tub seat between our legs. Miles nudged my hand with his thigh, holding himself tight like he was trying not to laugh.

"It's funny. I would have bet big money against Olive ever jumping in that lake with you," Glenn baited.

We both turned back to Glenn who was peering at us with a knowing smile on his face.

"She's not exactly the daredevil type, if you haven't noticed," he added, folding his arms.

Miles nudged me. "Olive? Care to rebut?"

I smiled sweetly at Glenn, though the motion pained me a bit. "Nope, he's right. I'm not the daredevil type."

"Told you, man. I always tried to get her to go skiing with me, but she flat-out refused. The craziest thing I could ever get her to do was a double feature of two movies on a school night." He laughed and rolled his eyes. "Remember that, Olive Oil?"

I did remember he had always wanted me to go skiing with him. I also remembered that it wasn't skiing he had been pressuring me for that night. Two action movies back to back along with a giant tub of popcorn sitting between us was the only way I could get his mind and his hands to focus on something else besides me.

I hated how Glenn seemed so sure about me. Fine, I *didn't* want to jump in a frozen lake. Crazy, I know. But it galled me, him sitting there on his high horse, smugly bringing up things from our past. And that's all it was. The past. Even though he was correct. Sue me if flying down a mountainside on two toothpicks wasn't my idea of a good time. I had plenty of books that gave me the same thrill. But regardless, who was he to assume he even knew what I was or was not interested in? We'd dated nearly four years ago. He didn't know me anymore, and I resented the fact that he acted like he did.

I swallowed before moving my hand up stiffly to Miles's knee, and with a raised chin and haughty expression, I said to Glenn, "Actually, we have plans to do lots of things this week."

His expression looked amused. "What's that? Stay inside and watch movies? Write poetry? Read a book together?"

Miles shrugged and looked at me, a gleam in his eye. "Well,

probably some of that. I think Olive's introduction to *The Terminator* is long overdue."

I wrinkled my nose. "We'd have to watch *Jane Eyre* to cleanse our palates after that."

Miles smiled. "Great, I'll be about ready to fall asleep by then."

"You two are poster children for adventure," Glenn said, amused.

This I could confidently contradict. "Miles is actually a certified Outward Bound instructor."

Glenn failed to look overly impressed. "I've heard of that. Isn't that where you take kids hiking? Or rafting?"

"Yeah," Miles said, squeezing me closer to his side. "We do a lot of white-water rafting, and rock climbing as well. We teach a lot of safety basics."

"My parents took me down the Colorado River in Arizona when I was a senior. You just can't get any good whitewater this far northeast."

Miles raised his eyebrows. "Have you ever done any out here?"

Glenn shrugged as though nothing mattered. "No. I wanted to go right for the big stuff."

"Well, you're missing out. There's a few great runs around here."

Glenn huffed in disbelief like it was all funny to him.

Miles suddenly turned to me. "You ready?"

I was most definitely not ready, if the sudden bolt of panic coursing through my body meant anything, but somehow, the frozen pond seemed better company than Glenn at the moment. I grasped the hand Miles was offering me and immediately began shivering as we made our way out of the hot tub.

Suddenly, we were running—correction, Miles was running and pulling me behind him while I squealed. My hand in his was the only warm part of my entire body. If I thought too hard about what was about to happen, I'd never do it. Though my brain was refusing to acknowledge the humongous frozen pond growing closer, my body seemed to have a good idea of what was expected and began to pull back.

"Nope!" Miles shouted as he dragged me along behind him, the pond twenty feet from us now. "You can do this!"

When we got five feet away, I dug in my heels. "Wait! Wait!" I yelped, sheer panic making my words come out in bursts and jumbles. "Let's think about this for a second. Let's just do the bingo. We don't need to do the blackout. I've got to—"

"No thinking. Just jump," Miles yelled, pulling my hand with his toward the small dock. But this time, my hand broke away. He turned, and for a split second, we both stared at our empty hands before his eyes flicked over to mine and narrowed dangerously.

Swimsuit bottoms and jiggly thighs weren't even on my radar at the moment as my body did a breakaway one-eighty and bolted forward. It was five degrees out, I was dripping wet, and I was about to jump into frozen water. With Miles Taylor. My brain was working fine now, and my fight-or-flight instinct came out swinging. I needed to end this madness. I had a book and a hot bath waiting for me. Adrenaline made me fly. I was Usain Bolt crossing the finish line.

Until two steel arms wrapped around my waist, halting me mid-stride. My back instantly warmed as it pressed against his stomach, blocking the chill from the night air. Oh gosh, it felt good to be held, even like this. Even by him. I had almost forgotten, but those arms also wanted to throw me into a frozen pond, so I lost all dignity, flailing about like a toddler throwing down a tantrum, squealing and shouting and offering up new negotiations. Finally, I broke away from him. When he regained his balance, he reached for me once more, but I held him off.

"Don't throw me in." I stood crouched, giving the impression

I could dash away at any second, which was laughable because my body was quite literally shutting down in the cold.

His hands paused mid-air in their reach toward me. He peered at me carefully. "Are you going to jump in on your own?"

My chest heaving, I glanced at the pond, the dark water hole shimmering from the outside light from the lodge. Ice chunks floated nearby. "If you try to throw me in, I will grind up your body, fry you into donuts, and feed them to your students."

His mouth twitched, but he lifted his hands in a gesture of peace. "You know, you're a lot different here than you let on at school."

"Shut up."

Now that I wasn't fighting for my dignity, I took a few tentative steps onto the dock.

He settled in beside me, his shoulder brushing against mine as we both stared down into the dark abyss complete with chunks of floating ice.

"Why haven't *you* jumped yet?" I asked. "I would have thought you'd be on round four by now."

"I don't usually stop and think. I just do it. You made me stop, and now I'm thinking that this sounds like a terrible idea."

"It *is* a terrible idea."

He chuckled softly. "Big chicken."

"I don't see *you* jumping in."

"Your chicken-ness is rubbing off on me."

"I'm helping you to see that there are other ways to enjoy life that don't involve doing dumb things."

A grin split across his face. "But I'll bet you don't remember anything special about the nights you read your book until 9 pm and then went to bed."

The cold was beginning to pierce through every part of my body.

"I'm living the dream," I said, shivering with each word.

He held out his hand to me. "When's the last time you had a chance to jump in a frozen lake with your good friend Miles?"

I snorted. "Who?"

"I'm not completely past the idea of pushing you in to get this over quicker."

"Fine. I'll jump. At this point, the water can't be any colder than I am right now."

"That's optimistic."

We counted down from three. When we got to one, Miles grabbed my hand and shouted, "Hold on tight!"

The snow-covered dock was a blur beneath us, and then we were falling.

FOURTEEN

"I knew you would do me good in some way, at some time--I saw it in your eyes when I first beheld you."
- Charlotte Brontë - *Jane Eyre*

IT FELT LIKE A THOUSAND NEEDLES JABBING EVERY INCH OF MY skin. When I came up for air, my mouth opened and closed like a gaping fish, but I couldn't seem to catch a breath. The shock was too great upon my soft book-reading, coffee-drinking, movie-watching body. Miles grabbed my arm and pulled me toward the dock. I wasn't sure how he was moving, because I had become a frozen statue.

His movements did seem slower, but he was able to lift himself out of the water before he turned back to me.

"Come here."

"Is this what hypothermia feels like?" I asked through chattering lips. I attempted to heave my body out of the water—the keyword being *attempted*.

"Not yet, but you've got to move faster." He leaned down

further, hooked his hands underneath my armpits, and hauled me up and out of the water like I weighed nothing more than a sack of flour. Another point for his secret muscles. I hadn't been aware that he had grabbed our towels and brought them with us, but suddenly, he was wrapping me in fluffy blue cotton and herding me back toward the hot tub.

"I'm…going to…kill you," I sputtered. The fierce-sounding words in my brain came out as an incoherent gurgle of short breaths.

"What?" Miles asked, wrapping his arm around my shoulder as we hobbled up the snow-covered pathway together. "Did you just say you loved me? And after such a short time of dating, too. I'm surprised at you, Celery Stick."

I couldn't find the energy needed to push him away, so I allowed his body to press against my side as he propelled me forward.

Glenn was drying off with a towel next to the hot tub when our frozen limbs arrived.

"Well, I'm impressed you got her to jump," he admitted, pulling a sweatshirt over his head. "You must be a better man than me."

My teeth clattered almost violently as I brushed past Glenn to climb up the stairs. My body seemed to sizzle when I stepped into the heated tub and sank down with a deep sigh, allowing the hot water to cover my frozen limbs.

"She did it all on her own," Miles stated generously as he climbed in after me, settling in across the hot tub from me.

Glenn snorted at that, not believing Miles any more than I did. He turned to go, giving us a halfhearted wave as he slunk out of sight.

Our chests were both heaving as our limbs began to thaw. My heartbeat ran rampant in my chest. I couldn't believe I had done that. My mind was racing as fast as my heart. Glenn had been right when he said I wasn't a daredevil, not even close, but —much to my surprise—I felt amazing right now.

The emotions and adrenaline zipping through my body at that exact moment needed an exit, somewhere to go, or else I would explode. I felt myself smile broadly. I had a hard time believing that the girl who jumped in the frozen pond (i.e., was basically held at gunpoint) was me. Now that it was over, and I had survived, and my ice-cube fingers and toes were beginning to regain feeling, a sense of wonder and pride overcame me. And then I did the last thing I ever expected to do in front of Miles. I tilted my head back, gazed up at the dark sky, and laughed.

And then I kept laughing. Like a certified maniac.

I felt like all the cool heroines in all the books I read who did daring things like it was no big deal. If there was a ladder, I'd walk across the ridge pole to show up Josie Pye. Give me a gun and a sleek car, and I think I could put up a good fight in a car chase. I imagined myself being an amazing, ultra-cool assassin who could make a sandwich at the same time I fended off an attack. Where the heck was Machu Picchu? As soon as I found out, I'd be on the first plane to climb it. I leaned my head back on the side of the hot tub and simply let myself live in the moment of pure, joyful, and unadulterated elation.

Soft chuckling broke through my amusement, and I slowly turned my head to see Miles watching me with a smile on his face.

"You'd better be careful," he said softly. "Some people feel their first adrenaline rush and then spend the rest of their lives chasing it."

Our eyes held for a long moment as we sat in a contemplative glow. A long sigh escaped both of our lips at the same time as we adjusted ourselves in the hot tub seats. My limbs were starting to feel heavier now as the rush of the moment began to dissipate.

"Is that what it's like for you all the time? Doing all the crazy things you do?"

He contemplated my question. "It used to be like that. The first time I went skydiving, I almost peed my pants. But by the time I landed, I was ready to do it again. Same with rock climbing. The fear is usually only because you haven't done something before."

"What got you into all of that?"

"My family would do a river trip every summer growing up, but it was mostly just fishing. I rock climbed a bit in college, but I'd never done any white water or skydiving until a few years back."

"What made you want to?" I asked.

A shadow passed across his face before it was gone. He raised his eyebrows. "Who wouldn't?"

I raised my hand.

"You don't count. Let me guess, you were the kid all decked out in helmet and pads every time you rode your bike."

My eyes narrowed. "Safety first."

"I'll bet you hated slip 'n' slides…"

My lips turned upward at a memory that came flying back to me. I wasn't sure why I decided to share it with him, except for the fact that my body had relaxed by this point, and my mouth must have followed suit. "My mom has this video of me and my sister in the front yard when we were little. We had just gotten a new slip 'n' slide. I had backed up, like thirty feet, and did a huge running start toward it. Full-out run. When I got to the slide, I stopped, sat down, and then scooted myself with my hands all the way down."

Miles grinned broadly, and I felt a hint of pride at having caused that reaction in him.

"I can see it all perfectly."

Leaning back, I gave him a once-over. Okay, it was a twice-over, but the newly discovered muscles were distracting. "I'll bet you were the type to climb to the top of all the trees and scare your mom to death. And you were probably doing stunts on motorcycles by the time you were eight."

He laughed. His feet brushed against mine in the water for a moment before I pulled them away. "I wish I were that cool back then. I was more like you, actually. Spent most of my free time reading in the hammock. The bigger stuff came later. Though, I did love a good slip 'n' slide. And not sure I'd consider climbing trees too dangerous."

"What books did you love as a kid?"

"*Lord of the Rings, Harry Potter, Percy Jackson*—"

"Such a cliché."

"Not clichés. Classics, Miss Secret Romance Books Hidden on Her Kindle."

I blushed at the memory. "It was for research," I insisted.

"Let's do a quick recap. I walked into your classroom to ask you a question, and you didn't even hear me because you were so engrossed in your billionaire-baby-vampire romance."

"I was fact-checking."

His smile widened. "For what?"

"One of my students wrote a paper on it, and I had to make sure she had actually read it."

He laughed again, pinching the bridge of his nose as he did so. "I think all your classic books are just a disguise. Are you ever gonna tell me what else you have on your Kindle?"

I kept my face passive, but my heart rate spiked. I would slice my right arm off before anybody saw what was on there—especially Miles Taylor.

"Nothing that would interest you."

"Probably right. And I get in trouble for *The Terminator*?"

"Yes. There couldn't possibly be a single redeemable thing in that movie that should instigate a discussion in a school setting."

"Clearly you've never watched it."

I shook my head and looked back toward the pond, ready to change the subject, but Miles beat me to it.

"What happened with Glenn?"

I groaned, tilting my head at him. "Really? Why? We just got rid of him."

"Can't blame your fake boyfriend for being a little curious about your exes. Why'd you break up?"

I scoffed. "Can't you see why?"

"I can see. But I want to know what *you* saw."

Tucking my hair behind my ear, I thought about what to say to Miles. I was completely over Glenn. Had been, in fact, for nearly three months before I had the guts to end it. The only thing that made me agree to this fake dating was that Glenn's ego wouldn't let me go. Glenn had clearly been glad he showed up at the hot tub tonight. He had wanted to watch me fail. To prove himself right. If Miles hadn't been here, he would have been much more of a nuisance toward me this week. I would have been living next door to him in Chloe's cabin. I didn't want to feel grateful that Miles was here in the hot tub with me instead of Glenn, but the thoughts came anyway.

He adjusted his position in the water, his foot brushing against mine again for a second and causing me to snap out of my thoughts. He was watching me, patiently waiting for me to gather my thoughts.

"He was just…kind of a jerk."

When Miles didn't react, I added, "He always...had a way of making me feel small." My words came out shy and unsure, as if I had just accidentally given him more of myself than I should have. But when I looked at him nervously, he was nodding.

"I can see that. He looks like the type who has a habit of doing that to everybody he's around."

I nodded. "Sorry about him."

He smiled. "I can handle him. How'd he take the breakup?"

I cupped a scoop of water in my hands and watched the

water escape. I had given him a crumb, and now I was tempted to offer a bite as I felt myself relax a tiny fraction in his company. "In true Olive fashion, I couldn't find a decent excuse to break up with him, so instead of facing the problem straight on and just doing it, after college, I made sure to pick a job two states away. Long distance really wasn't his style. So, while I technically broke up with him, it was all done very...strategically."

"How did you end up dating him?"

"He was my neighbor growing up. He's a few years older so never had much to do with me, but when we connected during my final year at UNH, he asked me out. I was pretty flattered at the time. We dated about six months total, but I'd say the last three, I wanted out."

"So why'd you stay with him?"

"He was nice." I shrugged. "At least, at face value. He could put on a good show. My parents loved him, so I kept brushing off all the little comments, thinking I was overreacting. He was always flipping things around in conversation to make something my fault. But it was all done in such a friendly way, with a smile, like he was just teasing. I didn't have a concrete thing to hold onto that would be a good enough reason to break up. So, I just avoided the problem and secretly sent out applications out of state."

"Sometimes that's the only way to get rid of guys like that."

We sat in contemplative silence for a long moment, me reliving brief moments in my history with Glenn and cringing. I hadn't known what it felt like to be around Glenn until I got away from him. Only then could I put into words just how he had made me feel. One thing it did teach me, though, was that I never wanted to feel that way again.

"You know that you're not...small, right?"

I startled and raised my eyebrows at Miles. His eyes widened, and an embarrassed smile flashed across his face. "No,

I meant...you're not—" He put his hands over his face while we both began to laugh.

"I meant that...even though you're kind of annoying, personality wise...you're big time. Top-notch."

I was still trying to hold back my laughter when I took in his gaze, piercing and direct on mine. Though he was across the hot tub from me, tingles began at the base of my stomach and worked their way outward toward every limb and nerve ending on my body.

"Thanks," I said, turning my attention back to the water. Things suddenly felt a little too intense for a fake-date situation. "You could have fooled me with how you treat me at school."

Another smile touched his lips. "Well, the joke's on you because I only tease people I like."

It didn't mean anything. I didn't *want* it to mean anything. He liked a lot of people. But for some reason, his words kept me warm the whole frigid walk back to my cabin.

FIFTEEN

"Merry Christmas little fella. We know that you're in there, and that you're all alone."
Home Alone

A LOUD BANGING NOISE WOKE ME WITH A GASP AND A START. I looked around the small log bedroom in a state of confusion before I heard Miles's cheerful voice from outside.

"Rise and shine, Celery Stick! We've got a lot to do today."

Not for the first time, I found myself wishing that my bedroom wasn't right next to the front door on the porch. My first choice had been the other bedroom down the small hallway, but it was locked for some reason, which disturbed me greatly, but when I asked Miles about it, he only shrugged.

Another loud knock—this time at my window.

I checked the time. 7:30 am. Technically, I went to bed at 10 pm, but in girl-with-a-Kindle time, it was actually closer to 2 am, which made this wake-up call much worse than he probably imagined. The previous night of a frozen pond and accidentally laughing and telling Miles too many things had left me exhausted. I flung the covers off my body, immediately regretting it as the damp chill of the winter morning touched my skin. I had left the fire on in the main room the night before, but it had since died out. I dressed quickly to the sounds of Miles singing his own special version of "Jingle Bells" outside my window. When I finally opened the door, I was wearing long, thermal underwear underneath jeans and a thick, cream-colored sweater. All that was accompanied by major bedhead and probably streaked mascara underneath my eyes because I had been too tired to wash my face the night before.

"7:30 on a Sunday, really?"

Miles gave me a quick appraisal with a lift of his eyebrows. He looked like he was about to say something when his brow quickly furrowed.

"I can see your breath," he said with some alarm.

He stepped past me, entering the cabin. "Why is it so cold?"

I closed the door and shrugged. "The fire went out sometime in the night."

He muttered under his breath and strode to the fireplace, stoking the white embers before opening a box full of chopped wood next to the fireplace. Wood that hadn't been there yesterday, to my knowledge.

"Did you chop that?"

He didn't answer and, instead, set about making me a fire. Within moments, a warm orange glow began heating up the cabin.

I dropped onto my knees in front of the fire and let the cozy warmth soak into my skin.

"Thanks," I said.

Miles sat on the couch somewhere behind me. "Alright. I was looking at the bingo card, and if we're going to hit all the squares for a blackout, we need to be prepared, so I made us a schedule."

I leaned back and took the papers he offered me, the top full of lines and times and dates, and my heart couldn't help but give a little sigh of happiness. "A schedule? Maybe I underestimated you."

"I feel like you're the type of person who gets motivated best with a list."

I looked at the paper, flipping to the next page, which held the actual bingo card.

"Since it's Sunday, the lodge will be doing some of the simpler, low-key activities. Cheese making. Roasting a chestnut. Cookie decorating. Crap like that. If we can survive the boredom, we'll be able to cross a bunch of stuff off the list."

As I perused the paper, it became very clear to me that the "crap like that" bingo squares were the activities I was actually looking forward to doing. They were all the things that could be accomplished in the warm lodge without exposing myself to any elements of the outside world.

"I thought I was supposed to be the Scrooge in this relationship. These all look like a blast."

"A blast, huh?" He smiled. "That definitely tracks."

My body had sufficiently thawed from the fire, so I made my way over to the couch, sitting on the other side of him. "Just because you're not risking death or frostbite doesn't mean these activities are crap."

He plucked the papers from my hand. "Roasting a chestnut? Making cheese? You categorize these under the *blast* category?"

Okay, *blast* was probably pushing it, but I was in this now, and I was going to prove my point.

"You probably grew up doing all this stuff. I have no clue how cheese is made, so it sounds fascinating. I've also never roasted a chestnut. And decorating Christmas cookies is always fun. Anyone who feels otherwise has no business being my fake boyfriend."

"Alright," he said. "You'll have to convince me."

I didn't appreciate the look in his eyes when he said that, so I looked at the paper again. "And Monday, we'll do the gingerbread competition."

He groaned like a man being tortured.

I swatted him on the shoulder with the paper. "This was all your idea. I'd be very happy to forego the entire blackout thing."

"Eh, once we get to tomorrow night, I'll be fine."

"What's tomorrow night?"

"The barn dance and mistletoe kiss. We can knock out both at the same time."

My stomach immediately clenched at the thought of kissing Miles. Again. Although the puckered grandma kiss we had shared wasn't one for the books, I had a feeling that if I ever really allowed Miles to kiss me, the effects could be devastating. "A sweet little kiss on the cheek sounds perfect. The kind you'd give your mom on Christmas morning."

He put his hands behind his head, a smile beginning to form on his face. "If you think I would kiss my girlfriend on her cheek under mistletoe, you've got another thing coming."

I raised my chin, not allowing his words to distract me from my purpose, which was to keep us in line—or more specifically, *him* in line. "I don't think it's a good idea."

"Why?" He looked genuinely curious.

"Things will…get into our heads."

"What are you worried about getting into your head?" Miles asked. He had crossed his leg over his knee and was now looking at me innocently.

I scowled at him. "Nothing."

"Good. All I know is that we have a fake-dating agreement. We have to do everything on the list." He peered closer at the bingo card and held it out to me, pointing to a square. "And it says mistletoe kiss right here."

"Fine," I said. "But if your heart gets broken, don't say I didn't warn you."

Miles gave no sign that he heard me, except for a slight pause before he continued reading off the schedule. "Tuesday, we'll milk cows, drink fresh chocolate milk…"

He droned on, but my mind was stuck on the "fresh" part of the chocolate milk. I didn't have any sort of dairy allergy–thank goodness, because I was a big fan of pizza and ice cream. But straight milk was a different matter altogether, especially if I had to squeeze it right from the udder with my own two hands. I couldn't quite stomach the thought.

He cleared his throat, snapping me out of my worried thoughts. "One more thing for tonight."

"What?"

"My parents want to have us over for ice cream sundaes tonight after the lodge closes."

I froze, wide-eyed. "What? Why?"

"Because they want to meet my girlfriend." He grinned cheekily.

"I've already met them both, and I'm not really your girlfriend."

"That's not the line we're feeding everybody here, though, is it?"

"What did you tell them about us?"

I couldn't be sure, but it looked like his face might have reddened a tiny bit. "Just that I knew you were coming and wanted to surprise you. And them."

"I don't want to."

"We're going."

"No."

"It's part of our cover."

"No."

We were still having the same argument hours later, after a day of learning to make cheese, roasting a chestnut, and, of course, decorating cookies. Miles had been a decent sport through it all, though I did have to remove all the candy from sitting in front of him and force him to decorate more than one cookie. By the end, it was almost as exhausting as decorating with two-year-olds. Although, two-year-olds probably wouldn't sit that close to me, or rub my back, or play with my hair to annoy me when all of my concentration was on piping a border around my cookies. Suffice it to say, I was officially wiped out from the day of holiday fun, and the idea of keeping up the ruse in front of his parents was almost too much for me to handle.

"On second thought, I think I'm about to come down with that violent stomach bug." I tugged against his arm as we stepped onto the pathway that led toward the farmhouse.

Miles didn't even slow, just kept pulling me along beside him. "You're so strait-laced at school. I had no idea you were such a liar."

"I don't want to be with your parents like this. They think we're really dating."

"So do your parents."

I didn't know why that was different, but it felt different. My mom wanted to set me up with Glenn Foster. Miles's mom was a sweetheart who probably chained herself up to save trees in her spare time.

"I just don't want to lie."

Finally, he stopped and turned to me. "Then don't lie."

"What?"

He shrugged. "We're here together, so technically we're on a date. We hung out all day. We were together last night, so this is basically our third date. We're dating."

"But we're not," I insisted.

Laughter sprang into his eyes as he moved closer, leaning toward me slightly. "Should I do something to make it more official?"

My mouth suddenly filled with moisture at his words. Or perhaps it was the way he kept glancing pointedly toward my mouth. Or maybe it was the quirk of his teasing lips while he was, no doubt, watching me internally freak out. I took a step back and placed a hand on his chest to keep him from moving closer.

He only chuckled. "Listen. It's just ice cream with my parents. There won't be a lie detector test, I promise. They probably won't ask us anything about it."

For the record, that was a bold-faced lie.

SIXTEEN

"Because when you are imagining, you might as well imagine something worth while."
L.M. Montgomery - *Anne of Green Gables*

FROM THE MOMENT MILES USHERED ME THROUGH THE FRONT door, we were greeted with hugs and smiles from his parents and a surprise cheek kiss from his mom. A passerby would have never guessed we had just seen them all day at the lodge. The Taylor home was earthy and inviting. Soft browns and creams and greens trickled seamlessly through each room. Though not the latest styles anymore, the house felt comfortable. Clean and tidy, but also lived in. The kind of home you could bring children to and not worry about them touching every little thing. In the living room, Miles tossed our coats onto the back of a couch and followed his parents toward a swinging door. We passed by several inviting picture frames filled with images of a young Miles that I vowed to examine closer upon our exit. Miles leaned forward to push the door open for me, pressing his hand lightly against my upper back to propel me forward.

Heat zinged my skin. He kept his hand there, guiding me into the kitchen and into a well-loved chair. The rustic oak table in front of us was littered with ice cream cartons and every topping imaginable. He sat next to me as he stretched his arm out across the back of my chair. His thigh brushed against mine and stayed there so casually, shooting electrical shocks up my veins. His parents took the seats across from us and began dishing up ice cream. Jett wandered into the kitchen from another doorway and grinned at me as he grabbed a bowl of ice cream and loaded it with crushed cookies and chocolate sauce before sauntering back out of the room, in true teenager fashion.

"We're so happy you came, Olive," Sandy said, beaming at me. "It's been years since Miles brought a girl home. Not since —" She broke off abruptly, her eyes flitting toward Miles briefly before she recovered quickly. A look passed between the two, but the moment was gone as quickly as it started. "I just think it's so fun that Miles hid the whole thing from you. And us."

Jack laughed. "I was even quizzing her on our tractor ride about setting her up with my son, Miles. Had no clue they were already dating. Call that intuition. I had a feeling about her the second I saw her."

"So did I," said Sandy.

I gave the best smile I could muster. Their words were causing me to fidget and rendered me unable to meet Miles's eyes.

"How did you hear about us, if not from Miles?" Sandy asked, scooping a carton of ice cream.

I chuckled lightly. "A scheming mutual friend."

"Remind me to give Millie a hug when we get back," Miles said, looking over at me with an expression that could only be described as sweet, which reminded me that we were now acting.

"How's the blackout going?" Jack asked while his wife filled my bowl with four large scoops of vanilla ice cream. I mean, I loved ice cream as much as the next girl, but I couldn't remember the last time I'd had that much. I was a polite, one-scoop-only type of girl in a public setting.

Once finished, she passed me the bowl. "Help yourself with whatever toppings you'd like. Don't be shy now."

"So far, we're right on track," Miles said, accepting his bowl —five large scoops in his. "Olive was begging to do the polar plunge last night, so everything else should be easy." I smiled and poked him hard in the leg as I contemplated between slathering my ice cream with caramel sauce or maple syrup. "And she's excited to drink fresh chocolate milk straight from the barn."

"No, I'm not!" I announced boldly, making them all laugh.

"You're not excited? It's our special chocolate milk for guests," Jack said. Though his words sounded hurt, he had a delighted twinkle in his gaze that reminded me of his rascally son.

I tentatively poured a tiny bit of maple syrup on my ice cream. Another nudge from Miles made my arm pour about three times the amount I had anticipated into my bowl.

At my withering stare, he only grinned boyishly, whispering, "Trust me."

We settled in to enjoy our dessert. Miles and I sat on one side of the table with his parents lounging across from us. He had removed his arm from my chair so he could eat, and it felt like something was missing. Which was crazy. I also hated to admit it, but the extra maple syrup really took the ice cream to a whole new level. I eyed the extra candy bar toppings and whipped cream sitting in the middle of the table with fondness but refrained.

"Do you make your own maple syrup?" I asked.

Jack beamed at me. "We used to, but it became too hard to keep up when we expanded. We buy most of what we use here from Morse Farm down the road. Has Miles taken you there yet? You can walk all through their trees and see the whole process. 'Course now, everything is covered in snow, but you can still tour the place and try some samples. Make sure Miles buys you a maple creemee."

I smiled. Growing up in New Hampshire, I wasn't ignorant of the process of making maple syrup, but for some reason, I had always found the maple farms fascinating. "It sounds amazing."

Miles looked over at me, eyebrows raised. "It's a date."

I swallowed and looked down at my now dwindling bowl. Miles reached across the table, his arm brushing mine for a second while he added more crushed cookies to his ice cream. Tentatively, I waited for him to put the spoon back before adding a few to my own bowl.

"So, Miles told us a little about how you two met, but how did it officially happen?" Sandy asked me, beaming.

The smile on my face froze as I glanced at Miles. He raised his eyebrows at me and nodded toward his parents as if to say, *Go right ahead and tell the story, Celery Stick.*

Crazy how well I seemed to know his smirks and pointed smiles.

"Well, he finally just wore me down," I said with a shrug, giving him a teasing smile. "He kept asking and asking."

Miles's eyes narrowed at me, though he smiled good naturedly. "Can you blame me?" he said to his parents.

"What do you like about Miles?"

I stared at Sandy, trying to keep the horror off my face. Who asks a question like that?

As if she could sense my discomfort, she smiled sheepishly.

"I'm sorry if that's a weird question, but I love hearing the good stuff. The stuff that pulls two people together."

"We're only dating, Mom. It's pretty new," Miles said, adjusting in his seat.

She blanched a bit, and her face began to turn red. "I know. I'm sorry, don't answer that question if I'm pushing you too far. I just…it's so fun to have Miles bring a girl home."

Bringing me home was a bit of a stretch, being that I was the one who created the whole mess. I laughed softly and took another bite of ice cream, expecting the conversation to move on, but when I looked up, I met Sandy's hopeful eyes again, and my heart dropped. I couldn't bear to not answer this question for her.

I swallowed my bite, made even more delicious with the addition of cookie pieces, and said generously, "There are lots of things to love about Miles."

The man in question reared back in his chair slightly before turning to look at me. Probably surprised by my statement. Heck, I was surprised by my statement.

"Really?" Miles said, leaning in close and putting an arm around the back of my chair. "Do tell."

There were warring emotions inside of me as I looked into the earnest and sweet face of Sandy Taylor. I should play this straight. Search deep into the creativity of my brain and come up with something I could say about her son. But the amused anticipation vibrating from the man at my left also triggered my snarky side. The side that desperately wanted nothing more than to put him in his place. My mouth opened…

"Well, he's an…author. And I love books, so…"

Sandy's face fell before good manners schooled her lips back into a smile.

"Yes, we love that about him, too. He was always so creative, even as a child. He used to get all his friends in the neighborhood, and they'd play in the treehouse for hours, making up plays and having pretend sword fights. It's no wonder he writes such fun adventure books."

I stole a glance at Miles, satisfied to see a ruddiness on his cheeks. He looked at me and glared slightly, as though he were embarrassed.

A satisfied smile lit my face. My kind words caused him to be embarrassed. That might be better than snarky.

"He's also loved by all the staff and kids at the high school. He even won an award for being the coolest teacher. The kids really adore him." I started off strong, bent on rubbing the ridiculousness of his award in his face, but by the time I got to the last statement, my voice took on a softer tone. Truth rang from my lips. The kids really did love him and…I'm not sure why that just barely hit me. Of course they loved him. He was cool and fun and taught them things in interesting ways. My mind was racing, and my mouth would not stop. "He brings donuts after school every Friday and I always hear him talking with the kids in the hallway. He has a way of making them feel special and he remembers personal things about each of them. The Friday donuts have been really…good…for some of our students."

I trailed off, meeting his eyes with a furrowed brow as a small puzzle began to be put into place.

Jack smiled proudly. "He's always had a soft heart. We used to find him feeding all kinds of stray animals. He'd bring them home and try to take care of them. Can't stand the thought of anybody going hungry."

I blinked. Why had I never put those two ideas together? I hadn't realized they correlated until I began speaking. I just thought he'd been trying to buy the students' love so they'd want to be in his classroom rather than mine. But…sudden memories of a faculty meeting where we had been discussing the kids we knew weren't getting enough to eat on the weekends came to mind. There had been several ideas thrown out to help, but to my knowledge, nothing concrete had ever been done. Was this Miles's way of helping to feed the kids who might not have enough food? And why hadn't I ever thought of it like that?

I looked at him again, but this time, he was staring down at the table, brushing away a crumb. He ran a hand through his hair, clearly uncomfortable. Looking toward his parents, he said, "That's enough. Should we play a game? Rummy? Thirteen?"

"First, I want to hear what you like about Olive. It's only fair," Sandy said, her blue eyes twinkling.

Honestly, I was starting to feel a bit sick, probably due to the half gallon of ice cream swimming down there, but still, we had to put a stop to this.

"There are too many things to name," Miles said, smiling easier now that the attention was off him. I relaxed when it seemed like he was going to play it off with a general statement. That is, until I felt his hand clamor up the back of my neck, giving it a light squeeze. Then, he kept massaging—slow, torturous touching that broke my body out into chills. Was there some sort of fake dating class Miles had taken? The touching and sweet glances, they came so naturally to him. It was disconcerting.

"She's hilarious," he said.

I huffed out a snort. Surely he wasn't serious. He found it hilarious to make fun of me, but that didn't mean that *I* was funny.

"She'll do anything to help out."

I reached over underneath the table and gave his thigh a warning squeeze. I knew what he really thought of that particular trait of mine. Quick as a blink, his left hand reached over and grabbed mine, keeping it there, resting against him. For a moment, I struggled but finally had to relent when it was clear I wasn't getting my hand back without a fight.

He continued. "Sometimes she can be too nice, but her heart's in the right place."

That wasn't true either. I did things for people, but rarely was my heart in the right place about it. I mostly just wanted to avoid drama. Keep the peace.

"But one of my favorite things about Olive is that her students, even the boys, come out of her class feeling alive."

I stilled. My heart began pounding, and I wasn't sure whether I wanted him to stop talking or keep going.

"She has them read books I'd never have the guts to bring into my classroom, but by the end, they all love her for it. It takes a special kind of teacher to read *Jane Eyre* to a bunch of teenage boys and have them enjoy it. But she does it. She's the kind of teacher her students will come back and visit in twenty years because she meant so much to them."

The room evolved into silence for a few moments. I was fighting a stinging hotness in my eyes that I could not, for all the holy love, allow to slip past. For all I knew, Miles was singing a tune for his parents. Playing our cover like a fiddle. Feeding our lie. Fanning the fake flame.

And…well done.

Miles cleared his throat and removed his arm from the back of my chair, his hand brushing across my shoulders as he did so. Good heavens, what was *with* the shoulder thing? Suddenly, it was hotter than a blaze in this house.

"Has anybody beaten my score yet?" he asked casually.

The weird feeling between us eventually dissipated as his family broke out the card games. Apparently, the Taylor family were big card sharks. My family had played more board games than cards, but I picked up the games quickly. They were the kind of players who teased and joked with others but never got angry when things didn't go their way. It made settling in with this family easy and enjoyable, and I even found myself teasing Jack about not giving up the card he wanted. I didn't tease much with Miles, however. Every time he shot a look or a teasing smile my way, I felt my face go hot. It was as if the conversation earlier had broken me. I had shown too much.

There was a natural rhythm between the four of us that made my heart ache. How many nights, growing up, had my family sat around our own table, playing Monopoly, or Risk, or my personal favorite, Scattergories? The joking back and forth, the camaraderie, the fake-outs…it made me miss my dad so much it hurt. But more than missing him, it made me miss us. The four of us together. Our family unit.

The hour grew later, and Sandy, ever the hostess, brought out a cheese-and-cracker platter and put on soft Christmas music as she ushered us into the living room. I had missed seeing the tree when we first arrived but now beheld it in its full glory, decorated in reds and golds with twinkling white lights and situated proudly in front of the window.

She and Jack sat on the sofa, leaving only the loveseat for me and Miles. He led me to sit down and sat next to me, leaving no separation between us. Miles Taylor was pressed up against the side of my body, his arm around my shoulders again like it was the most natural thing in the world. It should have felt natural at this point with how much we'd been touching, but it still sent a shock straight to my nerves. I tried to slink further into my seat, playing at a more casual pose without actually touching Miles, but couldn't find the right fit. Sandy was watching me with a questioning smile on her face, so in the name of fake dating, I placed a tentative hand on Miles's thigh. His lower thigh. It was mostly his knee. He flexed his leg under my hand.

"I don't want to call you a chicken, but I will." His whispered breath puffed into my ear. "You're stiff as a board."

I gave him a sardonic smile before snuggling more deeply into his side. His finger curled against my shoulder, and we sat that way while I listened to Miles and his dad talk about his plans for his latest book.

"I'm close to being able to start drafting with all my ideas so far, but I'll get started writing after Christmas. I wanted to give myself a breather for the holidays," Miles said.

"Have you read his books?" Sandy asked me, eyes shining.

I stiffened, but before I could cobble together an answer, Miles squeezed me closer to him. "If I can get her nose out of the classics, mine will be the next on her list."

I relaxed into his grip and leaned forward to pick up a picture album from the coffee table in front of me.

"Ohhh, you'll love that one. I just pulled it out the other day. Miles as a little boy was about the cutest thing you'll ever see." Sandy beamed.

And he was. Literally the cutest kid I had ever seen. It wasn't fair, actually. He had been as skinny as a beanpole. His teeth as an adolescent youth had been janky and crazy, but I loved how he smiled wide and proud in his pictures. His eyes were bright and held the same twinkle they did now. The impish smile and messy brown hair did something to my maternal instincts. I forced myself to not linger there. For his part, he took me seeing his formative years all in stride, laughing good-naturedly about his braces and the headgear, all the while holding me close with one arm and laughing late into the night with his parents.

And when it was all said and done, Miles walked me back to my cabin.

"So, your mom kissed me on the cheek."

He laughed. "You gotta watch her. She'll drop one on you before you even know it's coming. Did you have fun?"

I smiled. "They're really nice. They seemed pretty happy we were there."

"They're just excited I brought a girl home."

That phrase felt so out of place with what I had always imagined about Miles. While he didn't seem like a Casanova, per se, he was...to nearly quote *Pride and Prejudice*...one of the most handsome men of my acquaintance. And that wasn't me having any sort of crush on him. That was me stating pure, platonic fact. He had perfect hair that repeatedly fell into his eyes. The man could wear a five o'clock shadow like a cowboy could wear a tight pair of jeans. And his jeans…well…I won't go into the way they fit him like a glove. Thank goodness I was so completely disinterested or else I could have been in trouble. Plenty of women in my position would probably fall for a man just like him.

"Huh. That surprises me, actually."

"Why?" The look he gave me seemed genuinely curious. And now I wondered if I should have kept my mouth shut.

"I just always imagined you bringing home beautiful blonde women who probably eat kale regularly and hike Mount Everest on the weekends."

His face fell into a wide smile. "I don't think that's how Mount Everest works."

I shrugged, pulling my hand out from my pocket to scratch my cheek.

"So, you've been imagining me with other women, huh?" he said. I could feel him smiling, though I kept my eyes averted.

"No."

"You said it."

"Why would your parents be surprised that you brought somebody home?"

He gave me a crooked grin. "Until now, I hadn't found a woman I wanted to bring home."

I glared at him, hoping my flushed cheeks could be blamed on the wind. "Miles."

He shrugged. "I haven't dated much lately."

The cold breeze picked up, ruffling my hair. "Why?"

There was a long moment before he responded. And it was then that I realized he seemed to know a lot more about me than I did him.

"I was dating a girl a few years back, but..." He trailed off for a bit, the hitch in his voice causing me to look over at him. "It's just taken me a while to get back on that horse, I guess." He gave me a boyish grin, trying to play down the emotions he had obviously felt at the start of the sentence, but he didn't fool me. Before I could ask further, he changed the subject. He settled back into his teasing self, dropping me off at my cabin and making me laugh even as I closed the door in his face.

SEVENTEEN

"Dear old world," she murmured, "You are very lovely, and I am glad to be alive in you."
L.M. Montgomery - *Anne of Green Gables*

We had crossed plenty of small items off our list yesterday. Miles had a few errands and chores to do for his dad this morning. Suddenly missing Chloe and the girls, I surprised them at their cabin that morning for breakfast. The lodge had complimentary muffins, juice, and fruit every morning, but Chloe had brought her own food for the cabin that she knew her girls would eat. With her morning sickness, she rarely made it out of the cabin before 10 or 11.

The girls were very excited to see me, and I spent the first ten minutes playing with them on the floor, which evolved to me letting them paint my nails a fashionable rainbow of orange, yellow, and brown.

When I got them settled with a few puzzles, I meandered

into the kitchen, where Chloe sat at the table, sipping ginger tea. The sink had dishes waiting to go into the dishwasher, and cereal and bowls were scattered around the table as though she had mustered just enough energy to feed her charges with nothing left over for cleanup.

"How are you feeling?"

She smiled wanly. "I'm doing okay. Hopefully, it will just be another week or two of feeling like this."

"You make pregnancy sound so fun." I made my way to the sink and began putting the dishes into the dishwasher.

"It can be hard, but it comes with the best payoff. You don't have to do those. I can get them."

"So can I," I said. "Where's Ben?"

"He went to grab some Almond Joys and frozen burritos from the store."

My eyebrows raised. "Almond Joys and frozen burritos?"

"The heart wants what it wants."

I snickered. "Your poor heart must be sick, too."

"All I want is a burrito I can microwave and then cover in ketchup, and some Almond Joys to polish the whole thing off. It's literally all I can think about."

"Yikes."

"So, how are things going with you and Miles?" Chloe asked, taking a calculated sip while she studied me.

I closed the dishwasher and made my way to the table to pour myself a bowl of Lucky Charms, contemplating my response. She only halfway believed that we were really dating, so it wasn't a huge stretch to just divulge my whole secret now. But if I told Chloe it was all fake, it would feel fake again, and there was a dangerous warmth growing inside of me when I thought of Miles. It had been kind of nice to think of him as something like a friend. He still drove me crazy and was having way too much fun pushing the lines of our fake relationship, but I wasn't ready to come clean just yet.

"We had ice cream sundaes with his parents last night, and his mom kissed me." My family members were not kissers, so to say I had been surprised at his mom planting one on me was an understatement.

"Wow. Is she better or worse than her son?"

I snorted. I should have known Chloe would have no interest in the boring details I was willing to give her.

"Nice pivot," I said through a mouthful of cereal.

"Thank you. I could be puking at any moment, so I need you to get right to the good stuff . Besides, nobody could really tell from that pathetic kiss you gave him at the lodge earlier."

"I'm not into PDA. I told you."

"With the right guy, you will be."

My skin betrayed me as it blushed hotly under her perceptive gaze. I promptly changed the subject, which only made her laugh.

❦

"SO, WHAT ARE WE DOING HERE AGAIN?" MILES SCRATCHED HIS head as I led him down the cereal aisle at Shaws, the local grocery store in Montpelier.

"Listen, Taylor, if you want to win this gingerbread competition, I can't just use whatever sub-par materials come in the kit. We have to get creative."

"You know we don't have to win to get it checked off our cards, right? We could just slap some frosting down on the kit and call it a day."

I finally found a box of Golden Grahams and handed it to Miles, grabbing his arm to herd him into the next aisle. "You made me jump into a frozen pond, so you will be wearing an apron and holding a hot glue gun for me without complaint."

He looked interested. "Just an apron? I'm suddenly intrigued."

I pushed him away as I finally found the fresh herbs. "My cousin makes these amazing gingerbread houses every Christmas. They're next level. We'll win for sure."

He bit back a grin and gave me a slight bow as I handed him a plastic container full of fresh rosemary sprigs. "I love it when you're bossy."

We checked out a few minutes later and piled into Miles's white truck with our bags.

"I was planning to pay for all of that," I insisted, settling into the passenger seat as he started his truck.

"I know. You told me several times."

"Then why didn't you let me?"

He looked over at me, his eyes seeming to soak me in from my hair all the way down to the tips of my wet boots. "Because I wanted to," he said simply.

All the retorts I had about being an independent woman who could pay for my own groceries went right out the window. To be honest, I didn't have super strong convictions about being an independent woman—no offense to Beyoncé—but it was more the fact that I hadn't wanted Miles to pay for my things because that *would* feel like a date. I didn't need this situation to get any more confusing than it already was. But his brown eyes held nothing but kindness, a sweetness that I hadn't been expecting.

"Well, thanks," I sputtered, looking out the window as we pulled back out onto Main Street. For a long while, I was taken aback by the beautiful small town of Montpelier. Trees and hills provided a perfect backdrop to the shops and old historic buildings that lined the streets. Coffee shops, book shops, a toy store and even a record store were interspersed with delicious bistros and restaurants. Beautiful churches and a library finished out the street. Even in the winter, people were out walking the sidewalks, holding shopping bags and chatting with friends. There was an excited buzz in the air, and I could feel it even inside the truck—a small-town glow, like I'd just stepped into a Hallmark Christmas movie. I couldn't believe places like this were real.

"I can't believe you got to grow up here. It's so idyllic."

He looked at me, slowing the truck at a stop light. "You want to get out? Go for a walk?"

"How did you know I wanted to do that?"

"The drool smear you left on the window."

I swatted his arm. "Don't we need to get back for the gingerbread thing?"

"It's going on all afternoon. We could walk around and grab lunch if you want. I need to find my mom a Christmas present anyway."

I folded my arms. "Last-minute shopper? And for your own mother of all people."

He laughed. "I am the world's worst present giver, so this actually might be good to have some help."

We sat smiling at each other until the light changed. "So…*do* you want to walk around for a bit?" Miles asked again, a sweet hesitancy in his voice that did something to my insides.

"Yeah."

Whatever this holiday glow was, I wanted part of it. I hadn't felt this way in so long. Miles found some parking in front of the library, and we both got out, the smell of pine trees and snow feeding my soul the second we exited. The lodge smelled very similar, but there was something about this small town that felt different. We spent the next couple of hours wandering down the streets, stopping for lunch at a small bistro that was absolutely delicious. But my favorite was Miles pointing out landmarks and rehashing memories and old stories, like when he and his high school buddies jumped buck naked into the Winooski River running through the town. It had been in the middle of the night, but still. I found it hard to believe he wasn't a daredevil as a kid, even though he insisted he wasn't.

"Everybody does a few crazy things growing up," he said as I tried very hard not to imagine him jumping naked into a river.

"I never did."

He looked over at me as we crossed the street, headed toward the bookstore a few blocks ahead. "No?"

"Nope. You heard my slip 'n' slide story. I never did anything crazy." And lest he think I regretted that, I added a quick, "And I liked it that way."

His eyes narrowed. "I don't buy it. What was your family like growing up?"

I raised my arms. "Where do you think I got it from?"

"Russ seems pretty adventurous."

My foot caught on a hidden rock beneath the snow and sent me stumbling. Miles grabbed my elbow until I had righted myself.

"You good?" he asked.

"Yeah."

"I'm sorry. I spoke without thinking. I know Russ isn't your dad."

We walked a few moments in silence. Per our agreement, he wasn't pushing me to talk about anything, but he was giving me an opportunity if I wanted. And for the first time in forever, I found myself wanting to talk.

"Russ likes adventure. But my mom and dad never had much money growing up, so we never went on any big trips or anything. Our one splurge was going to the movies as a family a couple times a year. Mostly, we stayed home. We played a lot of games. We had this thing called quiet Saturdays…" I started chuckling at the memory. "Where every Saturday afternoon, my dad would make us all stop what we were doing, and we had to read a book for two hours."

"Two hours?" Miles asked incredulously.

I laughed. "It was his way of stopping all the chores so he could get some guilt-free reading time in."

He laughed. "My dad isn't a big reader, but my mom probably would have gone for something like that."

We arrived at the bookstore, and Miles opened my door while he motioned me inside. Breathing in the scent was heaven to both of us, if the contented look on Miles's face could be attributed to books. To my surprise, a table near the entrance of the store was dedicated to Miles's *Landfall* series. Complete with a sign that read *Local Author*.

I turned to look at Miles, rubbing his neck and looking uncomfortable.

"Is this why you wanted to come here?" I teased, moving to pick up one of his books.

"I didn't think they'd still have this up," he said.

"Is that our famous Miles Taylor?"

We both turned to see a red-haired woman striding excitedly toward us.

Miles broke out into a grin, stepping forward to give her a hug. "You're embarrassing me, Cathy. You still have this up?"

"Of course we do. It's not every day somebody from this town becomes a famous author." She beamed up at him. Looking at me, she asked, "Is this a girlfriend?"

"Yup." Miles smirked at me. "This is Oliviana."

I gave him an exasperated look before shaking Cathy's excited hand.

"Well, it's so nice to meet you," Cathy said.

"You, too."

"Will you sign a few books really quick?" she asked, looking up at Miles imploringly.

Miles signed everything they had in stock. We roamed the shop for another twenty minutes before we found what we both deemed the perfect book for his mom. A light snow began to fall on us as we meandered back toward his truck. There were bells in the distance, and the sound of Mariah Carey's "All I Want for Christmas Is You" humming through the town speakers. The only thing that could have made this moment more perfect was to be holding hands with somebody. Where were the eyes of my mom and sister when we needed them?

I was kidding.

Miles checked the clock in the truck when we got in. "It's 2:30. The contest closes at 4:00. How much time do you need to make the gingerbread house?"

"Assuming I have good help, we can do it in an hour."

"Assume away, Celery Stick."

"Why do you ask?"

He motioned up the hill we were climbing. "I'm in the mood for a maple creemee, and we're about to pass Morse Farm."

"Your family can sure put away the ice cream."

He raised his eyebrows. "Is that a challenge or a yes?"

"No whining with the gingerbread, and you have to do everything I say. And we can only stay for ten minutes."

"Yes, ma'am." Miles gave a mock salute as he pulled into the maple farm.

Forty-five minutes later, Miles dragged me nearly kicking and screaming back to the truck. It had been too much fun sampling the different grades of syrup, watching the videos on how they run their operation, and walking the beautiful snow-covered grounds. The soft-serve maple creemee I held in my hands was a delightful bonus to the most magical afternoon.

We rushed back to the lodge where I discovered Miles to be a halfway decent help. Having a time limit probably motivated him more than anything. I used the hot glue gun provided to build the house and then put Miles in charge of gluing the golden grahams onto the roof, giving it a thatched look. I covered the sides in white frosting, then strategically placed our rosemary sprigs in the eaves and down the roofline. We made windows and pathways with some of the candy bars we'd bought and, at precisely 4 pm, set it on the judging table along with seven or eight other completed houses.

"Okay, over-achievers." Chloe came up next to us, admiring our house in disgust. "You couldn't just use the stuff in the package like everybody else?"

Miles leaned across me to address my sister. "For the record, I voted for the package."

"Such a whiner," I said.

"I knew I liked you," Chloe said to Miles.

"Where are the girls?" I asked, looking around for the kids.

"We made ours at home, meaning the girls helped me for about three minutes before they began eating all the frosting, and Ben put them down for a nap while I finished."

The judges (Jack, Sandy, and Jett) began walking around the tables, admiring the effort of their guests.

"You really are pretty good at those," Miles said, his eyes raking over our very chic, white house that definitely stood out from the crowd.

"You don't get talent like this by careening down a mountain strapped to a pair of skis," I said.

"I think I've now successfully done both," he teased, pulling me in for a friendly side hug while the judges deemed our house the winner.

I couldn't put my finger on what made our afternoon feel so different. Miles was still Miles, but he'd been...sweeter. He felt more genuine. While in town, we didn't hold hands or touch beyond Miles grabbing me and pulling me backward once so I could appropriately gawk at the store window display decked out for Christmas. I guess it was because we weren't surrounded by people at the lodge who we needed to convince we were dating. But for a moment, our defenses had been down. My walls and his diverting humor had been put on the back burner while we made way for easy conversation and friendly stories. It felt as comfortable as it had strange—and with Miles of all people. It had only been two days since I'd arrived at the lodge, and three days earlier, I was under the impression that I strongly disliked Miles Taylor. My head seemed to enjoy this friendly direction we were headed, but my heart couldn't help but be wary. *Proceed with caution,* it said.

EIGHTEEN

"To be fond of dancing was a certain step towards falling in love."
Jane Austen - *Pride and Prejudice*

"Hiding out, Celery Stick?" Miles appeared suddenly at my side later that night. I was sitting at a table in the lodge, looking out at the crowd of dancers. Miles waited for no invitation and settled into the chair beside me. After our big gingerbread win, I had gone back to my cabin to shower and get ready for the dinner and barn dance. They called it a barn dance, though it was located in the lodge.

"Are you just worried your dancing skills will pale in comparison to mine?" He looked at my face, and his brow immediately furrowed. "What's wrong?"

"Nothing."

My eyes were on Mom and Russ on the dance floor, acting like lovestruck teenagers. Russ dipping her and kissing her neck was disgusting enough, but the way she laughed like a fourteen-year-old girl with her first crush made me physically ache. I couldn't help but wonder if my mom ever thought about all of the nights dancing in the kitchen with my dad. Though my dad hadn't been much of an adventurous soul, he'd had a romantic heart. There were so many nights when Chloe and I would pretend to gag as he zipped her dramatically around the dining table, kisses loud enough to drown out our squeals. Did she remember that? I wasn't sure how a person's emotions dealt with two loves in one lifetime, if that was truly what Russ was to her. People seemed to do it all the time, but my mind couldn't grasp the sudden change. I could feel Miles following my gaze.

"Your mom looks happy," he said after a long moment.

The last thing I needed was for Miles to tell me how wrong I was to feel what I was feeling, so I just said, "Yup. She does."

He looked at my face again, but I refused to meet his eyes. He leaned back, his arms folded and his long legs sprawled out in front of him.

"How long have they been married?"

"Four months."

He nodded, looking at the happy couple slow dancing to "I'll be Home for Christmas." "And how long since your dad passed away?"

I drew in a quiet breath, surprised at the hotness in my eyes. I widened them, forcing the sting to retreat. "It will be a year next week."

The air grew thick around us—almost stifling. I felt him considering me, but I remained a statue, my gaze a blur of Russ and Elaine.

"It happened right after Christmas?" His voice was incredulous and soft, like a whisper feathering across my skin.

I couldn't move or speak to acknowledge him, a dam inside of me threatening to burst. But there was nothing else to say, and he must have known that, because for the first time since I'd known him, he didn't press me for anything else. So, we sat there for a long while, shoulders touching, staring at the whirl of laughter and people around us.

"Wanna dance, Olive Oil? For old time's sake?"

I blinked up at Glenn's sudden arrival in front of us. He was holding his hand out toward me, waiting for me to take it. My body tightened at the thought of dancing with him. Good manners had me wondering if I should say yes, but I had no desire to deal with Glenn right now.

Miles wrapped an arm around me, his fingers caressing the top of my shoulder. "Sorry, man. She was just about to dance with me."

Glenn chuckled to himself, running a hand through his hair. "Okay. Olive's loss. Again." He gave me a pointed look that gave the impression he was trying to play off his very honest thoughts as a joke but ended up failing miserably. He walked toward the drink table where he proceeded to lean against the wall with folded arms, wearing a carefully crafted bored expression.

"Maybe I had the shoulder thing all wrong. It's kind of hot," Miles whispered into my ear.

I leaned forward immediately. His arm fell loosely to his side while he laughed. "Not for you?"

It *was* hot, but he wouldn't hear that from me.

He stood and turned back to face me, holding out his hand. "Alright, I guess we gotta dance now. You ready?"

I stared at his hand warily.

"I could go grab Glenn, if you'd prefer," he whispered. His fingers wiggled, indicating I should allow him to pull me up, which I did, but when I went to remove my fingers from his hand, he only held mine tighter. I knew he was supposed to be my boyfriend tonight, but watching my mom felt like a punch in my gut. I didn't want to act anymore. I was too disheartened to care about much at the moment. But I could see Glenn and his parents on the other side of the room, watching us, so I forced myself to snuggle up tighter against Miles's side and allowed him to lead me to the dance floor. A handful of other couples were dancing around us. I was grateful Russ and my mom had sat out and were currently laughing with another older couple from a neighboring cabin.

Once on the floor, we turned to face each other. My head barely topped his shoulder. My limbs felt heavy and unsure. I had gone dancing with roommates in college a couple of times, and that had been enough for me. My body didn't know quite how to move to the beat, but thankfully, the song was slow, and Miles didn't seem to be an expert either. I held my other hand out, expecting this to go how I was taught in middle school, with my right hand in his left and our other hand at the waist. Miles must have missed that school lesson.

His lips twitched, but he ignored my hands. "I didn't realize you were a ninety-year-old woman, Carrots."

Without warning, I found myself pressed completely against his stomach, his hands circling my waist with nowhere for mine to go except up—to those dang shoulders again. My fingers clung to his muscles there, feeling them move every so often as he led us in a very slow sway across the room. My chest was literally smooshed against him, and I wondered if he could feel my pounding heartbeat. I tried to gather my wits and bring us back to some sort of safe ground.

"If we're going to be fake dating, can your fake girlfriend request that you stop all the vegetable tray references? Even if it's just for one blessed week?"

"Well, you can sure try, Celery Stick."

I shook my head, a smile sneaking across my lips as I felt the weight of the night slowly leaving my body.

"Alright," Miles began, "the mistletoe make-out is the last thing to cross off for tonight."

"It did not say make-out."

He pulled away to stare down at me, his eyebrows furrowed in mock confusion. "Pretty sure it did."

"Miles."

"Pickles."

Both of our noses wrinkled.

"Too far?" Miles asked.

"Yeah."

"My bad. Anyway, let's plan our make-out—"

"Kiss," I insisted, swallowing hard. I had been hoping that particular bingo square would have been blown up and sunk by another battleship by now. But perhaps I was thinking of a different game.

He leaned down conspiratorially and whispered, "There's mistletoe everywhere. Should I just set you down on top of the table and go for it? Should we do it in front of Glenn?"

Fire heated my face. I felt light and giddy at the same time I felt my walls go back up. It felt so wrong to be talking like this with him. I didn't understand how he could be so casual. In two more weeks, our next semester would start, and we'd be back to normal at school, him still annoying me but, this time, with kisses and dances and touching between us. It wasn't good for anybody.

"Or I could pull you into a dark corner?" He went on as though he had no thought in the world about our close work proximity nine months out of the year.

"How about a nice, friendly kiss on the cheek?" I countered. "One where we can go back to school and face each other with our heads held high, knowing that we chose the high road."

His mouth split into a grin. "The high road? What road do you think I'm offering you right now?"

I pushed lightly against his laughing chest. "Maybe I'll just have my mistletoe kiss with somebody else."

I didn't really mean that. The thought of asking Russ to give me a fatherly kiss on the cheek under a sprig of mistletoe was definitely out of the question. After some groveling, I was pretty sure Glenn would be game if I asked, but obviously, I couldn't—and definitely wouldn't—do that. But for whatever reason, I didn't want Miles to think he had me so easily. Maybe I *could* kiss a stranger. There was a small handful of unattached men at the lodge. I read books about heroines kissing strangers all the time. It could be exciting. Maybe even romantic.

"You'd fake cheat on me?" His voice sounded incredulous.

"It would just be a friendly cheek kiss," I insisted. "It's how they greet each other in France and Italy. It wouldn't be cheating."

His eyes narrowed, considering me while I writhed under his scrutiny. My gaze caught on his full bottom lip before I swallowed and tore my eyes away. Miles's problem was that he was too attractive for his own good—and mine. But that was fine. There were lots of attractive men in this world. I could handle it. He could be platonically handsome. I didn't need to hyper-focus on that. Now I just needed to convince myself that kissing a random stranger would be preferable to the guy currently holding me in his arms.

A challenge lit his eyes. "Okay. But I get to pick."

I'm sure there were only two or three unattached males in this room, so I didn't think having him pick would be detrimental. The song ended, and in a flash, he led me off the dance floor. When we settled against a wall, he leaned in close, arm around my shoulders, as we scanned the room.

"What about him?"

He motioned toward a large cowboy with a handlebar mustache and a ten-gallon hat, sitting on the stage, playing a guitar version of "Little Drummer Boy".

"Who's that?"

"That's Frank. Don't get your cowgirl hopes up. He's actually a plumber in town, but he moonlights as Frank the Cowboy for the guests here a few nights a week. But I happen to know he'd be very okay with a mistletoe kiss."

I swallowed. "That's quite the mustache."

"It's a specific type of woman who can hold onto a man like that. You up for it?"

"I don't think I'm woman enough for Frank the Cowboy."

"Poor Frank. Strike one."

He began scanning the room once more. I tried very hard not to notice the feel of his arm around my shoulder. It felt so casual and yet territorial at the same time. And it was beginning to mess with my head.

"How about your ex-boyfriend glaring daggers at me right now?"

I followed his gaze back to Glenn, who glowered our way for a long moment before turning his attention elsewhere. Poor Glenn. If there were any other single girls here, I had no doubt he would be dancing up a storm right in front of my nose.

"I think he's more in the mood to meet you out by the flagpole."

"I guess we could go see if he'd be up for some kissing afterward."

"Don't you dare."

"Okay, that's strike two."

"What happens on strike three?"

"You're out."

I growled lowly. "What does that mean for this dumb game you're playing?"

He smiled. "It means that if you can't find somebody in the three *very* decent options I've given you, you have to kiss me."

It took some effort to keep my face passive and my blush absent from my cheeks. I wasn't sure I succeeded. Miles began searching the room once more.

"Let's see…my last pick. I'd better make it good. How about that guy?"

I looked at Miles and then at the man he motioned to, who

was very much in his middle age and very much sweating by the fire. I hesitated. No. I most certainly did not want that guy. But was it a better alternative than kissing Miles Taylor on a Christmas vacation? No. But…

"Yuuup. He's the one."

A smile grew on his face before he released me and began to move away. "Okay, I'll go get him for you."

My hand shot out in a panic, grabbing the sleeve of his coat and pulling him back toward me. Not allowing myself to think, I took aim and closed my eyes. His lips were much softer than I had remembered from our fumbled kiss on the first night. For a moment, we just stood there, our lips pressed together. I had never been the type of girl to kiss much in public, and at first, I was very aware of the room around us—the eyes that might have been watching. Speaking of eyes…I opened mine a peek and found him staring at me. I jolted and began to pull away, but Miles stepped forward into my space, his hand at my back, increasing the pressure of our lips until mine became pliable. Moldable.

Ever so slowly, Miles drew my body closer until we were pressed together. With one hand lightly at my neck, his thumb brushed gently over my jaw. This time, my mouth opened to his, and he responded instantly. His lips toyed with mine, pulling and playing…teasing. And then…he wasn't teasing any longer. His other hand on my back pulled me close until there was no space between us. By this time, my brain had caught up and was flashing red lights, telling me to slow down. Pull over. Get out from under his lips.

In a state somewhere between morbid curiosity and satisfaction, I nestled closer. I curled into his warmth. I needed to stop this. I hadn't intended for it to be like this. The mortification of facing him after a kiss like this was more than my mind could fathom. But my body begged for just another second. His chest pounded beneath my hands as they wound their way up to his shoulders. I felt his hand at the back of my neck, sending tingles down my spine as he lightly gripped my hair. We were fake dating. I could blame this all on that. People were watching. It was helping our cover. Glenn was probably watching. My family was watching. They needed to see this. I leaned in for one last second, feeling his strong body against mine just a bit longer before my brain overruled my body, and I stepped out of his arms.

Holy crap.

Miles blinked and raised his eyebrows ever so slightly. I glanced away, flustered by my reaction to him. I didn't know where to look, so obviously I looked everywhere but directly at Miles. My shirt had gotten twisted somewhere in our… exchange…so I tugged it back down. Miles seemed as lost for words as I was. From the corner of my eye, I watched him run a hand through his hair. We both watched silently as my mom and Russ began heading our way.

As if by mutual agreement of not wanting to talk to anybody, he slowly pulled me back out onto the dance floor. The tune was a jazzy version of "Jingle Bell Rock," but we kept to our own beat, which was basically tone-deaf and a bit…muddled.

"As far as I can tell, there was only one problem with that kiss," Miles said finally, his voice a bit deeper than usual.

I glanced up at him warily, acutely aware of his fingers pressing into me, absently toying with my shirt at my lower back. "What?"

A broad smile crossed his face. "You misjudged the mistletoe by at least thirty feet."

"What?" I whirled around, looking up toward the rafters where I had just kissed Miles. He was right. There was no mistletoe. Looking around, I spotted it under doorways and windows and a few strategic and obvious places around the center of the room. But I couldn't have been farther away from the green parasitic plant if I had tried.

"Was that just a warm-up for you? Should I move us closer for round two?"

"It counts," I said indignantly. For some reason, I had the urge to laugh but held it together.

He grinned, tilting his head toward me. "It doesn't."

"It does," I insisted.

"You know, for such a rule follower, you're sure willing to sell your lying, cheating soul for this."

The laugh I was trying so hard to keep hidden bubbled out of me just then. I drew my hand up to my mouth in an attempt to stop it, but it was not meant to be. Life for me was dangerous when I had so many emotions and so much blood currently coursing through my body.

A smile lit Miles's face as he watched me, no doubt pleased at the effect of his words. I did my best to stifle my reaction.

"It counts," I said finally.

"It *so* does not. We're gonna need a redo before this week's over."

And in case you were wondering, those were the words on repeat in my stupid, dumb head as I fell into a restless sleep later that night.

NINETEEN

"Good-night, my-" He stopped, bit his lip, and abruptly left me.
Charlotte Brontë - *Jane Eyre.*

"So, I just squeeze it?"

It was 7 am the next morning. I was standing in a barn next to Miles, his dad, and a 1500-pound Holstein cow who kept whacking me on the side of my head with her tail. Miles moved to stand between me and the tail and handed me a small plastic cup with a squirt of chocolate syrup inside, which seemed to be some sort of satanic ritual with the Taylor family.

"Squeeze and pull." He mimicked the downward squeezing motion again with his hands.

I took a deep breath and sat on the stool, staring at the plump udder, now at eye level, in dread.

"What's her name?" I asked, stalling shamelessly.

Jack Taylor laughed. "Depending on her mood, we call her a lot of things, but the polite one we tell people is Snowflake."

"Hey, Snowflake," I whispered as I leaned in closer, my hand inching toward the lady's privates. "Sorry about this."

Miles chuckled as he squatted down next to me. "You're doing her a favor. I promise, she's used to it."

My hand stalled, so he took it and placed it on the cow. "Now just squeeze it gently and pull it toward your cup." He held his own cup filled with chocolate syrup under a different teat and squeezed, easily filling his cup with frothy white milk.

"Show off," I muttered.

"Chicken," he countered.

I repositioned my hand to where it felt the most comfortable. It had a soft, rubber-like feel that was slightly disturbing. I squeezed and pulled. Nothing happened. I tried again. Same.

"Keep going. It's like sucking through a straw, it takes a few pulls to get the milk coming."

After a few more failed attempts, Miles once again placed his hand over mine and helped to guide my hand. Very soon after, milk was streaming into my cup. Miles removed his hand and let me keep squeezing. A smile leapt onto my face. I hadn't expected to feel so proud. I had just milked a cow. Who would have thought? Laura Ingalls Wilder had nothing on me.

Miles grinned at me. Once I had enough milk in my cup, he held out a plastic spoon.

"This might be a good time to tell you that I hate milk."

When I didn't take the spoon, he leaned over and stirred it himself. "Good thing this is chocolate milk, then."

"No. I hate all forms of liquid squeezed from a cow's"—I glanced down to the cow munching on grain beside me—"lady bits."

Miles and his dad had a good, long laugh over that while I stood there stiffly, chin up, taking in the fascinating scenery around the barn, before meeting the watering eyes of Jack, and a small laugh broke free.

"It's on the bingo card," Miles said, clinking his glass to mine in a toast. "On three."

"I don't want to."

"Suck it up."

"Milk is gross."

"One."

"Miles, no." I grasped his shirt in panic until I felt his muscles against my fingers, and I dropped my grip awkwardly. "I milked it. Isn't that enough?"

"It's fresh. It'll taste better than anything you've had."

"I don't want to!" My voice sounded pathetic and immature even to my ears, but I couldn't help it. The cup was warm in my hand. *Warm.* I honestly hated the taste of milk, and I highly doubted that the warm frothiness I watched spew out directly from a hulking, stinking bovine would help me to suddenly like it. Bile rose up in my throat, and I fought to swallow it down.

"Two."

"I'll do another mistletoe kiss," I bargained breathlessly in a panic, glancing toward Jack, making sure he was out of earshot, filling some buckets with grain for the cows to munch on while in the barn.

Miles was about to say three before he stopped short, humor in his gaze. "I know you will because you missed the first time."

"I didn't miss."

He snorted. "The mistletoe was nowhere near us."

"You didn't notice either."

He leaned in closer, mischief running rampant all across his face. "Who said I didn't?"

My mouth dropped open.

"Three."

He clinked his plastic cup against mine and drained it in seconds, leaving a frothy line across his lip that he casually licked away. For a second, my eyes traveled downward across his lean body full of lines and hidden muscles and wondered if milk really was the key to doing a body good.

He leaned in close, bracing himself with a hand on my shoulder. The second his lips brushed against my ear, I froze. "Carrots, you're a wild woman now. There's nothing you can't do. You jumped into a frozen pond. You had a non-mistletoe kiss with a hot guy. You just milked a cow. You can do this. I know it. You can drink these two ounces of milk."

I pulled back from his laughing face and scowled at him. He had been doing so well.

Jack made his way back to where we were standing with a grin on his face as he nodded toward my cup. "You haven't drunk it yet?"

I stared into the cup. Before I could let myself overthink what I was about to do, I brought the cup to my lips, closed my eyes, and chugged.

The moment the milk hit my throat, I gagged, the warm foam too much for my sensitive palate. Warm, frothy brown milk spewed out my mouth and nose, spraying both Jack and Miles. I coughed and sputtered a bit longer before facing the men. Both were wiping at the excess moisture across their faces and bodies.

"I told you."

The men began to laugh. "You did tell us," Jack said, giving his face one more wipe. "We should have listened."

Miles was grinning when he leaned forward, brushing a drop of milk from my cheek with his finger. "But at least we get to count it."

"You sure about that?" Jack teased, leaning forward to finish milking the cow. "I don't think she swallowed any of it."

"It counts," I insisted strongly, and for once, both men gave me no grief.

"You don't have a Christmas tree," Miles said as I opened the door to him and his incessant knocking exactly two minutes after he had just dropped me off from the cow-milking debacle.

According to the list, today we were supposed to cross off the milking of a cow, drinking chocolate milk, and watching a Christmas movie.

"What?" I asked, moving back to let him inside again.

"I just realized. The lodge never prepped this cabin to have a tree. Nobody was supposed to be in here. We need to get you a tree."

Honestly, I hadn't even thought about it. In my mind, this Christmas was a wash. Maybe next year I'd be more open to a real Christmas, but this year...I had a cold, dead Scrooge heart, and a Christmas tree wasn't going to help that.

"I'm okay. I promise. Besides, it's not part of the bingo thing."

He looked at me, his hand sweeping across his chest in mock offense. "My mom would murder me if I knowingly let a guest spend the week here without a tree. I'm adding it to the list. Today. After lunch."

It was pointless to argue, so I didn't.

"Fine. Should we just run to the grocery store and grab one off their lot?"

He looked mortally wounded. "I'm going to pretend you didn't say that."

After lunch, he picked me up, wearing more dang flannel that was beginning to mess with my head. I'd always thought of flannel as something old men wore, but this was...different. It was flannel I had touched during a kiss. Not just touched either. My greedy fingers roamed all over it. It was a soft and sturdy fabric. The kind a girl could depend on to keep her warm. He looked like the cover of a book Chloe would love. Curse her and her endless lumberjack comments.

He handed me a pair of black gloves and pulled a white beanie onto my head, slinging it low across my ears. I pulled on the gloves, marveling at their warmth, and followed him like a stray puppy down the cabin steps and directly west into the woods.

"Did you buy these gloves?" I asked hesitantly, noticing the tag still on them. I hoped they were a pair his parents had been gifted or something. A pair they just had laying around the house.

"Can't take my freezing-cold girlfriend Christmas-tree hunting without gloves."

"I have gloves," I said, trying to keep up with his long stride.

"I know. But you need gloves that don't look like you ripped them off a three-year-old."

He tossed me a smile over his shoulder and seemed to realize he was moving too fast, so he slowed down and grabbed my now warm, grown-up-glove-covered hand into his.

"Just in case anybody sees us heading to the woods," he stated, holding up our clasped hands. My eyes narrowed, but I allowed the touching breach to continue—for our cover.

"What's in your pack?" I asked, referring to the bag slung across his shoulder.

"A bow saw."

"Is this the part where you kill me in the woods?" I asked, slowing my footsteps dramatically.

He stopped and turned to face me. "There's a lot of things I could do with you in the woods. Should I start naming some off?"

My breath caught. "Well, I don't see any mistletoe out here, so…"

He leaned closer, his flirting game on level one thousand, and whispered, "I'm not a big traditionalist."

Having sufficiently rattled me, he smiled and began moving again.

I told Miles I liked about fifteen different trees on our walk before he finally deemed one perfect. I held the tree while he sawed the base, and soon we were making the trek back toward my cabin with Miles dragging our capture behind him.

He was on another level today, teasing me mercilessly like he just couldn't help himself. For ten minutes straight, he rehashed every line of the infamous email, one jab after another. My mind couldn't keep up as he used his wit and way with words to render me utterly outraged one moment and blushing and speechless the next. He brought up the letter, the nicknames, the hams, the missed kiss, and every other interaction between us that he could possibly twist into some form of a flirtation. One after the other, until I was left with unanswered retorts fluttering around in my head but unable to think fast enough to gather one and let it fly. As we walked side by side, my fingers clenched into a tight ball as I tried to school my emotions. He was Miles unleashed, and I couldn't decide if I should laugh, or push him, or punch him or—

Reader, I spanked him.

Instantly, I knew I had done wrong. The entire forest seemed to hush, fading away into quiet spectators watching this unfold. My hand shot back, and I stared at it as though I had never seen one before. The other hand covered my mouth. My eyes went bug-eyed. Miles dropped the tree and whirled around with a stunned expression on his face. Actually, to be more accurate, he was looking at me like I had just handed him a one-hundred-dollar bill.

"I didn't realize we were at *this* point in our fake relationship, Oliviana."

I couldn't move. My mouth gaped open, desperately wishing to bring a few seconds back on the clock. Rewind. Redo. Of all the people to get handsy with, it had to be Miles. My palm burned. I could only imagine what his…derrière…felt like. Well, I knew what it *felt* like…taut and firm…the perfect amount of bounce—*FOCUS*, Olive.

His eyes were dancing. Okay, he was *just* fine. Him and his…butt.

He bit his bottom lip in an ultra-attractive way as he took a step toward me, which I immediately countered by stepping backward.

"You just spanked me." He couldn't even get the sentence out without laughing.

"It…" I swallowed hard, my hands in my hair. *What*? Olive. *WHAT*? "You deserved it."

"If that was being bad, I never want to be good."

An embarrassed smile broke across my face before I leaned forward to push his annoying, laughing body away from mine. He held fast to my arm. I was out of protests, dismayed at how my traitorous body let me revel in the feel of his hands tugging me closer.

"I need to talk to you." His gravelly voice and our sudden proximity read like a warning sign to me.

"What?"

"I've learned a couple of things about myself the past few days."

"Should I be scared to ask?" *Don't look directly into his brown eyes, Olive. Don't!*

"Maybe."

Against my better judgment, I looked at him square on, nervous, until he broke out into a wide grin, the scope and attractiveness of his smile literally taking my breath away.

I took in some air for my lungs and shook my head. "What have you learned?"

He held up a finger. "Number one, I'm not really a fake-dating kind of guy. As in, I hate it."

My shoulders dropped while my mind immediately began to race. Did that mean he wanted out? That would make things awkward if we broke up here—embarrassing for me, anyway. Glenn would love this turn of events. Unless Miles let me do the breakup. Maybe instead of a breakup, we could just say he was called back in for work. Well, no, we work at the same place. Maybe we could…

"Number two."

His strong voice gave me pause in my thoughts enough to look back up at him.

"And this is something I've suspected for a while but has since been proven true."

"What?"

"I've got a thing for pretty, uptight English teachers."

I blinked as his words fell over me, but nothing made sense. He was staring at me calmly, almost nonchalant after this major bomb of a revelation. I stood like a statue, unable to move, though my body was a kaleidoscope of activity on the inside. There was something amiss with his words, a puzzle I wouldn't be able to finish without this missing piece. And I needed all the pieces to make sense of his words.

I swallowed and held up a finger, mimicking Miles. "Follow-up question."

He nodded. "Shoot."

"You said pretty uptight English teachers." The words were coming out mumbled, like I was in a daze, which I totally was. "Were you meaning an English teacher that's moderately uptight, or was there a comma in there somewhere?"

He cocked his head to the side as he regarded me with an expression somewhere between amusement and a tenderness I could drown in. "The statement could probably go either way. This teacher is definitely pretty uptight, but I did, in fact, mean that statement with a comma after pretty. But now that I'm really thinking about it, beautiful would have been a better adjective."

Suddenly, I noticed how close he was. Much too close. Much too comfortable. His eyes were roaming my face before landing on my lips. I made the mistake of catching his gaze, and it was…

in a word…smoldering. Oh my gosh. I needed to remember to ask him if he had a pen name or something—for romance books he must secretly write. He didn't put anything like this into his adventure books. I mean…from what I've heard…they're not romantic.

Shoot. Shoot. Shoot.

"Well," I said, my chin raised high, determined to keep us on track. "I've enjoyed my cabin, but that's about it."

He breathed out a chuckle. "Such a little liar." He slowly gathered me tighter until his arms were wrapped comfortably around my waist. It was December in Vermont, okay? I was going to lock in that heat source, so I allowed him to embrace me. I was half tempted to lean my head against his shoulder. I couldn't tell if that would be better or worse than actually looking at him.

"Who can see us?" I asked. We were within view of the lodge now, but currently, my view was blocked by his shoulder.

"Nobody."

"What? Hey!" I pushed myself out of his arms only to have him pull me back again. I'd give myself a solid D- for effort in resisting him.

"I would never *fake* date somebody I didn't already want to be dating."

The hair on my arms stood at attention with his words. Why was he whispering?

I drew in a breath and tried again to step out of his arms. He let me go a little, but not all the way. "You can't tell me that."

"Tell you what?"

"That you…that you…" I was lost for words.

"That I like you?"

"Yeah. That you like me." I whispered the words like the idea was crazy. Because it *was* crazy. It had to be.

His lips curled into a smile. "Why not?"

"Because it's only Tuesday. We've got three more days here. I don't want this to be more awkward than it already is. We work together." My eyes narrowed onto his, trying to look intimidating. "Take it back."

By this time, pure delight colored his eyes. "Take it back? Like we're five?"

"Yup." I folded my arms, trying to bargain with my racing heart. *Heart, if you slow down, I promise I'll try running again. Later. In the summer. Maybe.*

He scoffed. "You want me to wait until the end to tell the girl how I feel? I refuse to be a cliché. Like a real man, I told you in the middle."

"A real *what?*" I countered, trying to buy some time.

He pulled me closer. "I think you know."

"You don't really like me."

"I do." All the hairs on my body stood at attention. I ignored them.

"No. You can't. And I absolutely don't date people I work with. Been there, done that. I've made that *very* clear."

"That's not what you told your sister."

"I was desperate!" I stamped my foot. A definite sign of a mature woman.

He went on talking, almost as if he hadn't heard any of my protests. "Honestly, it was surprising how likable you were once we got you out into nature. Although, that could be the spanking talking."

It took me a moment to formulate words after that, with Miles's all-knowing eyes watching me with growing amusement. "Well, I reject your statement. You've just flustered me. That's all."

"Huh," he mumbled, stepping closer, his coat pressing against mine while his hands found my waist. "So that leaves me three days to convince your lying heart otherwise?" He leaned in closer, his mouth a whisper away from mine. The heat from his breath smelled minty and warm, and I wanted nothing more than to get lost in it. To breathe it in and…kiss him.

Oh no.

His mouth became my only focus as it moved closer, lips parted. I had tasted those lips the night before, and by the way my mouth filled with moisture, it definitely remembered. I'd probably get the shakes before long if I didn't just do it. I couldn't think at all anymore and, instead, closed my eyes to block it out, my lips parting the slightest bit. Then I waited.

And waited.

I opened my eyes to find a triumphant Miles. Still too close to me. Still making my breathing erratic. He slid his lips away from mine, brushing them ever so softly across my cheekbone until he reached my ear. Chills raced down my entire nervous system and a soft heat billowed from his mouth as he whispered, "Game on."

With a kiss on my cheek, he reached back down and grabbed the tree with one hand and my hand with the other and proceeded to pull us both back to the cabin.

And just like that, my body filled with all the clichéd emotions I found in the Hallmark Christmas romances I secretly watched every December. My heart was pounding, my stomach was fluttering, and the hint of a smile was begging to be released from my lips.

TWENTY

"No profit grows where is no pleasure ta'en."
William Shakespeare - *The Taming of the Shrew*

We got back to the cabin, red-faced and embarrassed—or wait, that was just me. Miles clomped along at my side, dragging the dead pine tree behind him and whistling "Baby, It's Cold Outside" the whole way back.

Once inside, I put a pot of coffee on. Miles busied himself finding a stand and an old strand of lights from the creepy basement, which was fine with me. I needed a moment to regroup.

Miles's revelation changed everything. It all felt different when I thought we both hated each other. I thought of the way he held my hand when we jumped into the pond and then half-carried me out, the way he paid no mind to Glenn, the way his hand felt when it pressed against the small of my back, the way our toe-curling, stupid, un-mistletoe kiss played in my thoughts, and the softness in his eyes as he told his parents—

excuse me—lied to his parents about the things he liked about me. Yes…we definitely…hated each other.

Shoot.

If I did happen to admit that he was attractive and could be charming when he wanted to, it only made it that much worse. Besides the fact that we worked together, he was a walking Bear Grylls. Way too adventurous for me. He'd get bored in a matter of days when I refused to do all the things he loved. Because this girl would never go skydiving. Never. I had zero desire to rock climb. Here, where Miles had fewer distractions, I was just something new to occupy his attention. He was bored. I needed to remember that.

It was easy enough to remember while we decorated our tree—*my* tree. Not *our* tree. I found myself getting a tiny bit excited by the smell of fresh pine in the cabin. The glow of the white twinkle lights he draped across the tree sparked a fury of childhood memories that had me biting my lip to keep my eyes from watering. He'd found an old box of Christmas decorations that he and his siblings had made in elementary school. Soon, I was laughing at a picture of an earnest, beaming, bucktooth Miles from second grade. He had grown into his teeth quite nicely. There was a homemade brown cinnamon ornament with his tiny handprint inside. It was all so sweet. Really, it was. The soft sounds of Bing Crosby and Frank Sinatra wove a spell over and around us. That was all it was. A spell. But my resolve to not fall for Miles Taylor was still firm. Look at me, a pillar of strength.

Of course, that was before my own personal Bear Grylls tucked me gently underneath a blanket on the couch, lifting my feet to rest against the coffee table. Then, he put in an old DVD copy of *Home Alone* that he'd also found downstairs, bringing me a cup of cream with a dash of coffee, just how I liked it, and a bowl of freshly microwaved popcorn before he plopped next to me on the couch. It seemed we had both decided to forego dinner at the lodge this evening in lieu of crossing off our Christmas movie bingo square. He was close enough to share the blanket. *My* blanket. Close enough for me to feel the heat radiating from his arm, which was definitely pressed against mine. Miles with socks on, black jogging pants, a gray shirt, and an adorable grin, looking much too comfortable lounging in my space, was a definite breach against my defenses. But I could keep it together. *One* of us had to. He leaned forward and took a sip of my coffee, making a face before setting it back down on the table.

"For a girl who can't stand milk, your coffee preferences are a head-scratcher."

"Those three tablespoons of coffee completely change the chemistry of the cream," I insisted, re-focusing my attention on the movie, which made it easy when we both quoted the lines as they were being said.

"I used to watch this movie all the time as a kid. Even during the off-season," Miles said, looking much too cozy with his head resting on the back of the couch, his arms folded across his chest and his feet crossed at the ankles.

I gasped. "That's sacrilegious!"

"Such a rule follower." His statement held no heat, but he bumped my leg with his and set fire racing to my heart.

After a moment, I added, "I used to watch it every Christmas Eve with my dad. It was his favorite."

We were both quiet for a long moment. "He sounds like a good guy," Miles said.

I smiled. "He was. But do you just think so because he liked the same kid show you do?"

His feet nudged mine softly. "If I had my guess, it was his favorite because it was yours."

Warmth spread across my entire body as his words seeped

into my heart. In the twenty-five years I'd been alive, never once had that thought crossed my mind. As a kid, I had never questioned my dad's taste in the movie. *Home Alone* was pure cinematic gold–who *wouldn't* love it? But now I could perfectly see my sweet dad settling in beside me on the couch once a year to watch two bumbling thieves try to rob a child of his Christmas...because *I* had wanted to. It was our thing. Of course it was for me.

Moisture filled my eyes as I kept my gaze forward. I knew the Christmas tree was a bad idea. Too many feelings and emotions wrapped up in the tradition. I was aware of Miles watching me for a long moment before he turned his attention back to the TV. Good. That was better. I needed to get my thoughts back on track. In this cozy setting, it was difficult to remember that he was the annoying teacher across the hallway.

I certainly didn't give rise to the feel of his arm pressed against mine. Nor did I care or get worked up every time I felt him move or stretch or re-adjust his position, which always seemed to bring him closer to me. Honestly, it was ridiculous that he was so close when there were three other seats on the couch. There were other blankets. Nobody could see us. I blamed the Christmas tree for my not scooting away from him. It seemed to emit some sort of warm Christmas glow about the cabin that left me incapable of moving an inch.

Our hands brushed against each other under the blanket. I stilled. The hands would definitely be a problem if he—

A warm finger reached out and unclasped my pinkie sitting clenched together in a fist on my lap. I drew in a breath. The kid in the movie—his name suddenly left me—had just dropped his groceries on the sidewalk when Miles went for finger number two. Warm heat from his fingers grazed mine, and I found myself not objecting when he seemed to get tired of his own game and grabbed my entire hand, locking his fingers inside and moving it to rest on his leg. He didn't look at me, but I could sense his smile. Tingles erupted down my spine as he played torturously with my fingers.

I cleared my throat and remembered that I was a pillar. I didn't remove my hand, but I did say in a very firm voice, "My hand is cold. I'm just letting you warm it up. That's all."

A throaty chuckle. "Good to know, Spanks."

An embarrassed laugh sputtered out of me at the new nickname. I moved to elbow him in the ribs. Before I knew how it happened he had released my hand, draped his arm around my shoulder and drawn me into his body. My head curled into his chest, and my feet (of their own accord) tangled with his on the coffee table. As naturally as if they'd been designed to do it, our fingers clasped together across his stomach.

I remember Kevin not eating the delicious-looking mac and cheese. I remember him blowing out the candles at the table. But the rest was a blur of the senses. The glow of the Christmas lights flickering across the room, the smell of pine and cinnamon, the feel of my feet resting against Miles, and the way his thumb moved softly against mine. And above all, I remember feeling the strong, sturdy beat of his heart pounding through his chest and the way he tucked me tightly against him.

It was 2 am when I awoke to a fuzzy blue screen and hurriedly uncurled myself from his body. Aghast that I had let myself get that comfortable, I shook his arm to wake him and shoo him out the door. This was getting out of hand. Dang you, Christmas tree. And Frank Sinatra. For the most part, Miles obliged, but he took me by surprise when he turned abruptly at the door as I was following him out, causing my body to run smack into his chest. I made the mistake of looking up, and our eyes held for a long moment.

It happened in slow motion. I blame the fact that I had just woken up. My defense system had a minor relapse. I had spent too much time cuddled up to him, and now my body seemed to crave his touch. My body was the problem. This couldn't actually be *me* falling in like with the enemy across the hallway. His hooded eyes fell to my lips, and he swallowed. He leaned down slowly, as if giving me all the time in the world to resist if I wanted to.

I didn't.

Soft lips touched mine like a breath exhaled. Instead of stepping back to end the kiss, my hands clutched tightly at his coat as I moved forward into his arms. My fingers found their way to his jawline, feeling the motion and the strength there as his mouth worked a kiss over mine that felt so divine I lost all words. His hands were pressed against my back and in my hair, his light touch causing me to tremor in his arms. Our kiss was slow and sensual. Indulgent. While he wasn't exactly forbidden, he tasted that way. Sweet with a bite of danger. One that left me pulling away in a confused state of quaking hands and uneven breaths.

He brushed at a strand of my hair that had come loose in our tangle.

"Are you going to freak out about this tomorrow?" he whispered, a hint of a smile on his face.

"It's starting now, actually."

The smile turned into a grin. "Better throw all my chips on the table, then." Before I could resist, he balled the sweater at my waist and pulled me to him again. His hands found my face, drawing me close as he kissed me once more. Where the first kiss had been soft, almost achingly so, this kiss was all heat. A heart-pounding passion licked at the air igniting sparks between us. It was disconcerting the way he so quickly rendered me incapable of doing anything but come alive the moment his lips touched mine. Though I couldn't help but think I would regret my actions in the morning, my arms wound tight around his neck as he did a very thorough job convincing me of the blurring line between us. He drew back, his brown eyes blazing into mine. He pressed one more satisfying kiss to my lips before he turned and bounded down the stairs. The darkness swallowed him up the farther he moved from the soft, yellow glow of the porch light.

"Goodnight, Olive Wilson."

TWENTY ONE

"Love? I'm not in love. You're crazy. And if I ever did fall in love, it sure wouldn't be with a vampire—even if he is rich beyond my wildest dreams, with gleaming white teeth and the most piercing blue eyes that send chills down my spine. Nope. Not me. You've got the wrong girl."

Velda Stark - *My Vampire Billionaire Baby's Daddy*

My new plan to treat Miles as though he had an infectious disease was quickly waylaid the next morning by a knock at my door. It was 8 am on Christmas Eve. I had hardly slept a wink the night before because my mind was too busy replaying the kisses—that should never have happened. The early morning hours did wonders for re-strengthening a person's resolve. I quickly shimmied out of my unattractive flannel pajamas into a pair of black joggers and a sweatshirt before yanking open the door. To my surprise, I found not Miles, but a small basket filled with cereal, a blueberry muffin, a carton of milk, a pack of my favorite coffee blend, and an orange. Leaning against the house was a stack of freshly cut wood.

A note stuck out of the side of the basket. Glancing all around, knowing Miles was most likely watching me, I couldn't help but pluck the note and read it.

Spanks,

I have to take all the kids in the lodge sledding at 10 this morning. I'd love for you to come with me if you're interested. (i.e. You HAVE to say yes. It's for the blackout). I'll pick you up in a horse-powered sleigh at 9:45. Please dress like you will be going sledding and having fun.

Love,

Your man with the fine pair of hams (as you well know)

I YELLED OUT TO THE SNOW-COVERED FOREST, "I DON'T LIKE sledding!"

The forest yelled back, "Everybody likes sledding!"

"I don't like being cold!"

"I'll take care of that!" This time, the forest voice had a flirtatious edge to it, which I didn't appreciate. However, my traitorous heart still skipped a beat as I picked up the basket and retreated back into the cabin.

Then, I yanked the door back open and yelled, "Thank you!" I slammed the door before the forest could reply.

Once inside, I paced the floors, snacking on bites of cereal and the most delicious blueberry muffin as I tried to find a way to get out of going sledding. The last time I remembered going sledding, I was probably eleven or twelve. I was the youngest child, and we lived in the country. My sister had outgrown sledding, so I quickly followed suit. And I never really missed it much. I remember my gloves always soaking through, leaving my hands red and chapped. My coat never seemed warm enough. And deep down, I just wasn't a thrill-seeker. Leave the cold and snow to the heroines in my books.

That being said...even if I *wanted* to go, I had no clothes to wear. The best I could do was my thermal underwear underneath my black joggers and a sweatshirt underneath my parka. But the joggers would get soaked through. Miles would take one look at me and hopefully have some pity.

Miles did take one look at me when I stepped out onto the porch at the sound of his snowmobile, but I didn't find any pity. Immediately, he killed the engine, climbed off the machine, and moved toward me, a determined look on his face.

"You can't wear that. You'll freeze."

I sighed, as though the news devastated me. "I know. I'm as bummed about it as you are."

He gave me an annoyed look before opening my door and motioning me inside. "Don't worry. I've got just the thing for you."

The fake in my voice dropped immediately. "What?"

He grinned as he passed by me, striding toward the kitchen. "What kind of boyfriend would I be if I didn't take care of my woman?"

I stared after him. "The fake kind."

He ignored me and walked past the kitchen and opened the door that led downstairs. "I'll be right back."

I paced the floor, sipping on my coffee, trying to achieve some sort of Zen with deep breaths and warm, caffeinated liquid gold warming my body from the inside. He returned all too soon up the creaky steps, holding a pair of tan, insulated coveralls hooked to suspenders.

My eyes widened as he held them out to me. "No, thank you."

He motioned for me to take them again. "We had a deal, Oliviana."

I never thought I liked my name. But the way he said it

caused shivers to run chaotically down my spine. It was low and gravelly and made me instantly wish I went by Oliviana constantly.

"I don't have the right clothes for this."

"Hence me handing you these insulated coveralls."

My fingers finally accepted the garment, and I held them up against my body.

"They'll be a little big, but with the suspenders, they should work. I wore them in junior high."

"Why do you keep your old clothes here still?"

"My parents still have some random things downstairs in storage." He flicked his head toward the bedroom. "Go change. I'm on the clock. Gotta meet at the lodge in ten minutes."

I made my way toward the doorway. "Don't wait for me, then. I can just meet you there."

"If you're not out here in three minutes, I'm breaking the door down and carrying you over my shoulder, whether you're dressed or not. And I would enjoy every second of that. Don't think I won't do it."

And that was how I came to be sitting behind Miles on a snowmobile, my fingers white-knuckling the rails behind me as we flew across an open field. Apparently, I had dressed quickly enough for a detour on the way to the lodge. My body ached from being bumped and jostled, but I refused to cuddle up against Miles's back. There had been more than enough unnecessary touching between us already. The last thing I would give him today was cuddles. I could hold onto the machine just fine, thank you very much, COWORKER.

My stomach dropped as I peered over his shoulder. We were flying toward a steep hill, bare of trees.

"Hey." I pointed toward the right side of the hill, where the trail upward sloped more gradually. "That way is less steep."

"What?" he called out, pressing on the gas.

"That way is less—" I yelped as we began our climb, the

incline forcing me to cling desperately to the side before flinging forward to wrap my arms around Miles. His hand pressed against my hands grasping his waist. Instantly, he slowed and turned our machine around, driving around the base of the hill toward the gentler incline.

"Good thing you caved. That was close."

I tried pulling my arms from his waist, but he held them firm against his body, my heart thumping wildly. "No way. I earned this."

In retaliation, I squeezed him so tight he gasped before reaching behind to tickle me. I squealed and let out a giggle.

A *giggle*.

The sound stopped as quickly as it came. The grown adult woman inside of me blanched to even think about that word. I wasn't a character in a middle-school *Baby-Sitters Club* book. Grown women didn't giggle. But I could think of no other word to describe the high-pitched yapping that exited my mouth. In a panic, my brain rushed to think of something else to describe it, tapping into the well-used thesaurus in my head. Chortle? Snigger? No. There had been no sarcasm in the sound. My body tensed as I felt Miles still, and the machine slowed to a halt. I knew I would have my reckoning if I didn't think of some excuse. Desperately, I searched for another word that fit. Chuckle? No. It wasn't breathy or sexy. It was pure, unadulterated, girlish delight that came barreling off my lips. I knew it. And judging by the satisfied look in his eyes when he turned to face me…Miles knew it, too.

"You'd better watch yourself," he said, his low voice sending tingles scattering down my spine. "That kind of stuff isn't helping my case against you."

There was something soft in his gaze, something like velvet that made my skin turn hot despite the cold temperature. Just when I thought I would burn to the ground, he leaned in close and whispered, "You could bottle that laugh and make millions."

And then he kissed me. Just once, quick and sweet on the lips. It was over before I could blink. The sudden warmth his lips brought to mine was gone before I could appreciate the heat. My heart landed in a puddle in my chest. It all felt too casual, too familiar. I had felt the devastating power of his kisses. And now he was making me feel unsatisfied at the quickness of this last one. But this kiss also felt different. He kissed me as though he had the right, as though he was marking his territory in my heart somehow. He turned back around and had us moving once again. I wasn't sure how I felt about it all. I couldn't begin to articulate my feelings. But when I had the chance to remove my arms from around his waist, I didn't. In fact, some might say I snuggled even closer.

When we pulled into the lodge, a red tractor with tracks for wheels was sitting outside, rumbling. Behind it was a black trailer. The long trailer had make-shift benches inside with a railing surrounding the perimeter. I wasn't sure what I expected when Miles said we were going sledding, but this wasn't it. It seemed like everybody staying at the lodge had shown up for this—except Glenn, thankfully. Chloe and Ben and their girls stood next to my mom and Russ. I beamed and hopped off the snowmobile to greet the two three-year-old marshmallows decked out in pinks and purples racing toward me.

"Aunt Owive!" Ivy exclaimed, putting her chubby hands on my cheeks to force me to look at her.

"Yeah?" I said brightly, stealing a quick, wet kiss from her heart-shaped lips.

"We're going swedding!" Her bright eyes were shining, and I couldn't help but grin at her.

"I know! And I love your pink coat." I turned toward Holly and picked her up in a hug. "Are you excited too?"

Holly was busy staring at something behind me. When I turned to look, I spotted Miles making a crazy face at the girls, but when he saw me looking at him, he stopped immediately, making his face passive again. The girls snickered. Miles and I made a game of it for a bit, me pretending to be confused and looking back at Miles while he made faces at them behind my back.

"Who's that?" Ivy asked, pointing at Miles with stars in her eyes. Looked like Miles had added another girl to his fan club.

"That's..." My voice trailed off, suddenly feeling shy and confused. How bad was it on the sin scale for an aunt to lie to her completely trusting three-year-old niece?

"He's my...friend, Miles."

Miles got off the snowmobile and knelt down beside me in the snow, leaning forward toward the girls so he could whisper something in their ears. Their faces lit up with delight as they looked back and forth between us both.

I gave him a wary look. "What did you tell them?"

He wore an impish smile. "The truth." He stood up, brushing the snow off his knees. "I've got to go help my dad load up the trailer. I'll be right back."

I squinted playfully at the two girls at my feet when he walked away. "What did he say?"

An eruption of giggles was my only answer before Ben and Chloe came walking over.

"Hey," Chloe said. She looked perkier than she'd seemed the past few days. When I commented on her bright eyes and relaxed countenance, she said, "I might be turning a corner. I don't know for sure. I don't want to jinx myself, but I ate breakfast this morning and didn't feel like I was going to throw it all up afterward."

Immediately, I felt guilty for moving into the other cabin. I should have been there helping her and Ben with the girls while she was still so sick.

She leveled me with a stare. "We're just fine, I promise. Ben can handle the girls while I'm not feeling well." She flashed him a smile. "Actually, it's been good for him."

"If she was half this bossy with you growing up, Olive, I feel sorry for you," Ben teased before pulling his wife in to give her a kiss on her cheek.

She laughed and swatted him on the rear, giving me yet another reminder of the man who my eyes kept searching out.

"Is it alright if I go help the men, boss?" Ben asked, giving his wife a salute.

"Dismissed. But only if you promise to bring me a warm chocolate chip cookie at some point today."

"Another craving?" I asked her once Ben left.

She looked at me surprised. "Not really, just a basic daily necessity."

I laughed and called toward Ben's retreating back, "Make that two cookies, Ben!"

He turned to scowl dramatically before tossing us a wave.

Suddenly, Chloe leaned in close to me, looking at something off to the side of me. "Another point for Miles."

I immediately looked toward where he was standing near his dad and a few other men, keeping the pathway clear while Jack backed up the tractor to just the right spot to hook up the trailer. He talked easily with the men nearest to him, making everybody laugh. He must have been telling a story, because his arm gestures were animated and dramatic. When he was done, his gaze flicked to mine. I jumped a mile out of my skin before I remembered I had a question for Chloe.

"What point? What do you mean?"

She motioned toward her girls with her head. "He's good with kids."

"Mommy, Aunt Owive and him kissed." My heart dropped as Ivy pointed toward Miles like she had just told a big secret.

My face heated up immediately before I remembered that, as

my boyfriend, that was something very normal.

"I think the whole state of Vermont heard about that." Chloe raised her eyebrows at me. "For all your declarations against PDA, you sure didn't waste time getting after it on the dance floor."

She meant the dance kiss, not the porch kiss, which was the kiss my mind seemed to want to return to frequently. I schooled my emotions into what I hoped was an alluring grin. "I might be coming around."

She folded her arms and watched me for a moment. "Something was off about you two at first. I'm not sure what it was, but I don't feel that way anymore. You haven't stopped looking at him since you got here. And he's completely gone on you."

My smile dimmed. "What?"

She nodded toward Miles, who was now walking our way with Ben. "That is a man highly smitten. And a lumberjack, no less. I couldn't have planned this better myself."

I couldn't retort because Miles was nearly upon us. He held my gaze as a mischievous smile etched across his face as he grew nearer. He looked down at Ivy and Holly, waggling his eyebrows before taking my face in his hands and giving me a loud, noisy kiss on my laughing lips.

Holly and Ivy cheered, and Chloe watched us, hiding a smile behind her hand.

"You two are sure heating up the place."

Any delight I was feeling vanished at Russ's words behind us. Turning, I saw him and my mom, holding hands and walking toward us. Russ looked ridiculous in a bright-blue polyester-type tracksuit and an ear warmer. My mom looked like she was trying to seem younger in her hot pink snow pants and coat. These newlyweds were going to be the death of me.

Miles put his arm around my shoulders, tucking me close. "She didn't pack appropriately for this trip. Gotta keep her warm somehow."

Russ laughed, rubbing his hands together. "Maybe we should try that." He pulled my mom close and dipped her body back with a dramatic flourish. He then set about putting his mouth all over my mom's lips. Chloe and I flinched and looked away, but the spectacle kept going for much longer than the quick kiss Miles gave me. Even Miles looked a bit stunned at Russ's bold display in front of me and Chloe.

"Get a room," Ben called out good-naturedly, trying to end everybody's torment. Although, if I was honest, that statement didn't help. Finally, Russ and my mom came up for air, my mom's pale face bright with embarrassment. She playfully slapped at Russ's arm and wiped at her face but wouldn't meet Chloe's or my eyes.

Thankfully, Jack called the groups of sledders over and explained what would happen. Everybody would jump onto the trailer behind the tractor, and he would pull the group toward the big sledding hill a mile away. Miles and Jett would each bring a snowmobile for the sole purpose of hooking sleds up at the bottom of the hill and driving them and their riders back up the mountain–the lodge's version of a rope tow. With that, everyone started piling onto the trailer. The day was crisp, and even I wasn't immune to the excitement in the air. I began walking with Chloe and the girls toward the trailer when a hand caught mine from behind.

I turned to see Miles, who began tugging me toward him as he did a very sexy backward walk thing, away from the group. Ben and Chloe kept moving, pulling the girls along with them.

"Unfortunately, the trailer is full."

"No, it's not." I glanced back and determined that our group wouldn't even come close to filling the trailer.

"It is. Sorry, ma'am. You'll have to ride with me."

"Eh, I'll just head on home, then. I've never liked sledding anyway." I gave a half-hearted attempt to pull free from his grip, but he didn't release me.

"How can you not like sledding? It's America's pastime."

"I was a hand-me-down kid and always had the gloves with the holes in them, and by the time I wanted to go, Chloe was too cool for it. So…" I forced myself to stop there. I didn't really think I had any deep-seated subconscious bitterness toward sledding, but it came out sounding like it.

Miles stopped. "What if I promise to make it fun for you this time?" He held my hand up in front of me. "You've already got better gloves now. And you have an extremely hot boyfriend that wants you to ride with him up the mountain."

"Fake boyfriend," I reminded him, though a smile began to peek out.

Just then, Jack honked the tractor, startling us both. We turned to see him and the rest of the group waving at us as he pulled the group toward the road. Miles shook his head. "Watching the little kids sled down this hill is one of the best parts of the whole week. I'd hate for you to miss it."

I tapped my chin. "Hmmm…can you make Russ go away?" I had meant it as a joke, but the words came out much more serious than I had planned and left the air between us unsettled.

His eyes were surprisingly gentle when he said, "I don't think you actually want that."

I could feel emotions brewing behind my eyes at his statement, but I pushed them away in favor of bringing back our lightheartedness. "Well, I didn't figure you'd ever be *that* handy."

His eyebrows raised dangerously. "Oh, really?"

Instantly, I knew what he was about, and I turned to run. I was in his arms with my back against his chest before I could make it one step. Our bodies fell backward into the soft snow. I landed with my elbow somewhere on his stomach and heard a satisfied groan from him upon contact. I scrambled off and began flinging powdered snow at him, not taking the time to make them into balls. He sputtered as snow hit him in the face, laughing as he made a dive toward me. He knocked me gently onto my back, snow leaking onto my neck through the collar of my coat. His body was carefully positioned above me and he held both of my hands over my head. Laughing brown eyes met mine. I couldn't keep the smile from my face if I tried. He was breathing heavily with snow and water droplets all over his face.

"You're going to pay for that, Spanks."

He picked up a handful of snow, which he proceeded to wipe gently all over my face. I was squealing by this point and squirming to get away. My cheeks were numb, but my heart beat wildly underneath my frozen exterior. Eventually, the snow in his hands had all been placed around my cheeks and face, and Miles remained hovering over me, his eyes seeming to take in every last freckle spread across my cheeks. Ever so slowly, his hand raised to his mouth, and with his teeth, he held his glove steady while he pulled his hand out.

My breath caught as he drew his hand softly to my cheeks and ever so slowly began to wipe the snow from my face. His eyes pierced into mine, and his warm hand melted the snow as he dragged it off my face. His touch was sensual and warm, as heated as his gaze, and I could do nothing but lie there as each rhythmic ministration left me spellbound.

His eyes drifted down to my lips before meeting my gaze once more. There was a question in his eyes, but before I could answer, a loud revving of an engine tore through the quiet moment. We both turned to see Jett riding the snowmobile out of the barn. He looked over at us and did a double-take before waving somewhat awkwardly.

Miles's head dropped down for a second before he stood and offered a hand to help me up. He ran a hand through his hair sheepishly before putting his glove back on.

"Enough trying to seduce me, Olive Wilson. We've got a sledding hill to get to."

TWENTY TWO

"You can be too old for a lot of things, but you're never too old to be afraid."
Home Alone

MILES KEPT HIS PROMISE. HE MADE SLEDDING THE STUFF OF dreams. He even managed to make it that way with my mom and Russ acting like teenagers, flying down the hill with their arms wrapped around each other. There were times when I rode behind him on the snowmobile as he tore down the hill, picking up sledders and tubes at the bottom, hooking them to the machine, and pulling them back up. He'd tease and joke with the adults and was gentle and sweet with the kids. There were other times Jack would man the snowmobile, and Miles would place me in front of his sled, jump on behind me, and wrap me in his arms as we flew down the hill. The wind in my face and strong arms holding me tight had me feeling very much like I had been living half a life until now. Even when we wrecked, snow and powder flying everywhere as we rolled the rest of the way down the hill, it didn't stop me from laughing until I cried.

But adventure for one not used to adventuring was exhausting.

Sledding was over. Jack had just hauled a trailer full of rosy-cheeked kids and their parents back to the lodge. I traded in my seat behind Miles's on the snowmobile to little Ivy, who had developed a healthy crush on him while sledding. He couldn't resist her charms asking for a ride and sent me an apologetic smile.

The arrangement was fine by me. And not just because watching him with Ivy—the careful way he held her and the way he leaned forward to try and listen to what she was saying to him, the ball on top of her big beanie smacking him in the face every time—did something to me that I wasn't sure I'd ever recover from.

But now we were back. My feet hit solid ground, and I had a second to breathe on my own. I needed to keep it together. Miles was a charismatic force of fun. But once out of his all-consuming presence, I couldn't help but feel that I was just an exciting challenge to him during a week of boredom. Get her to talk. Get her to sled and snow mobile. Jump in a frozen pond. He claimed he liked me, that this wasn't fake for him. And that could have very well been true...here on the mountain, in this cozy bubble we'd cocooned ourselves in. I could feel myself yielding. Being charmed. But the last thing I wanted to be was somebody's adrenaline rush. Because once the endorphins faded, the crash always followed.

Chloe and Ben jumped down from the trailer. Ben took a sleeping Holly out of my arms while an excited Ivy leapt out of Miles's arms and ran toward her parents—the little family making their way back toward their cabin.

I started to follow them when Miles rode toward me on the snowmobile, coming to a stop a few feet away.

"Come riding with me," he called.

My steps slowed. "What? We just went sledding. I'm officially tapped out of adventure today."

"I want to show you some places."

My eyes flicked between him and the snowmobile. There it was again. The allure of danger. And I wasn't talking about the snowmobile. Beneath his gray beanie, his hair draped messily across his forehead while his warm brown eyes were inviting and... I swallowed. "No, thank you."

"Why?"

"Because I don't trust you."

He looked mildly taken aback, and a small spot of pride burned in my chest at throwing him off his game. He turned off the machine and climbed down, coming to stand a few feet away. "Why? What did I do?"

"You...keep...making me do crazy things and...kissing me... and...rubbing my face all sexy, and I don't know what to do with that." My hands were currently flailing about in a panicked rush, but I couldn't seem to stop it.

He burst out laughing. "Rubbing your face?"

I lifted my chin, giving him a knowing gaze. "Yes."

He folded his arms, regarding me with great interest. "What do you *want* to do with it?"

I scoffed, my mouth gaping wide open. Seriously, the nerve. I wanted to go back to my quiet cabin, have a bath, read a book, and pretend nothing had happened so I didn't have to make any decisions about us or potentially get my heart broken and still have to face this man at work every day. It really was so simple.

When I didn't say anything, his lips fell into a half smile, and he closed the distance between us. Instantly, my heart rate sped up, and I pushed at his chest. "No more kisses. Nobody's around. You have to stop messing with me."

"You think I'm messing with you? I told you pretty clearly that I'm not messing around."

He did. But still, I kept my hands pressed against his chest, needing to get this out. "We're just trapped in this dreamland where Santa and Rudolph and Frank Sinatra threw up all over everything."

His nose wrinkled in distaste, which was so adorably distracting that a laugh sputtered out of me before I could stop it.

"It's all been weird, and cozy, and…"

Happy.

That was the word so close to leaving my mouth. Happy? Really? While my mom was here kissing another man? When I did the polar plunge and then spent all day sledding in the cold? Happy? That couldn't be the right word. But I couldn't deny the lightness in my heart, thinking over the past few days. Even amid the doubts and the questions, I was happy whenever I was around Miles. I felt strangely alive when he was near. But really…that would end, too. I couldn't keep up with him for long. He'd get bored of me, and then I'd be sharing a school with an ex-boyfriend—again.

Even though this particular man had proven himself to be much sweeter and more endearing than the last guy. And funny. And strangely insightful. And romantic.

Still a pain, though.

"Did you know your eyes do this sparkle thing when you laugh?"

"What?"

"Yup. I never noticed it until we came here."

I folded my arms, squirming under his scrutiny. His eyes roamed all over my face.

"You smile a lot at school, but it always stops right here." I stilled as he reached out his index finger and thumb toward my mouth, pressing the corners of it gently.

I stilled at the contact. He removed his hand and took a step back, though his eyes continued to hold mine.

"It always used to make me so mad to see you pretend so much. You'd smile, and take on extra jobs, and wash dishes, and get taken advantage of by everyone because, for some reason, you thought you needed to. And you'd be smiling the whole time, but it would never hit your eyes. But in the past few days, I've heard your laugh, and I've seen your smile—your *real* smile..." He broke off, shaking his head. "That's not something a guy can just unsee. It's a craving now, trying to make you laugh, or smile, or even get mad at me."

I opened my mouth to speak, but no words came out. My natural instinct was to deny it all, but I couldn't remember a time when I had felt so seen by someone. With so little effort, he had brought my hidden parts and pieces into full view between us. He had put words about me into existence that I hadn't fully realized about myself.

He took a step closer and put his hands on my cheeks, leaning down to meet my gaze. His eyes were so sweet and gentle and made me want to nuzzle into them. "So, I'm going to ask you one more time, Olive Wilson. Will you please come riding with me?"

Old habits died hard. Though my heart was suddenly wanting to burst free with sunbeams lighting the whole gray sky, I bit my lip to rein it in.

Miles growled lowly, and the dam broke away. I couldn't hold it back any longer if I had a hammer and nails. With a sudden laugh and a wide smile, I beamed in his direction. He grinned broadly, matching my emotion, and slowly pulled me in for a long, delicious hug.

"Do you want to try driving?" Miles shouted, turning his face to the right so I could hear over the roar of the motor.

"No, thanks." I looked again at the dark clouds above us.

Snow had been falling on us for a while, but it was coming down faster. The wind was picking up, pelting our faces with snow. "Should we head back? The clouds are looking dark."

He looked up. "I thought it was supposed to just blow over."

I glanced around, looking for a break in the clouds, but found nothing–just darkness casting a gray pall across the entire valley. We had been driving for at least an hour, me tucked behind him, my arms squeezing his waist. At first, Miles drove me around the outskirts of Montpelier, pointing out more landmarks and taking me past his high school and beautiful churches before taking a trail up a mountain. Soon after, we were in the woods, driving past houses and creeks meandering beneath the trees, until we reached a large field that seemed to spread out for miles. Snowmobile tracks covered the ground, but nobody was out except for us.

The snowmobile stalled while we stared out at the expanse of field. Miles revved the engine and looked back at me. "One last good run, and then we'll head back?"

My eyes widened as I peered over his shoulder. "Across that? How do you know it's safe?" Before now, we'd been riding roads and trails. This was a wide-open field in the middle of the mountains. There could be a cliff at the end, and we'd never know until we were plummeting over the side.

"This is my old biology teacher's hay field. I helped him haul hay on it one summer. It's just an old boring field." He pointed at the snow. "See the tracks? It's a popular spot for snowmobiling in the winter."

"What's past the field?" I asked warily, tucking my hands inside his pockets.

"There's a small drop, but I'll turn us around before we even get close to that."

"How will you know when we're close? It's all just one big snow patch to me."

"I'll know. You up for it, Adventure Girl?"

I squeezed my arms around his waist a little tighter. I was cold and a bit frightened about going off the trail but decided to trust Miles. "Do what you must," I told him before tucking my head against his back.

"You've got to look."

"What? Why?"

"You'll miss the best part."

"What part is that?"

"The feeling of flying."

My initial instinct was to say no. I always said no. But for some reason, I didn't want to disappoint Miles. I lifted my head. "Ten seconds."

"Thirty."

"Eleven seconds."

He laughed. "Twenty."

"Twelve."

"Fifteen."

"Ugh. Deal."

Miles gunned the engine, and the machine took off. Snow pelted against my face. My watery eyes wanted to shut, but I forced them to stay open. The wind snatched my new beanie off my head and carried it away before I could stop it. My hair flapped behind me, whipping every which way as we flew across the field. I inhaled a deep breath of crisp mountain air tinged with snowfall and pine and felt like laughing again. Had I really wanted to go back home and read a book? Hide away? I was still in awe of how fast we were going, but with Miles, I wasn't afraid. When my fifteen seconds were up, I continued to fly.

That is...until a jackrabbit jumped up in front of us from his hole somewhere near the earth's core. The rabbit saw us upon him and panicked, frozen with wide eyes as we nearly plowed into him. Miles jerked backward and instinctively swerved to miss him. The rest happened in slow motion. The sharp turn of the machine, the feeling of falling, hitting the ground, something heavy rolling on top of me, and then…a quiet stillness.

TWENTY THREE

"Come with me if you want to live."
The Terminator

"Olive! Are you okay?" Miles's panicked voice broke into the eerie silence.

I felt his hands rolling me onto my back. I stared at his face above me momentarily, dazed as my mind tried to comprehend what had just happened. In a flash, he had discarded his gloves and was feeling around my head and arms.

"Olive. Talk to me."

"I'm fine," I mumbled. "I think. Just disoriented."

Miles let out a string of mild expletives under his breath as he released me. I stared up at the snow in a daze as it fell onto my face. The world felt like it was still spinning around me.

After taking a few moments to regain my bearings, I sat up slowly and took in the carnage around us. The snowmobile was on its side, a few yards away, with a few random parts scattered around, sticking out of the white snow. I turned again to Miles, the thoughts in my head becoming clearer now. With some alarm, I took him in, sitting four paces away with his hands on his head. He was rocking back and forth ever so slightly.

"Miles," I said, unable to look away. Maybe he was hurt. "Are you okay? Are you hurt?"

He didn't answer me. By this time, my stomach was sinking with dread, my mind an anxiety-driven machine now. I rolled to my knees and scooted my way over to him. He was probably hurt and bleeding internally somewhere, and I'd never know until it was too late.

"Miles," I said again, putting my hand on his arm. "You're shaking."

He flinched under my touch and blew out a breath. "Sorry, I'm over it. I promise. That was just..."

His body movements were jerky, and he was mumbling to himself. I had never seen him this out of sorts. He was always calm and collected. Confident. This felt scarier than our crash.

"Miles." I put both of my hands on his cheeks and forced him to look up at me. "Are you okay?" I touched his stomach. "Does anything hurt?"

"No." He finally met my eyes and blinked. "I'm okay. Are you sure you're okay?" He did a once-over across my body.

"I'm fine."

He nodded, and the mumbling ceased. I stood up on shaky limbs. He followed suit, but his hands were everywhere—covering his mouth, touching his legs, buried in his hair—as though he couldn't handle being completely still.

The snow was coming down harder now. I tried to tuck my hair behind my ears, but the wind made it nearly impossible. The world seemed gray and very isolated from our viewpoint.

"Let's see if we can get the snowmobile started. The storm's picking up," I said, eyeing him cautiously.

Together, we walked to the overturned machine and worked to turn it right side up. Miles seemed to have gotten ahold of himself enough to climb on top. He fiddled with things and worked at starting the engine. I set about picking up all the parts scattered around us in case something was needed. It was mostly things from inside the pockets of the machine: sunglasses, a Coke can, and a few tools. Nothing that looked like we'd be stuck out here forever. There was a low growl when Miles turned the key. A clicking noise came next, and then… nothing. Miles hopped off, did some manly jiggling of parts, and tried again. This time, no growl or click. Just nothing.

We locked eyes. I gave him my most encouraging smile, though my nerves were on track to betray me soon. I checked my phone in my pocket. No bars. We were too far into the mountains. I had no service.

Miles checked his phone, too, but I could tell by the look on his face there would be no rescue mission coming to pick us up anytime soon. He looked around as if trying to gauge our odds of finding shelter.

The snow peppered my cheeks, and I cinched my coat up tighter on my neck and pulled my hood down low on my face, really missing that beanie.

"There's a covered bridge about half a mile across this field. Right next to the creek. That might be our best bet."

I mentally cringed. A covered bridge was a decoration piece for Vermont. Beautiful and touristy. Not something that would necessarily save us from hypothermia in a Vermont blizzard. But I didn't see any better option amid our surroundings, so when Miles held out his hand, I didn't hesitate a second before grabbing it. We fell into hurried steps across the field, not talking beyond an occasional grunt or his warning me to step over a rock. The tightness around his face since our crash had not lessened. His tension bled into me, making my steps and limbs jittery, so I said nothing and just followed alongside him.

The covered bridge was one of the smallest I'd seen. Rustic dark wood framed the outside. Upon closer inspection, it only had a couple of leaks from the roof that I could see. Except for the sides that allowed cars to pass through, it was closed in. Thankfully, there were two windows on each side of the bridge, giving us a little light amid the darkness. We moved toward the middle, wanting to get as far out of the wind and snow as possible. Once there, Miles let go of my hand, settled down on the gravel road beneath the bridge, leaning back against the wood.

I looked both ways through the bridge as though a car might drive through at any moment. But only black clouds and snow met my sights. I shivered, running my hands up and down my arms. I had worked up a little sweat with our brisk walk to the bridge, but now that we were here, the bitter wind whipping through the tunnel seemed to freeze me at my core.

Miles tugged on my hand, drawing my body down beside him. When I sat, he stuffed our clasped hands into his coat pocket, tossing me a small, tight smile as he did so. He appeared to be slowly coming back to himself, but it seemed forced.

"Thanks for your help back there," I said.

"In almost killing you? You're welcome." The words, full of sarcasm, spat out bitterly.

"No." I squeezed his hand inside his jacket. "It was an accident. That could have happened to anyone. It's not your fault."

He shook his head but didn't say anything. Instead, he leaned his head back against the wall and closed his eyes. Though he still held my hand, his actions left an unfamiliar distance between us. A bridge we hadn't yet crossed in our growing friendship these past few days. I wasn't sure what to say or do.

"I know I'm being a jerk right now. I'm sorry. I just need a minute."

"You're okay," I whispered.

My entire body went into maternal-instinct mode. I wanted to hold him, to make whatever was inside of him not hurt anymore, but I didn't know how to do that, especially with him. This was a man that I wasn't really dating in a really confusing way. So, I did the best I could and just sat there in the quiet, holding his hand.

"Do you want to talk about anything?" I asked after a few minutes, listening to the wind howl through our tunnel inside the bridge.

He let out a humorless chuckle. "I'll be fine. Tonight just dug up some bad memories."

"Bad memories?" I prompted lightly.

I began to think he wasn't going to answer before he mumbled, "It's…just this thing that happened a long time ago. Took me a while to get over."

"This thing that happened," I repeated slowly. "Care to expound on that, writer man?"

He smiled for a moment before it was gone.

"Was it in college?" I guessed.

A long pause. "High school."

Goodness, it was like pulling teeth. "With a girl?"

He took a deep breath and crossed his legs out in front of him at the ankles. "It's a long story. You sure you want to hear this?"

"If you want to tell me." I motioned with my hands to the blizzard swirling in the openings of the bridge. "I happen to have some extra time right now."

"Buckle up, then."

It took him a minute to start the story, but slowly, he began. "When I was a senior in high school, I was dating this girl. Kelly. I'd known her my whole life. I had a crush on her off and on growing up. We were friends, but I was always quiet and didn't think she'd have anything to do with me. She was…a terror. Wasn't afraid of anything. Lived every second going a hundred miles an hour." He chuckled dryly as though he was remembering something from long ago. "Anyway, our senior year, we ended up working on the school paper. She was one of the photographers. I'm not sure what she saw in me, but we started dating, and it got serious pretty quick. We started planning to go to college together, and we were even talking about marriage." At my surprised face, he amended, "Not right away, but you know, later. Down the road."

I nodded.

"Anyway, that March, we had one of the worst winters Vermont had ever seen. It might as well have been January. It was pretty crazy, but it made for good skiing. She had taught me to ski earlier that winter, and so, every chance we could, we hit the slopes. For our six-month anniversary, I wanted to surprise her, so I planned this big ski trip. Just the two of us. I wanted her to think I was more of a rebel than I used to be, so I convinced her to cut school that day, and we rode up to Killington Resort together. It was two months before graduation."

My hand covered my mouth to brace myself as he continued his story. The tension in the air was thick and dense with untold grief.

"Anyway, it was going to be our last run, and she wanted to do the hardest run. She'd done it before, and I wanted her to think I was pretty hot stuff, so we went for it. It was all going fine until about halfway down. I was behind her, watching her go off a jump. From what I could tell, she caught the edge of her ski and plowed right into a tree. It took her down immediately. I skied over to help." He paused, looking as though he was far away in his thoughts. His voice was low and steady. He wasn't speaking, as though the grief was fresh and painful. He was calm and matter of fact but with an air of regret and sadness lingering around the words. "I thought she was playing a joke on me at first. She liked to pull pranks, but usually she'd start laughing after a few seconds. But she didn't. Then, I noticed she wasn't breathing. It just looked like she was sleeping. But she was gone."

I sucked in a deep breath as I imagined a younger Miles watching all that unfold.

"I started doing CPR and yelling for help. The medics got there pretty quickly and took over for me, but she was gone. She was gone before I had even gotten to her."

"I'm so sorry," I whispered to him.

He blinked and looked away from me, biting his lip. Suddenly, his reaction to the events of the evening made sense.

"Sorry," he said, smiling meekly. "That's why I freaked out earlier. I thought, for the second time in my life, I'd been involved in killing a girl I cared about."

"What happened after that?"

He paused, staring into the distance. "She had been pronounced dead at the scene. And by that time, her parents had gotten there. That part was pretty horrible, too. They rode in the ambulance with her. My mom and dad had been visiting my aunt that weekend, so I had to drive my truck home. The ambulance had left, and her backpack was still in my car. And her lip gloss. I'd bought her a drink from the gas station on the drive up, and she wanted to save the other half of it for the drive home because she liked the taste of it flat. Just so many things like that. I was in complete shock. Shaking like a leaf. I definitely shouldn't have been driving." He blew out a breath.

Rubbing his eyes, he sat up straighter and cleared his throat. "I'm sorry. I'm good, I promise, I've made my peace with it all, but it's been years since I've talked to anybody about it. And tonight just brought it all back, I guess."

"It's probably good to get some of it out again."

Miles shrugged and cleared his throat. "What about you? What was it like for you to lose your dad?"

I stared at him for a long moment, jarred at the sudden change in the conversation but realizing that he needed a distraction.

"My experience was different. I had a couple of years to

prepare, so when the day finally came, it was almost a relief. He had been in such pain—those last few weeks, especially."

My mind flashed back to those days just before his death. There had been sadness and regret, but the memories were sweet. No matter how sad you are to lose someone, spending the last few days in the company of a loved one about to pass on were some of the most precious moments of my life. I was honored to hold my dad's hand those last few hours. The part for me that was difficult to think on was the days and weeks and months *after* his death. When life moved on without him.

With a shaky breath I kept talking. "But I get what you mean about the things left behind. I remember when they moved his body out of the house. I just walked around in a daze and looked at all of his stuff, just sitting there waiting for him. He'd had these brown slippers next to the bed for years. Before he was bad enough that hospice had to be involved, he was in the middle of a book. It was on his nightstand. Never got it finished. His coffee mug was in his spot by the sink. There were so many parts of him scattered all around the house, waiting for him to pick them up."

There was silence for a beat, and then Miles said, "Death sucks."

"Then, your mom puts the brown slippers in a box labeled *Walt,* along with Walt's shoes, and Walt's coat, and Walt's high school yearbooks, and moves them downstairs. Out of the way. Then, she puts the half-read book back on the shelf and washes the coffee mug. All that he was, now stuffed into a box because someone couldn't stand to look at it anymore." I was aware of Miles's eyes on me. I knew I should stop, but found I couldn't. "And then, a new guy moves in, and you find out your home is really just a house. Not a home. Lumber and nails. Four walls to a room. Out with the old, and in with the new."

Salty tears were streaming down my face at this point. I tried to wipe them away, but they were coming faster than I could keep up. I knew I would regret this happening in front of Miles, but there was no way I could hold it back any longer. The dam I had so carefully constructed around my heart had burst. I had wanted to say these things to somebody—anybody—for so long, but I never felt I could. My emotions were coming out in a wave, and I stood powerlessly in front of it as it moved to crush me.

From his place at my side, Miles reached over and wrapped his arm around my neck, pulling me gently to him. My body turned and curled against him, my head on his shoulder and my hand splayed out on his chest. He didn't try to whisper weightless words or shush me, for which I was grateful. For the first time in our arrangement, I didn't let myself think. I was all heart. And for a person not used to allowing myself to feel, the experience was both terrifying and liberating.

"I didn't want to feel anything this Christmas," I whispered into his shoulder.

He pulled back to look at me, brow furrowed. "Why?" he asked softly.

"Because of this." I wiped my eyes, scoffing. "Because I'm afraid once I start to feel, I won't be able to stop. I know my feelings aren't right. They're not fair. I should be happy for my mom. She grieved for my dad for two years while he was sick. But it's only been one year since he's been gone. One. All of a sudden, he's been replaced. We don't even talk about him anymore. We were so busy getting ready for him to die that I never got a chance to think about life with him actually being gone. And then, once he was gone, I never got to that place where I was ready for my mom to date again. Where I could accept it. And I *would* have gotten there, I know it. But then, five months later, here's big, loud Russ coming to family dinner and sitting in my dad's chair. Three months after that, they were married. *Thanks for the memories, Dad. We're done now. Moving on.*"

My chest heaved as I felt the tension leave my body. Miles continued to hold me, stroking my hair. Eventually, the tears dried up, leaving me at that awkward place of calm embarrassment.

I had just unloaded my most personal thoughts on a man I had claimed to not like five days earlier. An arm of trust had been extended, and I had yet to find out if that would break me in the end.

I tried pulling out of his embrace, but he held me tight, so I whispered, "I'm sorry. I shouldn't have gone off like that."

"Have you ever told anybody this stuff?"

There had been so many times I wanted to discuss things with Chloe, but she had so much in her life to distract her—namely, Holly and Ivy. A year earlier, her grief had taken a backseat to teething toddlers and sleepless nights. The addition of Russ to our family actually seemed welcome to her—a relief, even. Having my mom married became one less thing for her to worry about. We'd talked about Russ and the uncomfortable feeling of watching my mom with a new man, but I'd never let myself unleash all my feelings. My own effort at keeping the peace. I'd talked a little bit with Millie at work, but my job was where I wanted to forget and focus on other things.

"No. Can you tell?" My attempt at humor fell flat.

"I'm sorry."

"Thanks. I'm sorry for you, too."

His fingers ran up and down my arm for a few long moments before he said, "For what it's worth, Russ seems like a decent guy."

I laughed, the sound bitter to my ears. "He is a decent guy. That's never been the problem."

"What is the problem?"

"He's not my dad."

Miles nodded.

I drew in a breath, wiped away a rogue tear, and moved out

of his arms. "Listen, I know that I need to give Russ a chance. My mom seems happy now, and that's because of him. My brain knows all of this. I'm a grown woman. I'm not a kid still living at home. But I just…I can't convince my heart to let my dad go. I can't move on."

"Why do you have to let him go to move on?"

I opened my mouth to explain to him how things worked, but the words became scrambled in my mind, like they might not fit as well as they used to.

"I know you've spent the last year grieving your dad, and I don't want to make light of that. But you've also spent the last year trying to control your emotions. Even now, you're telling me how you *should* feel. That's bull. Your feelings are what they are. And there's a reason for it. You don't need to sugarcoat them. They're valid."

"But I need to be an adult about this. I've treated Russ like he was invisible for most of the time I've been around him."

"He can handle it."

My surprised eyes swung his way as a small bit of laughter bubbled out of my throat.

He laughed softly. "I'm not telling you to treat him badly, but Russ seems like a smart guy. I'm assuming he's divorced or widowed?"

"Widowed. His wife passed away five years ago."

"Yeah, see? He knows it's going to take time. I'm sure his kids have had to adjust to your mom being in their lives as well. But you have the right to feel all the emotions you're feeling without trying to push them away."

"On paper, I know this. But I feel like I should have things figured out as an adult. I should still be able to function in society and around my family."

"You have been functioning. But you've been grieving at the same time. Eventually, you have to decide to live again. And allow others to do the same thing. You and your family will always be grieving your dad. You'll always miss what could have been. What *should* have been. But life can come at you fast. Moments don't last forever. Sometimes we have to take opportunities when they come."

"What do you mean?"

"I'm wondering if that's what your mom might be doing with Russ."

My eyes glanced back up to his. "What?"

"She's picking her moment and choosing to live again."

I drew my eyes away from his, leaning my head back against the wall of the bridge. I couldn't accept his words completely, but I sat with them for a minute and felt them out in my heart.

"How did you get so smart with all of this?" I asked eventually.

"Two years of forced therapy. My parents made me go after the accident. I didn't want to, but they wouldn't accept that. It was only supposed to be for a year, but I ended up going for two. For the longest time, I couldn't get over the fact that I had taken Kelly out of school to go skiing. Nobody knew where we were. Her parents kept denying that it was their daughter on the ski hill, because they thought she was in school. And it was my idea. My fault. If I hadn't asked her, she'd still be here."

My heart dropped a tiny bit at that. I wondered if there was a part of Miles still in love with her. My selfish heart was now jealous of a woman who had been dead for years. I forced myself to push past the emotion.

"Any other day," I began, "everything would have been just fine. You wouldn't have second-guessed anything. But in that one moment, somebody else was in control. You couldn't have stopped it because, for whatever reason, it was her time to go. You were never in control of her life. Or her decisions."

Miles leaned his back against the bridge. I followed suit, our shoulders pressed against each other.

"Maybe you're in the wrong profession, Oliviana. You sound just like my therapist."

"Why is it always easier to fix other people's problems than it is my own?"

We sat that way for a while. The roar of the wind outside of the bridge provided a relaxing white noise as we both got lost in our thoughts.

"Do you think…do you think you'd be married to her right now if she'd survived?" I didn't really want to know the answer, but I couldn't look away from the train wreck of my thoughts.

He shrugged. "I don't know. My brain wants to immortalize her as being perfect because I've blocked out everything else. But looking back, our relationship was pretty immature, which makes sense. We were eighteen, and I hadn't dated much before. I was halfway terrified of her. So…probably not."

The pieces of Miles's puzzle were slowly beginning to come together.

"I remember you telling me a while ago that you didn't start doing all the extreme sports until a few years ago. Was it related to her? To Kelly?"

He smiled and absently rubbed at a spot on his pants. "For a while, the accident made me scared to get close to anybody again. It took me some time to get past the trauma and stop feeling guilty. So, I decided to try to live my life like I thought Kelly would. My own way to justify her death instead of mine. She wasn't afraid of anything except being still. She climbed every mountain chain in the Northeastern United States. When she turned sixteen, she begged her dad to take her white-water rafting in the Grand Canyon because she heard they had some of the best rapids. She went bungee-jumping and skydiving multiple times before she was even seventeen. She was fearless. I hadn't been brave enough to do all of that with her when we were dating, but she got me into skiing. So, after she died, I made a pact with myself to start living moments for Kelly, *espe-*

cially if it scared me. The more out of my comfort zone, the better."

"How was jumping out of an airplane the first time?"

He smiled. "Scariest thing I'd ever done up until I jumped. Then, it was amazing."

I shuddered.

"Did it work? Does anything scare you?"

"I don't think the fear ever goes away completely—especially when you're scaling a cliff with a ninety-foot drop beneath you."

I shook my head.

"The first few years, I forced myself to do the big, extreme things. To honor Kelly. But as I've gotten older, now I just do the things I want to do. The things that I think I'll legitimately enjoy but still push me out of my comfort zone. I try my best to pick my moments. If I've learned anything from Kelly it's that life comes and goes too fast. People are so casual with their time, especially when you consider that it can all be gone in a second."

I nodded along, thinking of all the Saturdays I spent curled up reading a book and my nights in a hot bubble bath.

As if he could sense what I was about to say, he continued, "And I'm not saying that going buck wild is the only way to live. I couldn't sustain that type of life. Reading books and swinging on the porch is living, too. There's definitely a balance to be had. I just think that getting out of our comfort zone every so often is when the magic starts to happen."

"Like jumping in a pond with ice chunks floating next to you?"

"Exactly." He turned and looked at me, his brown eyes scanning my face. "Do you have any regrets about jumping in?"

I bit my lip, thinking about that night. It had been scary. I wouldn't have done it without Miles pushing me, and I was definitely not lining up to do it again anytime soon. But just thinking about it brought back the rush of the moment, and I couldn't help but grin. "No, I don't have regrets. But don't let that go to your head. I'm not doing it ever again."

He laughed and nudged my arm. "Skydiving next week?"

"Not on your life."

We both chuckled softly as we sat there, each staring off into space until he spoke again.

"During therapy, I was encouraged to write down whatever I was feeling. That became a powerful outlet for me. Eventually, I began studying English at college, so taking a creative writing course seemed a natural step. The first couple of years, my writing was crap, but I kept at it and eventually got better."

"And now you have three books out with the fourth coming out next year."

He looked down at me, a curious gleam in his eyes. "You know, for somebody who claims not to care that much, you sure seem to know a lot about my books. I'd love to get my hands on that Kindle of yours. I feel like I'd learn a lot about you."

I grinned cheekily up at him. "I've got that thing locked down tight."

"I knew it." He tickled my sides until I was laughing and trying to squirm away. When he relented, he didn't release me. Instead, he maneuvered his body and mine so that he sat directly behind me, with me leaning back against him, his legs sprawled out at my sides. I turned slightly so my face could curl against his chest while his arms wrapped around me.

"You think I'm going to cuddle with you just because we're trapped in a covered bridge?" I asked, while my frozen right hand unzipped his coat just enough that I could slip my arms through and slide them around his waist. Even through his flannel shirt, the heat from his body kissed my skin. A sigh of relief came unbidden past my lips.

"You think I'm going to let you steal my body heat so you don't freeze?" he countered, pulling me even tighter against him. My body felt too twisted in its current position, so I turned even more to the side, letting my legs sprawl out over top of his right leg.

The wind whipped through the tunnel, and though we were just out of reach of the snow, everywhere around us looked to be freezing, except for our tropical oasis in the middle. I would have been perfectly content to stay just like that forever.

"So, you said you can't sit still. Was it hard watching the movie last night?"

He breathed out a laugh, ruffling my hair slightly. "Nope. That wasn't hard. I had a few other things to occupy my mind."

Heat warmed my cheek pressed against his chest. His heartbeat was a steady drum against my ear. I kept my face pressed against him and tried to contain the smile that threatened to burst free.

"I learned something else from Kelly too," Miles whispered in my ear.

For some reason, I stilled at his words. I was wrapped in the arms of Miles Taylor in the middle of a covered bridge in a storm. We were cozy and warm here, effectively blocking out the entire world. The air between us shifted to something palpable. I could almost hold it in my hands, though I was too scared to meet his eyes. Too scared at the emotion I might find there.

"What?" I whispered.

His voice was a soft rumble against my ear. "When I see something I want, I just need to go for it."

The storm whirled on around us, but the air between fell into a hushed silence, his words swirling around us with the wind. I had started the day wanting him to keep his distance. His confession the day before had terrified me. And I think he knew that. I had every excuse in the book to be wary of him, but he had spent this past week slowly disarming every one of my defenses. Miles Taylor was a good man. I think I had always known it, but he had caught me at a bad time. With the passing of my dad and losing Mr. Grady's steady presence at school at the same time, my world had been turned upside down in one fell swoop. Instead of letting me be and giving me a wide berth, like everyone else, Miles tested and pulled and nudged me into uncomfortable places. He noticed parts of me that I tried to hide away from the world. I had been so threatened by that. By him. I saw him as demeaning and arrogant, when now I could see he had been trying to help me stand up for myself. In his own way, he had been protective of me.

Before I could let myself overthink my actions, I lifted my head to meet his eyes. My hands slid up his chest, cupping his cheeks gently before I pressed my lips against his. He met my shy kiss with a softness, taking his time to linger and savor. His hands cradled my face, returning my kisses with a sweet tenderness that felt too delicious to be real. Slowly, the heat between our mouths began a dance that matched our pounding heartbeats. He wrapped his arms around me, tucking me close while he increased the pressure of our lips.

My hands found their way around his neck, diving into the feel of his hair. One of his hands cupped my cheek, caressing my skin softly while his mouth explored every inch of mine, wrapping me up in a romantic spell so enchanting he had me whispering his name in a breathy, embarrassing sort of way.

He pulled back to look at me, a sudden grin on his lips. "Yes?"

I stared at him, dazed and blinking, taking a moment while trying to form actual coherent thoughts.

"What are we doing?"

"We're having our moment. And it's about damn time."

"It's been literally five da—"

His mouth found mine again, breaking apart only for a moment when we were both smiling too wide for the kiss.

"It's been a lot longer for me," he whispered.

I met his intense gaze with a reluctant smile crossing my

lips. After he wielded a few more words to swoon me into silence, he pulled me onto his lap where he spent quite some time kissing me senseless.

WE WERE RESCUED SOMETIME IN THE LATE AFTERNOON. Thankfully, Jack had been aware of our plans to go riding and, when we didn't return at a reasonable hour, set off to search the few places he could think of that we might have sought shelter. He was visibly relieved to find us both okay. After shooting a few meaningful glances at his son as he helped us onto his snowmobile, I concluded that this ordeal must have brought up a few memories for him as well.

TWENTY FOUR

"Till this moment I never knew myself."
Jane Austen - *Pride and Prejudice*

Christmas morning arrived all too soon. The air bit at my nose as I made my way toward my mom's cabin. There was a peaceful calm about me. The gray clouds that hung low in the sky all day yesterday were absent this morning. The sunlight sent its rays down to sparkle on the snow before me. The howling wind from yesterday was silent, the calm after a storm. Somewhere in the distance, the loudspeakers hummed out a soft tune of "O Come, All Ye Faithful". Even though I still preferred to hide away in my own cabin, I walked forward with a purpose in my step, a determination that had never been there before. Though this had never been a moment I would have wished for, I was going to try my best to attempt to live it today.

The snow-covered sidewalk crunched under my boots as my thoughts turned to yesterday and how I had left my heart bleeding under the covered bridge in the care of Miles Taylor. I couldn't remember a time since my dad's death that I'd unloaded my thoughts on somebody that way. Earlier this morning, I had awoken to the sting of embarrassment, the dawn of a new day bringing to light my pathetic vulnerability. Then, not even five minutes later, I received a text from Miles.

MILES: IF I UNDERSTAND YOUR SELF-PERSECUTING MIND AS WELL as I think I do, you woke up about to die of embarrassment. Don't. Please don't. It was my sincere pleasure to be your listening ear. Everyone needs one. Thank you for being mine. Have a great Christmas morning with your family, Olive. I hope it's a good moment for you. I'll see you this afternoon. P.S...I left something by your door.

I FLUNG THE SHEETS OFF MY BED AND RACED TO THE DOOR, HALF hoping to see Miles sitting in a basket with a bow on his head. I was only slightly disappointed with what I found instead–a small basket filled with a large thermos full of freshly made hot cream with a splash of coffee, a book, and what looked like a well-loved DVD.

With a grin, I pulled out the book first—a beautiful hardback copy of *Jane Eyre* we'd spotted earlier in the bookstore. I opened the cover and discovered his inscription.

Olive,

For a cozy night by the fire. I'll let you read me to sleep.

Love,

Miles

I LAUGHED WHEN I PICKED UP THE DVD. THE COVER HAD FADED, and the clasp had broken off, but the face of Arnold Schwarzenegger as *The Terminator* was very clear. Attached to the back was a sticky note.

Olive,

For our next date night in. I'll change your mind, I promise. So much fodder for good literary discussion in this movie. Trust me.

Love,

Miles

I ARRIVED AT MOM AND RUSS'S CABIN AT 8 AM. ON THEIR FRONT porch was a large basket of Christmas brunch items from the Taylor family. There would be a big Christmas dinner celebration at the lodge later this evening, but each family had the whole day to spend together in their cabins. The basket contained the makings of simple but delicious breakfast foods, along with cheeses, specialty meats, and sliced bread for lunch.

I was the last to arrive, with a tired Chloe and Ben sitting by the tree while their two impatient three-year-olds rummaged through their stockings. My mom and Russ were both cheery and dressed in a matching set of flannel pajamas and robes when I stepped inside, depositing my small box of presents near the tree by the window. Mom came over and wrapped me in a hug, her warm scent of vanilla tickling my nose. When I pulled away from her, Russ and I glanced at each other awkwardly. I had never hugged him. And I didn't really hug him this time either, but as if by mutual accord, we went in for a brief side hug and a hesitant smile.

"Hey, kiddo," he said. "How's your cabin holding up? Do you need me to chop some wood for you?"

I bit my lip. Though Miles had talked a big game about leaving me to fend for myself, the wood always seemed to be replenished. A fresh bundle appeared almost magically every morning on the porch.

"No. Thank you. Miles has been keeping me warm."

Mom and Russ looked at me in surprise as my eyes widened in horror.

"No! That's not what I meant. I mean he's kept the fire burning."

Ew. No. Make it stop.

I shook my head in mortified frustration. "Let me start over. He chops wood for me every day and puts it on my porch. And then he goes away."

Russ started laughing, and my mom followed suit, though her laughter brimmed more with relief than actually thinking I was funny.

"Let me know if he gets out of line. I'll have a talk with him."

I stiffened at the gesture, but before I could think too hard about it, Russ clapped his hands excitedly and motioned us over to the couch and chairs in the living room, surrounding the tree. "Should we open presents now?"

Holly and Ivy squealed in excitement, jumping up and down. Chloe and I exchanged a look with my mom. I wanted to tell Russ that we always opened presents after we had a big breakfast. We would wake up early and check out our stockings first, before my parents began cooking a big breakfast of eggs, bacon, hash browns, and cinnamon rolls we'd made the night before. Then we'd sit down to eat before digging into any actual presents, dragging the whole morning out until we were all dying of anticipation.

Mom met my eyes. "Russ's family was never patient enough to wait until after breakfast."

Russ looked appalled. "Open presents after breakfast? What kind of self-controlled monsters are you people?"

Ben raised a hand. "I have to agree with you, Russ. My family always opened everything before breakfast, too. These people are crazy."

Chloe gave Ben a playful push. "We still do, at YOUR parents' house. My year for Christmas, we do it right."

Russ nodded theatrically to Ben. "Yes, the second we were all up, it was a race to the tree and a wrapping-paper frenzy going a hundred miles an hour."

"Yup. It's the best," Ben agreed, smiling smartly at his wife.

Knowing what I knew of Russ, I could very well imagine him in the middle of the fray with his kids, childlike excitement in his manners, just like he was looking at us now.

This didn't necessarily feel like climbing Mount Everest or scaling a ninety-foot wall, but it was perhaps a tiny step forward I could take. "I guess we could try it Russ and Ben's way. But if it sucks, we're eating breakfast first next year."

"Deal," Russ said.

Mom gave me a small, relieved smile, and we all sat down while Russ began handing out presents like Santa's elf. Russ's way wasn't half bad, except that the excitement of Christmas was over much earlier. We each walked away with a handful of presents, and to my surprise, my lame gift to Russ of a digital picture frame was received like I had just handed him keys to a sports car. If I wasn't careful, Russ's excitement for life and people might start to endear him to me. As it was, we ended up having a nice morning together. Different, but nice. I could at least say that much.

After our breakfast of fresh maple cinnamon rolls, cut-up oranges, and hot chocolate, Russ stepped into the bedroom, claiming he needed a nap after all that sugar. Soon after, Ben and Chloe left for their own cabin to attempt a nap for their own sugar-crazed children.

My mom and I sat next to each other on the couch, a brief moment of awkwardness between us at our sudden alone time. I hadn't really spoken much to my mom this whole trip once I moved to the other cabin. Some of that had been intentional. Wherever my mom was, Russ was somewhere nearby, and I hadn't wanted to deal with him. But now, for the first time since coming, I wondered if this Christmas had been strange for her, too.

"Have you had a nice time here?" I asked, almost bracing myself for her answer. Why was it all so hard? Why did there have to be so many emotions tied up into the holidays?

A smile touched her lips. "Yes. This place is almost magical."

I nodded. Even though it still didn't seem quite right to make memories without my dad, I thought of my time with Miles and couldn't deny the magical qualities of this place. I glanced again at my mom. She was still smiling, but it almost looked pained. It didn't reach her eyes. Like mother, like daughter, I guess.

"You and Miles seem pretty cozy. How are things?" She said the words but still wasn't looking at me.

Suddenly, I was tired of the fake. I actually wasn't even sure what *was* fake anymore. But it was time. "Mom, I need to tell you something."

She looked slightly alarmed but waved me on. I took a deep breath and blurted, "Miles and I were never really dating. We were pretending so I could get the Fosters off my back."

"What?"

I smiled a little sheepishly. "I'm sorry. But I *really* didn't want to get set up with Glenn."

"I don't understand. Why couldn't you have just told me that?"

"Because he was already coming. Next time, could you give me more than twelve-hours notice that you're inviting my ex-boyfriend to our Christmas vacation?"

"I thought you'd be excited to have an old friend. I knew you wouldn't want to hang out with us the whole time."

Well, that was true. "But he wasn't an old friend. He was an old boyfriend, and I broke up with him. And...it wasn't a good plan." I didn't want to dive into Glenn's less-favorable qualities, so I didn't.

Her mouth had been open as if to argue before she closed it and leaned back against the couch. "Well, then, I'm sorry. I thought the two of you were still friends. The way Glenn lit up when we mentioned you'd be there, I wondered...but I didn't know how you really felt. I just...I knew this Christmas was going to be hard, and I wanted you to have a distraction. Something fun to look forward to."

I hoped that, one day, Glenn found a girl who would find him an exciting distraction, but I was definitely not that girl.

Her brows furrowed as though she had just thought of something. "You two really aren't dating? I saw that mistletoe kiss."

"The anti-mistletoe kiss," I said. "Apparently, I missed by about thirty feet, so Miles says we have to do it again."

"What a tragedy," she murmured.

I shrugged my shoulders. "I'm not really sure what we are. The past few days have been fun." And sweet. And eye-opening. "But we work together. I don't think he's too concerned about that, but..."

"But you are?"

"Yeah. I've had a bad experience with dating coworkers, remember?"

"That doesn't mean that will happen this time."

I nodded, leaning back into the sofa, my arm brushing against hers. "How did you and Russ meet, anyway? I mean, I know you were at the restaurant, but how exactly did it happen again?" I felt a bit guilty even asking this. It was my mom. I should have known her and Russ's story, but it's amazing what details slip your mind when you spend seven months trying to forget it even happened.

A small smile broke out across her face. "It was a coffee shop, actually. He tried to pick up my order."

"What? How?"

"When they yelled out a very clear, 'Elaine,' he came up and bumped into me and claimed they had said, 'Russ.'"

I huffed out a small laugh, shaking my head, imagining his frank nature shocking my mother.

She opened her mouth like she was about to speak again, but then suddenly, her face crumpled like a napkin. Her hands moved to cover her face, hiding from me while her shoulders tensed against mine.

"Mom?" I grasped her arm in some alarm.

My touch seemed to unleash something from deep within her. Now, she was crying. She tried to stop once but only succeeded in moaning and sputtering a laugh, desperately wiping tears from her eyes.

"Mom," I said again. "What's wrong?"

"I'm sorry," she said, taking a deep breath. "This place and all the Christmas things…it's been fun, but I've had a hard time not reliving last year. It's been good not being home, but it's been hard, too. I miss him so much."

Pure relief filled my entire body. Her words filled cracks in my heart almost instantly. I needed this so badly, to hear her say she missed him. That she hadn't forgotten. Now, it seemed silly to even have questioned that. Perhaps she had been putting on a good face, too.

She cleared her throat and wiped at her eyes. "I'm sorry. I'm sorry. I shouldn't be doing this."

"Mom, I need to see you cry."

Her face looked up to mine. "What?"

I stared at her, collecting the thoughts that suddenly rang so true in my mind. It wasn't that I couldn't find it in me to be happy for her or even try to get along with Russ. After this week, I truly felt like I could do that. But I needed to know my dad was still a part of our lives.

"I need to see that you miss Dad. I've been dreading Christmas because I didn't want to feel like we were forgetting him. I don't go home anymore because Dad's not there. And it doesn't look like he's *ever* been there. Which...I get it, but you've got someone new, and you seem so happy all the time, and we never talk about him, and I..." I broke off, willing my emotions to settle, but this conversation had been too long in the making. There was too much that needed to be said.

Her hand grasped my arm. "I have been happy. Russ is a good man. He's brought fun into my life that I never imagined having again. But I've also been sad. I've been worried. I've felt guilty. I've been crying for your dad while married to another man. I've been trying to put on a happy face for you kids. I've been so many things that I don't know what I am anymore."

I turned to face her, both of us clasping the other's arms while we released our built-up emotions.

"Do you think you jumped in too soon? Should you have waited to get married again?" I blanched as soon as I said the words. Perhaps I was pushing things too far.

"No," she said gently. "You have to understand. I was so tired." Her voice broke, and she took a minute to wipe her eyes.

"You had every right to be tired, Mom. You had just buried your husband."

She shook her head. "No. It was more than that. I began grieving him when the doctor said the word terminal. It was the slowest and most torturous way to watch somebody you love die. Two years of getting your heart broken every day was almost more than I could take."

She leaned forward, wiping her eyes. The whiffs of her

coconut shampoo next to my nose made her seem so human somehow. It was easy to forget that moms could be human.

"I know. We were all part of that."

"Even with all of that, do you know what the hardest part was?"

I wiped at the hot stubborn tear making a run down my cheek. "What?"

"Watching my children watch their dad die."

Hot tears fell from both eyes now, drenching my cheeks. Her arm slipped around my waist and pulled me to rest on her shoulder. It got to be too much to keep wiping the tears away, so I let them come. I wondered if it was possible to cry all the tears out. I'd certainly had my fill the past twenty-four hours. I had always allowed myself to cry in private. But outside my doors, I was a rock. A machine. Holding myself rigid so as not to break. Any cracks or flaws at all and I would be done. Broken. I refused to be broken at work, or with my family. Only alone. Only at home.

But now I started to wonder if maybe being broken wasn't a flaw. Maybe it was a beautiful shard of glass that could one day be made into a vase again. Maybe the flaw gave it character. It couldn't be whole again, but it could be pieced back together—each unique shard helping to press and hold the others into place, some glue around the edges. Almost like new.

"When your dad passed away, I was devastated. You have to know that." She waited until I looked over at her, finding her through the blur in my eyes. "But I was also so relieved. For me. For him. He was finally out of pain. And our family could finally start to rebuild."

My dad's looming death had been this weight pressing down on our family for two years. I remember, at the funeral, being able to breathe deeply for the first time in a long while. In the end, his death hadn't scared me. It was the change of it all that frightened me, left me crippled. What would happen to our family now that he was actually gone?

"I know my relationship with Russ happened fast. I know you've all had a hard time catching up. And I'm so sorry for that. I didn't expect it myself."

"It's okay," I whispered. "I'm going to try harder to get to know him better—just as long as we still keep Dad around every once in a while." My words came out like I was half teasing, but I was very serious. For the first time, I could start to envision a path for myself that included Russ in my peripheral view. But I needed to know that my dad would still be a part of our lives.

"I just want to make sure we still talk about him. I want to meet up at his favorite restaurant to celebrate his birthday. I want to watch *Home Alone* every Christmas. And make Poor Man's Sloppy Joe's every once in a while, just because he would love it."

Mom laughed at that. "We all hated that meal—including him."

"I know, but lately, I've had a weird craving for it."

I draped my head gently on my mom's shoulder. The tears leaking from my eyes were of the peaceful variety now. We rehashed old memories and phrases my dad used to say. Through sniffles and smiles, she smoothed my tear-soaked hair, her fingers lightly brushing my cheek as we talked of moments with my dad that had stayed with us. Her words spilled out in a contemplative whisper, and ever so slowly, a healing balm began to spread over my dry, cracked heart.

"One thing I've learned through all of this, Olive, is that people don't fill up on love. There's no brim on the cup. Love overflows. It grows and bubbles over over. I used to believe there was something I would be trading to let another man into my life. That I would have to give away a part of my heart that belonged to somebody else. And then I met Russ, and I realized that a person doesn't reach the capacity for love. Love just is. It's all-encompassing. There's no trade-off. I don't have to sacrifice my love for your dad or you and Chloe to love Russ. He doesn't take any of your dad's place in my heart because the heart doesn't retract–it expands. My heart grew bigger for Russ. But I will always ache for your dad."

TWENTY FIVE

"I didn't mean to fall in love with my vampire billionaire baby's daddy, but I did. That's the thing about love, I guess. Sometimes all it takes is one little taste."
Velda Stark - *My Vampire Billionaire Baby's Daddy*

MILES KNOCKED ON MY MOM'S CABIN DOOR JUST AFTER LUNCH. A sigh of utter relief came over me as I scrambled up from my chair at the table and flew to the door to answer it.

He was a sight for sore eyes in his jeans and a flannel shirt underneath his coat. His eyebrows raised a tiny bit at the speed at which I flung open the door, but I quickly tried to play it cool.

"Oh, hey."

He looked at me a moment before peering past my shoulder to where my mom and Russ sat, working on a puzzle, *White Christmas* playing on the TV in the background.

"How's your morning been?"

"It's been…good," I answered truthfully. The three of us had passed a relatively nice morning playing games and working on a puzzle. Every so often, I'd been tempted to sneak back to my cabin, but every time, I heard Miles's voice in my head, telling me to try and live in this moment. So, I stayed. And if I was being honest, it *had* been enjoyable getting to know Russ a bit better and learning about his family's Christmas traditions–many of which he had tried to hold onto with his kids once his wife passed away but found it difficult to do with married kids, which gave me the realization that everybody gave up something to be here like this. Not just me. And we were all still alive. Still standing.

I also snuck away while the twins and Ben were napping and visited Chloe. It had been her turn to know the truth about me and Miles. The smack to my shoulder that Chloe dished out as I confessed didn't feel great, but I probably deserved it.

"You lying punk! I called it! I KNEW there was something fishy about the whole thing."

"I'm sorry!" I said, holding my hands out. "I panicked and needed an excuse to not be around Glenn."

"Why couldn't you tell me?"

I gave her a look. "Do you remember the whole shopping-trip debacle of three years ago? You can't keep anything from Mom."

She made a face. "Fine."

"Besides, I owed you a lie, remember?"

Her mouth dropped open before she burst out laughing. "If this is about—"

"Dirk McCoy. High School. You lied to me for WEEKS about that."

"Because you had a crush on him, and you would've killed me."

I sighed. "If only I hadn't been in middle school. I think we really could have had something special."

We laughed a bit longer until a contemplative silence came over us both. She turned to me, her eyebrows raised. "But…

what about all the kissing? With you and Miles? Was that planned? I may have missed the famous mistletoe kiss, but I was there for the sledding. That sure didn't look fake."

Heat tinged my cheeks, and I tried my best to hold back the smile, but I couldn't.

Thankfully, Holly had woken up with a start and began screaming, so she had to go. I slipped out soon after, and instead of turning toward my own cabin, I went back to my mom and Russ's.

Even though it had been a nice morning, I also learned that I could only take Russ's "dad" jokes for so long before wanting to bash my head into the wall. Hence, my excitement to see my fake-but-maybe-not-so-fake-but-quite-possibly-still-fake boyfriend.

"You coming to challenge us in a battle of Risk?" Russ called out to Miles.

I blanched. Risk? That game would take approximately ten thousand years.

Miles must have had that same idea because his face dropped a tiny bit. Thankfully, Mom stepped in.

"He's just teasing. You two go for your walk."

We took our leave before Russ could think of another game. I adjusted my mom's beanie over my ears as we stepped out onto the snow-covered sidewalk, each with our hands in our pockets, walking side by side.

"Look at you, getting all cozy with Russ. And not a single battle wound on you."

I gave him a look. "I've got a date with a bath and a book this afternoon as a reward for good behavior."

"That sounds nice. Need some company?"

"No." I bumped against his shoulder.

He chuckled softly. "Seriously, though, how was it this morning? Any improvements?"

"I think so." I gave him a sheepish smile. "I mean, I was still really happy when you showed up, so it must not have been that great."

His arm snaked out and pulled me to his side. "Oh, really?"

I laughed and attempted a half-hearted escape but not before he grabbed my hand and shoved our clasped hands into his pocket.

We walked for a few moments longer before I said, "But it was better. I feel like Russ and I broke past a barrier between us. It's not perfect. It probably won't ever be. His personality still drives me crazy, but he does love my mom. And it's kind of sweet to see."

"Good. When we get back, you should definitely play that game of Risk. Twenty-seven hours in somebody's company is a great way to bring people together."

"Don't even joke about that. How was your morning?"

"Good. My little sister got home late last night, so it's been fun having her here. Jett and I played on his new PlayStation for a couple of hours until it just got embarrassing for me to go on. And I had a good chat with Glenn a few minutes ago."

I stopped walking and faced him in horror. "What?"

Miles laughed and kept strolling, pulling me along with him.

"What did you talk about? Did you fight him?"

He grinned. "Almost. But he was leaving."

"He left?" I repeated.

"Yup. Said he'd wasted enough time here already."

"Aww, he always knows just what to say."

"But before he left, he asked me to give him a few pointers."

I looked at his face now, trying to decide if he was teasing me. "About what?"

"He has this book idea and wants to start writing it, but he just doesn't know if he can find the time in his schedule to get it done."

I snorted. "It must be hard to be so much busier and more

important than everybody else. Did you give him the name of your publishing house?"

"Yeah, but that's meaningless without an agent."

"What's his story about? Did he tell you?"

"I don't think he really wanted to tell me, but it definitely had dragons. And possibly a zombie character, but I might have misheard him."

"Ohh, that's a fun twist. Where are we going, by the way?" We were meandering through a trail in the woods out behind the village cabins. It was a pathway I hadn't been on before.

"You'll see," he said.

We walked a bit longer in silence while I took in all the beautiful trees. Once, I had traveled out west for a school trip and remembered feeling so exposed with the lack of trees everywhere. They had trees, but it was nothing compared to the dense thickness I'd grown up with. Everything was so open out west. And dry. Its own kind of beauty, for sure, but I craved the cozy, protected feeling only a mountainside of trees could give. And Vermont was full of them. This time of year, they were covered in snow but still cheerful somehow.

We rounded a bend and stopped at the sight of a small, red covered bridge atop a winding, frozen creek. I said a quick apology in my head to Vermont for thinking covered bridges were just decoration pieces. A warm, romantic glow filtered through me as I thought about the heated couple of hours we'd just spent in one the day before.

"So, we've come to the agreement that shoulders and covered bridges are the new sexy. Is that right?" I asked.

"Definitely," he said as we ambled toward the structure.

When we got to the bridge, he stopped us just before we walked inside. "With Glenn gone, I guess the ruse is up," he said softly, brushing a strand of hair off my forehead.

I swallowed and nodded, immediately feeling a tightening in my chest. "We've still got a few squares left on the bingo card before it can be totally over, though, right?" I asked, meeting his eyes.

He watched me, a small smile on his face as he seemed to concede that I definitely didn't want to talk about that right now. "I guess."

"Did you tell your parents?" I asked, my hands on my hips, very aware of his close proximity to me on this bridge.

"About the ruse?" When I nodded, he said, "No."

"Why?" I waited in dreaded anticipation for his answer.

"Because there's no ruse for me. They know I'm dating you right now, and that's true."

He inched a bit closer to me. I made the mistake of looking in his eyes and found them to be smoldering. I turned and began walking through the small bridge. He was at my side in seconds.

"Are they doing the drawing tonight?" I asked.

"No. Tomorrow morning at the goodbye breakfast, but we have to turn in our cards tonight."

"What all do we have left to do?"

"Make out under the mistletoe."

I tried holding back my smile. "It counted."

"Not even close, Spanks."

"You know, for being such a wild adventurer, you sure are a romantic. What would Tyrok think?"

He slowed, turning toward me, and I immediately realized my mistake. "What did you say?"

A beat of time passed, and I quickened my steps. "Nothing."

"You said Tyrok." He said the words like a predator catching scent in the wind.

I shrugged. "It's a common enough name."

"Name one person with that name." Just as we passed through the bridge, he leapt in front of me, walking backward until I stopped.

I took a step back and ran my hand through my hair casually. "My uncle's…second cousin's…nephew, once removed."

His smile grew wider and stepped closer. "Sounds like you're close."

We were dancing now, one step backward to his step forward, a challenge tinging the air, me desperately trying not to break. What was it about this cursed place that I somehow couldn't rest until I revealed all my secrets?

"Do you have something to tell me, Oliviana?" His voice was low and dangerous and sent a thrill from the top of head to my littlest toe.

I was almost trapped. Another step and I'd be against the wall just inside the bridge. According to the "gotcha" smile growing on his face, he was very aware of my plight, so I did the best thing I could think of and took off running back toward the village.

He caught me before I made it three steps. I squealed as his arms locked around my waist. Within seconds, he had lifted me and set me on top of the handrail running the length of the bridge, our eyes now level. He rested his hands on both sides of me. His body was warm and inviting and close. So close.

"Fess up and I'll make your punishment for withholding information quick."

"Not too quick, I hope." I grinned cheekily at him.

In retaliation, he leaned closer, bringing his lips tantalizingly close to mine, but every time I tried to sneak a taste, he pulled back. "How do you know the name of the main character in my *Landfall* series?"

"I've got a secret stash of Miles Taylor books under my bed."

A beaming bright smile broke out across his face at that. He looked as though he would devour me on the spot but held off, eyes narrowing.

"Since when?"

"Since I first learned you wrote them."

He raised a brow. "Pages worn and dog-eared?"

"One under each post of my bed, actually. They're just the right height to give me more room for my Glenn Foster collection."

He tickled me mercilessly for that one before taking my face in his hands and kissing me speechless. I was about to fall off my precarious perch on the handrail, so of course I had to cling to him. For my safety. My hands roamed up past his shoulders and into his hair. His hands eventually moved to around my waist. I gasped as his thumbs brushed against my ribs before wrapping his arms around me, squeezing me tight against him. When he finally released me to come up for air, he pulled me in close. Our heartbeats drummed wildly.

"What about your Kindle?" Miles asked. "Any secret copies on there?"

"I told you, I'm taking that information to my grave."

His warm lips kissed my jawline, pulling me into such a state of euphoria that when he nipped at my earlobe, it caused me to pant and flinch away, laughing.

"I don't have anywhere I need to be the rest of the day, so if you think your family will start missing you, you'd better speak up now," he said.

I wanted to tell him I was perfectly content to stay here as well, except for the fact that my butt was starting to go numb on the small handrail. I nestled in close to his neck and whispered one last truth, my lips brushing ever so softly against his ear.

"You're on my Kindle. And I've read your books more times than *Jane Eyre*." His reaction was instant, and for several long, LONG moments, we stood under the red covered bridge, wishing each other a *very* Merry Christmas.

But then, I pulled away, remembering something terrible. "And by the way, I'm so sorry, but I didn't get you anything for Christmas."

He snickered, leaning in for another kiss as though I had

stopped too abruptly. "You being obsessed with me and my books is enough, trust me."

"I feel like obsessed is a strong wor—"

Miles rudely interrupted me, though I felt his smile against my lips. Okay, okay, maybe I was a *little* obsessed.

TWENTY SIX

"The ledge of the cliff was within my grasp. With rasping breaths, I summoned the fortitude to leap upward to freedom. When my hand clutched the root of a tangling vine, I breathed the first sigh of relief in days. That is until the pirate wench, Rita, peered over the ledge and stomped on my hand. Laughing while I plummeted back down the mountainside."

Miles Taylor - *Landfall*

THE LODGE HELD ONE LAST DINNER ON CHRISTMAS NIGHT. FROM my seat near the door, I spotted Mom and Russ sitting by the Fosters at their table. With Glenn gone, there was no awkward, avoiding-of-the-eyes thing, which was nice. I waved to Chloe and Ben at the table next to them. Miles had wanted me to meet his sister, Lainey, so I found myself across the room, seated next to his family.

Lainey was twenty-three and worked as a wedding photographer in Boston. I couldn't help but notice the family resemblance in her lean build. Her eyes also frequently lit up in laughter, crinkling down the sides.

"So, let me get this straight," she said, leaning forward across the table, her long brown hair falling across her shoulder. "You both hated each other at school?" She glared at Miles. "How could you not like her?"

Miles drew his arm around my chair, brushing against my shoulders. "That wasn't ever my problem."

Lainey's green eyes widened in understanding as they focused on me. "Oh, *you* didn't like *him*. That makes more sense. Miles can be very annoying."

"*So* annoying. Right?!" I said in solidarity, turning to grin at Miles who frowned playfully. His hand moved to my side in an attempt to tickle me, but I grabbed it with my right hand, which was now crossed over my stomach, and held it there.

Lainey eyed our hands. "Well, it looks like you figured out how to live with each other."

I gave Miles a warning look before slowly releasing his hand. I really wanted to finish my prime rib and mashed potatoes. He didn't tickle me. Instead, he removed his arm from around my chair and dropped it onto my leg.

"Speaking of living, I heard you're staying in his cabin," Lainey said as I took a bite of mashed potatoes. "I hope he cleaned it for you."

My body froze at her words. After a moment, I remembered to swallow the potatoes stuck like glue in my mouth. I turned to Miles to see him issue a warning look at his sister. He met my eyes somewhat guiltily.

"*Your* cabin?" I asked.

"Lainey," Miles whined.

"She didn't know?" his unrepentant sister countered. "Why wouldn't she know that?"

I cocked my head to the side as I stared up at him. "Why am I staying in your cabin?"

He sighed. "It's technically still my parents' old cabin. They haven't updated it at all, and they don't have any plans to rent it out just yet. I just stay there most of the time when I come for visits. If I need a change of pace or different scenery, I come here and get some writing done."

"It's also close enough that he can freeload meals off of our parents," Lainey said with a smirk, taking a bite of her roll drenched in maple butter.

Jack and Sandy tapped on the microphone from their spot on the stage a moment later. Lainey and Jett's attention turned toward the stage, as did everybody else's in the room.

I turned to Miles, whispering, "Why didn't you tell me?"

He leaned over, his mouth brushing against my ear, sending chills up my spine. "I needed a bargaining chip, and you'd have never stayed there if you knew it was mine."

"You're right," I said. "So all that stuff downstairs? That's yours? You just, what? Chucked everything down there the minute I agreed to stay?"

He grinned sheepishly. "I threw most of my personal stuff in the second bedroom and just locked it. The stuff in the basement is stuff my parents left when they moved."

All this time, I had been sleeping in the bed Miles slept in when he visited. I don't know why that felt so different to me, but it did. Very much so. I had been imagining this place as a cabin people rented. Comfortable and cozy, but not belonging to anyone. It felt much more personal knowing it was the cabin Miles used. It was a mixture of mortification and gooey sweetness, and I wasn't sure which would win out.

"That was...so freaking sweet of you," I choked out.

Again, his lips brushed my ear as his voice whispered, "Well, I'm definitely not a saint. I got you where I wanted you."

My eyes narrowed. "In your old house?"

He gave me a roguish grin. "In my bed."

I smacked his arm, which only made him laugh and pull me

closer, planting a kiss on my head. Eventually, we focused on the stage where Jack regaled the crowd with funny anecdotes and old Christmas stories before relinquishing the stage to a band for some Christmas music. When Miles's hand dropped back down onto my knee so casually, squeezing gently every so often, a warm glow made an appearance like it always did. But this time, anxiety began to bubble up where it had laid dormant for a while—the chew-on-my-fingernails-and-stare-off-into-the-distance kind of anxiety.

This was our last night.

Tomorrow, we'd pack up and head back to New York. We'd drive back to our respective houses alone. The bubble would officially burst. It frightened me how quickly I had done a complete one-eighty in my affection for my coworker. It happened both slowly and quickly, as we were literally here for only six days. Our time together under the covered bridge, whispering secrets and sharing kisses. Our night cuddled on the couch, watching *Home Alone*. The teasing and flirting. Jumping into the pond together. The sincerity in his eyes when he looked at me. All those kisses. My heart wanted to lean into all of it. Believe all of it. But it was too good to be true–the kind of stuff that just doesn't happen to me. Not in real life, anyway. And as I looked around at the cozy lodge covered in mistletoe and garland, sitting next to Miles Taylor as his hand on my knee drummed to the beat of the local band performing "Little Drummer Boy," it didn't feel like we were in real life.

"Why do you look like you're on the verge of a freak-out?" Miles's voice rumbled softly in my ear.

When I could only stare at him helplessly, his brow furrowed. Wordlessly, he scooted his chair back and stood up, motioning me to follow. We were toward the back of the lodge, and only those seated at our own table took note of Miles taking my hand and leading me toward the doorway. Once we passed through the threshold, he kept walking, leading me down the hallway and into an empty room.

Miles flipped on the lights, lighting up a large room with shelves lining the perimeter and a bundle of shelves in the middle. It was a storage room of some sort, probably for all the tables and chairs and decorations it would take to pull off events for a large crowd. Empty storage tubs sat open, the lids flung off as if someone had just rushed in to grab something really quickly. The air had the briskness of a room with a closed heating vent. I rubbed my arms to ward off the chill. Miles closed the door, and the space grew smaller. He filled every inch of the room. I leaned on one side, against the wall between the door and a shelf full of bins, bracing myself for this conversation. He watched me with cautious amusement, mirroring my stance against the wall, both of us facing each other but not touching.

"Now, one more time," he said, "why are you freaking out?"

"I'm not freaking out," I said, wiping my sweaty palms on my pants. "I'm *concerned* a very normal amount for a rational woman."

"What are your concerns?"

His voice was so soft, so tender and sweet that I almost wanted to lie and tell him I had none and kiss him senseless right here. But when the kissing was over and we left tomorrow, I'd be right back where I started, which was, I'd say, a healthy 7 out of 10 on the freak-out scale.

"That this bubble will pop. Christmas is over. Tomorrow, we leave and go back to a place where you're not some sweet and sexy alter ego moonlighting as a hot lumberjack man."

"A hot lumberjack man?" He folded his arms across his chest, looking very pleased by this assessment.

I ignored him. "We have our rhythms at school. You do things to bug me, and I get mad at you for it."

"That all sounds perfect to me."

I stumbled on my rant. He kept breaking into my stride, leaving me not quite remembering what I was going to say next.

"Me annoying you and you pretending to hate it," he clarified.

"These feelings will all go away when we're back in the real world where we barely tolerate each other."

He took a step closer. "Let me explain something to you. I've always liked you. I've had a massive crush on you since the second I started working at the school."

I was all primed and ready to fire off more reasons at him, but instead, my mouth could only gape at him. "The second you started?"

"Yeah. You were like this big, brown-eyed, sexy librarian bombshell. Right out of my dreams."

Another step closer. One more step and I would feel the heat from his body. "And I can't imagine myself breaking up with the woman I've been into for nine months."

Okay, that was a pretty good answer, even if it was hard to believe.

"Well, why were you so rude all the time? Telling me what to do and making fun of me?"

He sighed, rubbing a hand over his face. "The first time we met, I just poked my head into your room to say hi, and you looked up from your desk and gave me the biggest smile. To say I was blown away by that moment would be a massive understatement. Your smile lit up everything. And I stood there with my mouth open like a freaking idiot because I lost all words for about thirty seconds."

Heat flamed my blushing cheeks at his confession. I remembered that moment so plainly. I was in the middle of reading essays at my desk when a knock at my door sounded. I looked up, and there stood the most attractive man I'd ever seen, grinning at me. I don't care who you are, there was no way a person couldn't return that smile. But our interactions after that initial meeting had been much more underwhelming.

"But then, I never saw that smile again—until we came to the lodge. From our first meeting, I had this idea of you as this vivacious woman, but I didn't see that in almost any of your interactions at the school. You lit up for your kids, and you were real with Millie, but I watched you with everyone else, and it felt like you were always sizing down for your audience. Your smiles were fake. You took on everybody's workload because you wouldn't tell them no. You cleaned up after everyone. You edited papers without getting paid. I didn't handle it the way I probably should have, but in my own stupid way, I thought I was trying to help you."

I thought of Miles in the kitchen, not letting me wash Jason's dishes, physically taking them out of my hands and putting them back in the fridge. I thought of all our other interactions together the past nine months. I had seen him as arrogant and bossy, but now…

"What's next?" Miles asked.

"What?"

"You've still got your freak-out face on. What else are you worried about?"

"We work together," I whispered. If he really wanted to know, I had to tell him all of my concerns.

He didn't even flinch. "It's not against the rules."

"What if we break up? I'd have to change schools. Or you would. I've already done that once, and I…really like it at Stanton."

His brow furrowed. "Why would you have to change schools?"

Were men really that dense?

"We work across the hallway from each other. Can you imagine how awkward that would be? What if it's a bad breakup? One of us would have to go."

A grin spread across his face. He was laughing at me, and suddenly, I wanted to punch him. I glared at him as I began to move away when his arm shot out, nudging me back against the wall, facing him. He removed his arm.

"I'm sorry. I didn't mean to laugh. How about this? If we ever break up, I promise I'll make it a manageable amount of awkward. Nothing too terrible."

A small smile managed to escape my lips, even as I tried to hold it back. I turned my face away. With a thumb and a touch as airy as a whisper, he turned it back.

"Hey," he said softly. "I know what this is. I've seen the movies. I write the books. The part where one of us gets scared. Our dark moment. And I get it. It's scary to go back somewhere when everything's changed." He grinned. "Especially with the fact that you have to face Millie again, knowing she was right about us. It'll be the worst."

Again, my stupid smile came back, unbidden. I shook my head and tried to press my lips together, unable to meet his gaze.

He took a step toward me, and my breath caught, though he still wasn't touching me. I stared at the top button on his flannel shirt.

"But what about this? What if, instead of breaking up with each other, we just broke up with all the fake parts of this week? Let's break up with the notion that any part of this has been fake. Because it hasn't been fake for one second to me."

I covered my face with my hands, unable to take the sweet fire in his eyes as he stared at me.

"What else?" he whispered. Warm hands slowly uncovered mine from my face. It was all so sweet, and his eyes were the kind of eyes I could get lost in. Inviting and warm. I wanted to wrap my arms around him so tight, but I couldn't. Not yet. I wasn't done, so I removed my hand from his and kept them lonely at my side.

"What if I've just been some sort of adrenaline rush for you while we've been here? You got me to do some crazy stuff here with you, but when we get back, I'll just be boring again. Grammar Queen, remember? I will never go skydiving. Ever. Really. If I survived you pushing me out of a plane, the first thing I'd do when I got back on the ground would be to kill you. And if I didn't survive, I would haunt you for the rest of your days. And I'll never go bungee-jumping with you." He took a step closer while I babbled on, a leaky faucet unable to shut off. "I mean, I could maybe try a white-water-rafting trip, but that's it. And only if it's not a super scary river. I'm talking baby rapids. Bumps, really, not—"

He reached out and clutched a handful of my shirt at the waist and began pulling me closer and closer until I landed in his arms. I had an impressive speech left to give but found the words hard to form when he leaned forward, his mouth hovering close to mine.

"*You* are a rush to me. Every time I make you smile, my heart rate goes through the roof. The way you blush and bite your lip and pretend to be annoyed when I tease you..." He patted his chest. "Straight shot of dopamine. Let's not even talk about what your laugh does to me. But you're not just my dopamine hit. You're my soft place to land when I come back down. I don't need you to go skydiving with me. Or rock climbing. I'm perfectly happy reading a book. Or hanging out watching a movie with you. But there *are* times when I'd want us to get out of our comfort zones. Make some memories. I want to pick our moments, whatever they are, and live them."

"What if it doesn't work out?" I asked again, my voice more stable now. Nervous. "All relationships start with pretty words."

He shook his head. "You can 'what if' your whole life away. Relationships are always going to be scary, whether we work together or not. There are always unknowns, but you've got to take a chance on something, or else you're going to spend your life wondering what could have been."

He was chipping away my defenses one argument at a time. I hadn't seen that coming. He made me want to forget all about the unknown and just trust him. He gave me so many reasons to do so, but there was one more thing I couldn't shake. The fact that our life the past six days in Vermont had been an anomaly.

"I'm just scared that this is all going to go away. We're out of our normal environment. I can't help but think that when we go back to New York, everything will go back to the way it was. Because that's how it's always been. What if we slip back into our old ways? Because that's where we're comfortable. This all happened so fast—and completely out of nowhere. Here it feels right, but what about there? I just can't help thinking that we need some space. To proceed with caution. Let's think about things for a bit to make sure that I'll still be what you might want…when we're not here."

I looked up at him, surprised to find his eyes regarding me thoughtfully. Our gazes locked while he just stared, as though his mind was busy calculating something.

"You know what?" he mumbled. "I think you might be on to something."

"What?" I asked, feeling anxious all of a sudden.

"Maybe you're right."

"I am?"

A hint of a smirk appeared on his lips. "I've given you too much here. You need to miss me."

I scoffed, happy to redirect my thoughts to something more lighthearted. "I think you might be overthinking my attachment just a bit."

His eyes narrowed as he brought his lips closer to mine once more. "Oh, really?"

Of their own traitorous accord, my lips parted, waiting for

his. They never came. His self-satisfied grin was extremely present, however.

"You need to miss me," he said again, this time with firmer resolve.

"Are you breaking up with me now? After all that?" Panic began to rise up in my chest. I didn't want to break up. I just needed time to think it all through.

He snorted, a smile touching his lips. The sparkle was definitely back in his eyes. "I'm not breaking up with you. This is me stepping back so you can decide what you want in the place you need to decide it."

My brows furrowed. "Huh?"

"Back at school. Back in the land where Rudolph and Santa haven't thrown up on anything." He threw up his hands for air quotes.

I tucked a wayward lock behind my ear. Relief flooded my body as he seemed to understand exactly what I needed. Feeling more secure now, I looked up at him cheekily. "What happens if I decide I can't stand you again? Do you still promise not to make it awkward?"

"I never said that. I said I'd make it a *manageable* amount of awkward."

A laugh bubbled from my throat as he wrapped his arms tight around me, pulling me in closer and pressing a light kiss to my forehead.

"I have meetings in New York City with my editor and publisher this next week, so I won't even be around to bother you. But I'll be there for the first day back at school, and we'll talk then. But as for me, you know what I want. And you know where to find me."

I looked up at him in surprise and a little apprehension. "The first day of school? That's…longer than a week. So, what, I'm not even going to hear from you? The whole ten days?"

He grinned, rubbing his hands together like a psychopathic

maniac. "The plan's working. You're missing me already. And nope. I'm not going to call you."

I placed my hands on my hips, getting annoyed. "Fine. I wouldn't answer if you did."

"Great. It's important that we're both dedicated to our space so we can think."

"Agreed."

Later that night, we walked back to the cabin side by side. Not touching. And it left me feeling unsettled. Like something left undone. Purposefully. I assumed it was the fact that we didn't make out in the storage closet like I had been anticipating when he pulled me in there. But it was fine. It was a great idea. If anything, this was just proving to me how much Miles understood me. It was sweet that he would be so thoughtful to give me space. I had gone almost twenty-six years without kissing Miles Taylor. Ten more days didn't matter one bit.

Of course, he had a strange twinkle in his eye when he looked at me. A determined spark on his face that I could only assume was similar to the look he might have when climbing a rock wall. It both terrified and thrilled me for reasons I won't go into. I had wanted a little time. He was giving it to me. But did he have to seem so cheerful about it all? Whistling as he walked me back to the lodge? Smirking to himself when we realized we had missed the time to turn in our bingo cards? We had only one square left unchecked, but he insisted we couldn't mark down a mistletoe kiss. And now, it was too late. Which meant I had suffered through all of the Bingo game horridness for nothing.

He walked me to my cabin door that night, and instead of inviting himself in and plopping down on my couch to watch his dumb *Terminator* movie, like I had assumed we would do, he shook my hand at the doorway.

Shook my hand.

"It's been a very life-altering few days, Oliviana," he said, releasing his grip on me and clasping both of his hands behind his back.

"It has," I agreed, folding my arms and leaning against the doorframe. "Do you want to come in?" I tried for casual, as though I didn't care if he came in or not. I was just being polite. It was technically his cabin, after all. But my voice caught on the last word, and it came out sounding a little too vulnerable.

For a second, he looked like he would take me up on my offer, but then he straightened, a fresh determination appearing on his face. "You know I'd love to, but I've got to pack for my trip."

He grinned and took a step backward on the porch. Suddenly, a ripe annoyance flooded my insides. I had wanted *some* space. That didn't mean he needed to give me *all* of the space. I just didn't want to proclaim my undying devotion to a man I didn't even like a week ago. That was all. There had been a lot of changes between us this week. Maybe a bit of reflection and going our separate ways for a few days would be a good thing. It was a very reasonable thought process. But the way he was going about it made me want to snap his overly attractive lumberjack face off.

Or kiss him.

"Wait." My fingers clenched in a ball as I strode out from the cabin, stopping directly in front of him. His eyes widened with delighted anticipation at my approach. Maybe two could play this game. He wanted me to miss him? Fine. I would make dang well sure he'd miss me, too.

I reached out and grasped the back of his neck with both of my hands and pulled his lips down to meet my own. I could feel Miles resisting for about one second before his arms locked around me, pulling me closer and higher until my toes didn't touch the ground. Though it was the middle of winter, instant fireworks flew between us. Knowing we wouldn't see each other for the next ten days made this moment that much more important. Giving him everything I could, I ran my fingers gently across his jawline, feeling him kiss me under my palm. He set me down on the ground, still kissing me. One of his hands found its way to my cheek, his thumb stroking my face gently before moving to trail across my neck, getting lost in my hair.

Though I didn't want to admit it—and I strongly suspected Miles didn't either—we both didn't want to end this kiss, which was why it went on for a good long while.

Finally, when the need for oxygen won out, I pulled back, air filling my lungs. Miles had a slightly dazed expression on his face for a moment before carefully hiding it away.

"I feel like you're playing your cards a little strong here," he mumbled, smiling at me. His arms were still wrapped comfortably around my waist.

"That's where you're wrong. I don't even know what game we're playing."

He laughed. With a look in his eyes of simmering passion, he leaned forward and pressed a kiss to my cheek before releasing me. "See you in ten days, Spanks."

TWENTY SEVEN

"I cannot fix on the hour, or the spot, or the look, or the words, which laid the foundation. It is too long ago. I was in the middle before I knew that I had begun."
Jane Austen - *Pride and Prejudice*

IT HAD BEEN FOUR DAYS SINCE MILES AND I SAID OUR GOODBYES at the cabin. Three days since the goodbye breakfast Miles was unable to attend due to his meetings in the city. Three days since we found out Mom and Russ had won the Bingo Blackout. I hadn't even realized they were participating, but apparently, they did so in secret. When they won the cruise package, they promptly gave it to Ben and Chloe for a babymoon getaway, offering to watch the girls while they were gone. Chloe and her hormones had her bursting into tears. Well, actually, there hadn't been too many dry eyes at our table. That was the second time in two days I found myself giving Russ a hug.

True to his word, Miles hadn't contacted me at all. Which was just fine. Great. He was a man of his word. Giving me space to figure things out. That was good to know. One point for Miles.

Millie had tried calling several times, but I avoided every one of her calls—and the five hundred messages she left via text. She was going to want details I didn't have for her. I was still a bit miffed at her audacity to set us up like that, as well as the fact that she had been right—played me like a fiddle, to be exact.

For some reason, I just wanted to soak in my bathtub and read something, which lately had been the first three books of the *Landfall* series by one Miles Taylor. I refused to judge myself for this. It had nothing to do with me *missing* anybody. The fourth book was coming out in May, and I needed a casual reread to remind myself of all the details I might have forgotten. (Full disclosure, I had forgotten nothing, which happens when you've read a book series so many times.)

So far, my days at home had consisted of me watching movies, cleaning, and immersing myself in the fascinating world of the dung beetle and their mates. Yes, I had brought the manuscript with me to Vermont and promptly forgotten all about it. It was actually a good thing I'd waited until now. My mind went into editing mode and left me with little else to think about. Although, I now had a few disturbing visuals of a mating pair of dung beetles rolling around in my head. But for the most part, except for the time I spent eating, breathing, taking a bath, and sleeping, I never once thought about Miles.

Tyrok had just climbed to the top of Mount Spurn, barely evading the pirates chasing after him, when my phone dinged with a text. The sudden sound caused me to jolt in the bathtub, the water sloshing against the side. I almost didn't look at my phone, thinking it was Millie, but it wasn't. If seeing Miles's name lit up across my screen didn't give away my feelings, the smile bursting across my face mixed with my pounding heartbeat sure did.

MILES: This is me not calling you.

ME: This is me not answering.

MILES: I don't wonder how you're doing one bit.

ME: And I couldn't care less if your having a good time in New York or not.

MILES: you're

ME: That was Autocorrect! Not me!

MILES: What part of our history makes you think I'd believe that?

ME: *GIF of Michael Scott's annoyed face*

MILES: *GIF of James Franco's winky face*

MILES: It's too cold for me to want to do much here, not that you care. I've mostly been sitting in my hotel trying to read an old book my "friend" recommended.

ME: Well a "friend" gave me an old movie for Christmas and I watched it last night. Not that it's any of your business.

MILES: You watched The Terminator without me?

ME: Are you reading Jane Eyre without me?

MILES: You're pathetic, Spanks.

ME: Ditto, Taylor.

MILES: I sure don't miss you.

ME: I don't miss you either.

MILES: P.S. Jane Eyre is growing on me. But I have to take A LOT of breaks while reading.

ME: Big words can be intimidating. Just keep at it. By the way, I still can't find one redeemable piece of literature fodder in The Terminator.

MILES: Now THAT is a wound straight to my heart.

ME: I guess my job here is done. Goodnight, you.

MILES: Goodnight, Spanks. I'll see you in six days, but I'm not counting.

ME: That soon? Wow.

MILES: I'm going to kiss the crap out of you when I see you.

I dropped my phone to the side of the tub so I could laugh and cover my face, finally allowing Miles's flirtations to go straight from my grinning cheeks to my heart.

ME: I'd like to see you try.

WALKING THE HALLWAY OF STANTON HIGH AFTER TWO WEEKS OF being away felt very much like no time had passed at all. The hallway still smelled faintly like B.O. and cafeteria food. The seniors still hung together down their hallway. The teachers' lounge already had crumbs littered along the countertops. Somebody brought muffins, I noticed. I didn't stop to clean anything, however, and kept walking toward my room. On my way, I passed Harvey's empty classroom, and I placed the thesis on his desk, happy to be rid of it.

There was a lightness in my step I hadn't remembered being there before. I had bought myself a new outfit with a gift card my mom had given me for Christmas. When I had gone shopping, for some reason, the typical grays and creams and blacks didn't call out to me as usual. Instead, it was a green floral blouse that matched my eyes that caught my attention. The material was both loose and fitting in all the right places and paired nicely with my gray pencil skirt that made my butt look like a felony (Millie's words, not mine).

Eventually, I had responded to Millie's texts. I didn't want her to think something had happened to me, though I refused, point blank, to give her any details about Miles. I told her all about the lovely cabin her "friend" had recommended, and I thanked her for her help. She had asked me out for coffee over the weekend, but I declined, telling her I had an appointment. She was not pleased by my answers, and I knew I wouldn't be able to avoid her today. I unlocked my classroom and strode inside, turning on the lights and my computer. Class started in about twenty minutes, and Miles still wasn't here yet.

"You're looking pretty today."

My body tensed. I looked up from my desk and spotted Millie leaning in my classroom doorway, raking me in with a very suspicious undertone in her mannerisms.

"Um, thanks?" I said.

Her eyes narrowed as she strode a few paces closer. "How was your…appointment?"

I swallowed, not meeting her eyes. "It was…fine."

"What was it for? Gyno?"

"No."

She took a few steps closer. Slowly. Like a cat sneaking up behind a bird just minding her own business. "Ortho?"

I bit my lip, really concentrating on the blank screen of my computer. "Nope."

She leaned forward, both hands on my desk, her face next to mine, drama teacher until the end, and said, "Cardiovascular?"

She said the words with so much heat behind them I couldn't help the grin that broke free.

"I KNEW it! I knew you wouldn't last a week with Miles Taylor at a Christmas lodge. Are you two in love yet? "

"Shhhhh!" I stood up and flung myself toward her, attempting to cover her mouth with my hand. She brushed me away.

"Spill everything right now, and I'll forgive you for ignoring me this whole week."

"You deserved every bit of that!"

She gave me a knowing look. "Oh, did I? Or will you be thanking me at the wedding?"

"Stop talking so loud," I insisted, cocking my head to see if I could hear Miles arriving. Still nothing yet.

"What happened?"

My mind raced for a CliffsNotes version of what I could tell her before students began arriving to the classroom. The whole thing sounded like something out of a dream. If I told her we were fake dating, she'd want to know why. If I told her it was because I used his name to get me out of hanging out with Glenn, she'd want to know why. So, I settled on the basic truth.

"We made an arrangement to put down our weapons for the week, and it was a nice break."

She put her hands on her hips and leaned closer, sniffing out the lie. "You two kissed, didn't you?"

It was apparent I would never do well in a drama class. I tried to keep my face passive, stoic, but at the word *kiss*, moisture filled my mouth, and my mind raced back to a cozy cuddle, watching *Home Alone*, and keeping warm inside a covered bridge, and the feel of his arms wrapped around me. The feeling I had craved all week. A smile came unbidden just then, and Millie's eyes lit up, clapping to herself.

"I knew it."

And then I told her everything and even graciously accepted her rubbing the whole thing in my face.

Slowly the kids in my class began to trickle in and Millie floated on cloud nine back to her own classroom. My morning classes passed by in a blur. Miles had been teaching next door all morning long, and I still hadn't seen him. He hadn't made a peep. Or made any sort of effort to see me. My girl brain whirled at the possible explanations. He realized during our time apart that he didn't like me. The space gave him the clarity he needed. Now, he was avoiding me, and our life at Stanton High was about to get awkward. I would have to move again. All of this was running through my head as I attempted to introduce *The Taming of the Shrew* to my classes. I was a sweaty nervous wreck of a mess, and to top it all off, I had worn a stupid new shirt full of colors and flowers, and he wouldn't even care.

The bell rang and I stood, talking in a blurred daze to my students as I shooed them out for lunch. I contemplated sneaking out my window and eating lunch in my car. Perhaps we could exist this way and never have cause to see each other. There were ways to make it work.

"You look pretty, Miss Wilson."

I looked down at the face of Erica Sanders, one of my favorite students. I blinked, taking her in as if seeing her here for the first time, her pink hair and all. Had she been in my class this entire hour? My hands and heart felt so jittery I couldn't name a single student that I had just spent an hour looking at. I forced myself to pull it together and held the door open for her to exit.

"Thank you, Erica. I apprecia—"

Across the hallway, another door opened. A student walked out with Miles trailing behind, stopping just inside his doorway. His dark gaze was on me, and I watched his eyes trail down my body and back up at the same time he said something to his student.

My heart raced underneath my skin, pounding into my ears as I locked onto his gaze. Smoldering air crackled between us as the loud bustle of the students in the hallway dulled to white noise. Ever so slowly, his face began to crack. A tiny smile at first, at the corner of his mouth, growing wider by the second. I tried my best to hold mine back, but my strength didn't last for long. Or at all. I didn't want it to. I was done holding back. This whole week, I had been terrified of this moment, of coming back and discovering that nothing had really changed. But now I knew. Our time here would be different because *we* were now different.

Ever so slowly, Miles closed his door behind him and began walking toward me. I straightened and took a few steps back, suddenly feeling nervous. His grin grew even wider as he stepped through my threshold. I drank him in. He had traded his flannel shirt for a polo and khakis. He was missing his gray beanie, but otherwise, I found him and the twinkle in his eyes completely unchanged.

He closed my door with a thud. Like usual, my room felt smaller with him inside, but that could have been the way he kept stepping closer to me until he had me nearly trapped against the wall. He wasn't touching me, but he was close enough that I could feel the heat.

"Hey there, Spanks." His voice was soft and gravelly and brought out every last goosebump on my skin. "Nice shirt." And then my emotions completely overwhelmed me. I burst out laughing and immediately covered my face with my hands. This wasn't real. No way could he be real.

He gently removed my hands from my face.

"No hiding your smiles. I work too hard for those," he said, cupping my cheeks gently in his hands.

I bit my lip, staring up at him, trying to suppress the sunbeams wanting to burst free. I thought about playing hard to get, but realized I was done with the games. "I missed you so much."

A grin split across his face as he moved in closer, his mouth dropping down to hover over mine. "Good. Are we done with the not-kissing thing? And not seeing each other? That was a stupid idea. I just about had to tie myself to my desk today to keep from bursting in here. Nothing's changed for me."

"Same."

This time, his smile molded into mine as he pressed my body into the wall with his own and proceeded to make up for every day we'd been apart. I was consumed by him and his overwhelming presence in front of me. His arms pulled me close, and his fingers messed up my hair. He drew heated kisses all down my jawline and cheeks before I clasped his neck and brought his mouth back to my lips. When I felt myself almost on the verge of losing control, I pulled away from him and took a deep breath, trying to think of something to calm our nerves.

"You're going to have to find a different name than Spanks. Especially at school."

He seemed affronted. "I will not. That's my favorite memory."

I leaned in closer. "Your favorite?"

"Well, one of them."

Then, we were kissing again. My plan didn't work. To an outsider, I was sure we really were disgusting in that twitterpated, obsessed-with-each-other, cheesy-grin stage, but I didn't care. What a difference a couple of weeks could make.

I pulled away from him, wiping my lips, my chest heaving. "I gave back the edits for 'The Mating Habits of the Dung Beetle.'"

"How'd it turn out? Was there anything good?"

"If I tell you, you can never go back to a time where you didn't know."

"Good point."

He moved to kiss me again before I stopped him. "And for your information, Harvey paid me for a job well done."

He reared his head back, looking at me in surprise. "Really? That's good. If you're interested, I made a couple of adjustments to my next book. I wondered if you'd be willing to go over it for me?"

"Well, I'm charging for my services now, so you'd better be prepared to pay up."

He pulled me in closer, his hands roaming my back while his lips hovered tantalizingly close to my own. "Are you open to alternative forms of payment?"

I smiled and pretended to think. "I could probably be persuaded."

"I've got a surprise for you."

"Okay." I leaned back into him, fully intent on resuming our makeout session.

"Down, Spanks. I've got to show you something."

"What?"

He lifted his arm. I looked up to see him holding a tiny, green, parasitic plant above us. "Thought I'd give you a chance to remedy the whole mistletoe debacle."

A smile bit my lips. "There was no debacle. It counted."

"It didn't."

"Well, either way, we lost the bingo game. It doesn't matter if we finish or not."

"Not technically, but…" He held out a card in front of my face.

"The bingo card?" I laughed.

"I know how much you love to cross something off your list."

I was almost to his lips. "I do love a good checkmark. But I don't plan to ever be finished with you."

"Prove it."

So, I did. Under the mistletoe in my classroom next to his, I gave him my lips and my heart. The moment was ripe for the picking, and I was finally ready to live it.

He pulled back from our kiss and grinned at me as his fingers found the light switch.

"Blackout."

EPILOGUE

"The future has not been written. There is no fate but what we make for ourselves."
The Terminator

IT WAS SUMMER NOW. WE WERE LOUNGING ON THE PORCH SWING at my little butter-yellow house. Miles was sitting upright and I lay across the swing, my head on his lap, rereading my favorite parts of *Jane Eyre*. A cool summer breeze ruffled my hair as we rocked gently. This was a favorite spot of ours—when he was home. He'd been off and running for what would be his last year of teaching with Outward Bound, trying to make the most of his white-water-rafting trips and rock climbing adventures while he could. He'd been picked up by his publisher to write a whole new adventure series and would need the extra time to write. The last book had come out in May, and so far, it was a smashing success. I liked to think that was due in large part to the last minute addition of a small love story featuring a charming heroine nicknamed Spanks.

Miles and I had made it through a whole semester as a couple. We tried to keep it professional in the workplace, but every so often, he would walk into my classroom while I was in the middle of teaching and plant a huge kiss on me before walking back out again—to the utter delight of my class. And me.

He might never love *Jane Eyre*. I might never understand his obsession with skydiving or *The Terminator*, but he also never lets me get away with a fake smile. My laughs were real and heartfelt around him. He was my wings, and I was his nest. He continued to help me see the best in Russ. He taught me to see that I had so much more love to give, and none of it deserved to be locked away.

He also pushed me to get out of my comfort zone, while still being respectful of the fact that my comfort zone was different than his. Together we discovered a love of kayaking. I kept us to more gentle parts of the river, but I found that I liked being in water. I was a decent swimmer and he planned to take me on a white water rafting trip later this summer. I might never become a full adventurer–I meant what I said about never going skydiving. Or rock climbing. Thankfully, he had good friends who enjoyed both.

It turned out I had been wasting my talents as an editor. After I returned Harvey's thesis, Miles helped me set up a website where I offered my services for a fee. I became the first editor for his new book, and while he didn't exactly pay me in cash, we managed to come up with an arrangement that suited us both.

I turned the page, almost to the part where Rochester admits his feelings, when something dropped out of my book. A clanking sound on the concrete followed. I slid off the porch swing, confused, and looked around for whatever it could possibly have been. Something glinted in the sunlight underneath the swing, and I tentatively reached out and picked it up.

It was a silver, oval-shaped ring, exactly from my dreams. A smile bit my lips as my heart began to race. I stole a glance at Miles.

He was now kneeling before me, an apprehensive smile on his face. "Spanks—"

He cut off when I glared at him and tried again. "Olive, I love you. So much. Will you marry me?"

I spent the next long moments thoroughly convincing him that I would. There were no more questions in my mind. No more doubts. I had given him my timid heart, and he made it soar. And in the words of the great Charlotte Bronte, from my second favorite book, "Reader, I married him."

The End

Read the next book in the series!

A Newport Christmess

By Jess Heileman

Love can be downright messy.

Read the rest of the Christmas Escape Series!

All standalone, clean, closed door

romances that can be read in any order.

Christmas Baggage

Deborah M. Hathaway

Host for the Holidays

Martha Keyes

Faking Christmas

Cindy Steel

A Newport Christmas

Jess Heileman

A Not-So-Holiday Paradise

Gracie Ruth Mitchell

Later on We'll Conspire

Kortney Keisel

Cotswolds Holiday

Kasey Stockton

Christmas Escape Bingo

Read all seven books in the series to get a Christmas romance blackout!

Broken elevator	Sleigh ride through the mountains	Allergic reaction	Snowstorm Power outage	A walk down main street
Candlelit house tour	Define the boundaries chat (multiple answers)	Ice Skating on a frozen pond	Mint hot Chocolate	"Highway to Hell" ringtone
Boat ride	"Fresh" chocolate milk	FREE SPACE	Reindeer Attack	Miniature Christmas Tree
Hot chocolate at a Christmas market	Trip to Ikea	Burning hot chocolate	Home Alone movie night (multiple answers)	Listening to Bing Crosby
An angry dachshund	Blanket fort	Snowy Beach	Mandalorian pajamas	Snowmobile ride through the mountains

AUTHOR'S NOTES

My husband was a travel nurse for a year and a half. During that time, our little family packed and moved and lived all over the country with him. One of our stays was three months in Montpelier, Vermont. We were tucked away in a tiny, run-down apartment during the spectacular fall and winter season and loved every second of our time there. I always knew I would write a story set in one of the most unique and breathtaking states in the country and when the opportunity came up to take part in this Christmas series, this little story was born. Though most of this book takes place in a fictional Christmas lodge on the outskirts of Montpelier, I couldn't help but give the reader a tiny taste of what the town is like. I used to go for walks down Main Street, talking to my mom or sister on the phone and telling them all about how amazing it smelled, the charming old buildings, all the local businesses, and how friendly the people were on the street. We shopped at Shaws grocery store, and my sons and I had weekly visits to the town library. But our favorite place was Morse Farm, where we would stop to sample the different grades of maple syrup, say hi to Rex and James (the resident goats), walk the beautiful grounds, and grab a maple creme.

I used to love the covered bridges all throughout the Northeastern states, but especially the bridges we'd find in our explorations around Vermont. I added a few extra bridges for the purpose of this story but thought they'd make a great decoration piece for a good kissing scene.

I grew up on a small dairy farm in Idaho. Once my cousin-in-law, Dave, came to visit so he could try milking a cow for the first time. The idea to bring a cup with chocolate syrup out to the barn to drink "fresh" chocolate milk was inspired by Dave–who did just that while the rest of us stared at him in a confused kind of horror. For the record, I, like Olive, hate milk.

The gingerbread house idea came from my other cousin, Lindsey. She is a talented designer and DIYer and makes the most beautiful gingerbread houses every winter.

Miles's corrected email is available to view up close and personal on my website at www.cindysteel.com.

Thank you so much for reading this book! It was so fun to write and I hope it provided you with a little Christmas cheer.

ACKNOWLEDGMENTS

It's an absolute miracle that books go from inside my head to something a person can hold in their hands. It's a process every step of the way. From the first sprout of an idea, to hashing out plot points and characters, to writing the first chapter ten different times wondering if I'm telling too much, to calling my mom and sister and friends about every little bump and win along the way. That's the secret to how books get made. It's all about the people you surround yourself with. And I happen to have the very best in my circle.

The Christmas Escape authors - Martha Keyes, Kasey Stockton, Kortney Keisel, Gracie Ruth Mitchell, Jess Heileman, and Deborah Hathaway. Thanks so much for letting me be a part of this series. I had the best time and now you're stuck with me forever because I love you all to pieces.

My sister, Lisa - Without you there would be no books. Thank you for being interested in my characters and for telling me when something stinks. But mostly, thank you for pretending you want to talk about my books even when you probably don't. You're the best.

Mom - Thanks for reading all of my books several times during the drafting stage and for telling me you love it every single time. You're the best mom ever!

Karen Thornell - You are one of my favorite people on the planet. Thanks for your friendship, feedback, encouragement and talking me down from all those author ledges.

Holli Jo, Whitney, and Karen - I love our critique group so much. Thanks for helping me hash out plot ideas.

All of my Beta readers - Jess, Kasey, Karen, Martha, Lisa, and my mom. Your feedback was invaluable!

All of my ARC readers - Thank you for taking another chance on a book of mine and for your excitement and encouragement. Also, thank you for your help in catching those last minute typos!

The Bookstagram community - This is the happiest place on the internet. From my first book two years earlier, you have been so welcoming and encouraging. I've made so many good friends in this community and it's been such a blessing in my life. Thank you!

Amy, Claire, and Autumn - You'll be able to tell what portion of this story you inspired. I don't necessarily thank you for always pushing me EXTREMELY out of my comfort zone, but I do appreciate the stories afterward.

Jana Miller - Thanks for helping me to find the balance in this story.

Jenn Lockwood- I still don't have a clue where commas are supposed to go, but thanks for fixing them all. You're the best!

Amy Romney - You have an uncanny ability to help me say in one sentence what I was trying to say in three. Thanks for your time and talents in making this manuscript shine!

Melody Jeffries Design - Thank you for the beautiful cover.

James, Stetson, and Dawson - Thanks for eating cereal for dinner, putting up with my glazed-over expressions when I'm working out a plot, and for making me feel loved every day. I hope to make you all proud.

And finally, thanks to the literary greats who have paved the way before us - Charlotte Bronte, Jane Austen, L.M. Montgomery, and William Shakespeare, to name only a few. It was a delight being inspired by your words.

ABOUT CINDY

Cindy Steel was raised on a dairy farm in Idaho. She grew up singing country songs at the top of her lungs and learning to solve all of life's problems while milking cows and driving tractors—rewriting happy endings every time. She married a cute Idaho boy and is the proud mother of two wild and sweet twin boys. Which means she is also now a collector of bugs, sticks, rocks, and slobbery kisses. She loves making breakfast, baking, photography, reading a good book, and staying up way past her bedtime to craft stories that will hopefully make you smile.

She loves to connect with her readers! She is the most active on Instagram at @authorcindysteel and her newsletter, but she occasionally makes her way to Facebook at Author Cindy Steel, and her website at www.cindysteel.com.